The Eyes of Coda

James Hirschfeld

Cover Design by Katherine Murdoch

Full Moon Publishing, LLC
Glade Spring, VA
Fullmoonpublishingllc.com

ISBN: 1946232041
ISBN-13: 978-1946232045

CONTENTS

ACKNOWLEDGMENTS

Mark and Loraine, thanks for rekindling my love of a good story.
To the Hirschy clan and the Florence collective, a massive thanks.
Kat & Katie, you are the best of the best.

CHAPTER 1-

Missidnyl, Oregon

It'd almost been two decades since I'd last visited my childhood home, and it was so much smaller than I remembered.
Each room was littered with childhood memories, and as I walked through the house they would spark up in my mind and play themselves out like old crackling rolls of film. My early years were full of love, my mother had always done everything she could manage in order to provide me with a joyful upbringing.

The house had aged a great deal, and the thick oak trees surrounding it had over the years cocooned it into a little wooden nest. The afternoon sunlight trickled in through the oak leaves outside the windows leaving a subtle orange glow throughout the house. I missed my childhood. And I wondered if I'd appreciated the feeling of boundless magic that a child feels when I'd lived here all those years ago. I wished I'd returned purely for the purpose of reminiscing my early years, to bask in the warm memories of the long years I'd spent in this old house. But unfortunately the reality was much worse.

Jessie Quiad, an old neighbor of mine, sat solemnly at the bottom of the steps that led from the old front door. I was unsettled by the very sight of her, and it sat badly in the pit of my stomach. Nothing about this situation felt good.

When I reached into the oldest compartments of my life's memories, I'd think of a little girl who was always happy. The kind of wide-eyed and outgoing happiness that some children seemed to radiate and infect those around them with. My memory could of course be wrong, but this is what intuition told me--and in a heartbeat I'll trust my feelings without hesitation. *In fact,* the biggest mistakes I've made in my life so far have been due to not giving feelings of this nature that very trust.

The last rays of the warm afternoon sun lit up her youthful golden ringlets of hair, she wore blue sandals, yellow shorts and a dirtied white t-shirt. However, her posture was tired and defeated. She reminded me of a marionette--held only by the strings that were attached to her.

I watched her through the stained glass window beside the old front door, and I could feel the blood pumping through my body with each pulse. I looked beyond her and towards the horrid, monster of a house that stood at the other side of my old street. *Her old place of residence.*

Without looking back towards me, Jessie rose from the steps and slowly began to wander in its direction. Orange beams of sunlight flickered and danced over her body as she moved forward.

I felt a mild spark of intuition and knew with certainty that I needed to follow her. I had a strong feeling that my theory *was* indeed a reality, *a bad reality.*

I headed out the front door and made my way up behind her, watching carefully.

For a moment her pace seemed to increase, and her soft footsteps along the asphalt almost mirrored the nervous beating in my chest.
I kept my cool and watched my breathing pattern, I couldn't let fear have its grip and get the better of me. I got a sudden paranoid idea that the faster my heart was racing - the faster Jessie would move.

She stopped abruptly, and stood motionless like a statue - just a few feet short of the cracked and eroded incline of the monster house's front driveway. I felt the gentle warmth of the sun on my face as I silently watched from behind.

Life and movement returned to Jessie after a few moments, she began to lean forward and reach out towards the house. Had I been standing on the other side of her, I've no doubt that I would have seen her eyes all puffed up and swollen with tears of

THE EYES OF CODA

resentment.

The house felt truly awful, it completely opposed the sweet and youthful nature of Jessie. It was cold, badly aged and utterly unwelcoming.

I tailed behind as she continued her journey up the steep driveway.

The knot in my gut grew tighter with each nervous step, it was like being slowly submerged into a deep, cold body of water.

She came to a stop at the front door, and shakily reached out for the handle. Her wonderful golden contrast to the house withered to nothing in an instant, the moment her petite little hand gripped the doorknob she became nothing but a bleak and lifeless limb connected to the old house.

Nevertheless, she swung open the large oaken door and I followed her inside.

I found myself in the living room. My long black shadow stretched across the ripped and battered carpet floor, nestled between the mellow orange sunlight that poured in from outside.

Jessie stood to my left, next to one of the many smashed out windows. Almost every inch of the carpet was littered with small shards of glass, they were like little translucent teeth - which at any moment seemed like they could fly at me like a whirlwind of murderous knives.

I had an urge to turn back and sprint towards my old house, lock the doors and get the tragic life of Jessie Quaid as far from my mind as possible. But I couldn't, because if I didn't help her - nothing would change. And that would haunt me until my last days.

My eyes were drawn to the far end of the room, and I became transfixed on what looked like masses of small insect nests. They covered the entire wall like some kind of insane wallpaper.

I hesitantly made my way across the room while keeping fixated on whatever disgusting blend of artwork waited for me on the other side of the room.

Though the closer I got, the more I began to realize what it was I was looking at. It was a collage of tiny, intricate paintings, a crazy mural of little eyes that all seemed to be looming down on me.

There were possibly hundreds of them, all of which were

painted with noticeable skill and precision.

It was deeply unnerving, mostly because I felt like they were real. Masses of eyes watching me with a sick curiosity, I shivered violently.

Amongst the sea of eyes, down towards the floor were the words,

'CODA IS KING.'

I froze. The cold breath of winter blew hard on my bones and found its way into my bloodstream.

Once upon a time, I had seen these words, During a particularly bad time of my life. On one of the many, many nights I'd spend getting as far gone as I could manage on a dangerous blend of unprescribed opiates.

And to see the words written here and now meant very bad news, this house was part of a dark and dangerous web.

I looked back at Jessie and into her small, innocent face for the first time in eighteen years. Her face looked like a heavy Grey led drawing that'd been lightly rubbed with an eraser; dark and blurry.

Though the true horror was her face beneath.

She hadn't aged, she was the same six-year-old child. Where I had aged and grown past the stages of adolescence - she hadn't.

Pity ripped into me, and the fear I felt was overcome with anger.

I looked back at the sick mural of eyes and tried to gather my thoughts, tried to calculate the situation and formulate some sort of plan. *What does this all mean..."*

I turned back to face Jessie again.

"Who painted this? Who did all this?" I asked. She stared at me desperately for a moment before moving towards a broken down, rotted out buffet covered in all sorts of distasteful ornaments.

I met with her at the buffet to study whatever it was she wanted me to see. I noticed a couple of old photo frames housing small portraits of what seemed like two happy little children. The left photo showed a playful looking little girl with an enormous grin lighting up her round little face, she had a pair of big soulful blue eyes that gazed out of the photo. The photo to the right of it was of a similarly grinning little boy who shared the same features as Jessie.

I felt a sensation similar to remembering a portion of a dream, and the longer I stared at the picture of the boy, the more rapidly my memories of him seemed to unravel, like a falling stack of dominoes. His name was Josh, and we were friends, good friends, my first friend.

For a moment I felt as though I was the same six-year boy I was when I'd last set foot in this house twenty-two years ago.

"Did Josh paint the eyes?". I asked Jessie.
She shook her head violently.

"Did you paint them?", once again she shook her head.

"Okay well... What is it here I need to see?".

She stared at me almost angrily for a moment before once again pointing towards the buffet. I continued studying the contents on the buffet awhile longer before I noticed a third photo frame, it was face down on the rotten wood-top with a camouflage of soot and dust covering its surface. I turned the photo frame upright and looked into it.

I stared at the Uncle of Jessie and Josh, a man with a thin tuft of dark brown hair between his two receding hairlines and a small cheerful face like a rodent; he was like a strange, skinny, shaved brother to Santa Claus.

I looked up at Jessie to see her gaze just off from meeting my eyes, her small blurred face was beetroot red and defeated.
Pity ripped into me for her, I looked back at Uncle Quaid - a wretched man that I had no pity for whatsoever.

I studied the horrific portrait of eyes a little while longer before I moved throughout the other rooms of the house, desperately searching for clues or hints as to lead me in the direction of Uncle Quaid.

Every room of the house was as putrid and rundown as the living room, shards of glass covering the carpet, every piece of furniture rotted to its last days of standing, and the overpowering odor of neglect filled the air of the house like a cologne worn by death himself.

Despite my blind, anger driven search, my eyesight was suddenly snagged on a door towards the back of the house,
I noticed a similar collage of eyes like the ones on display in the living room. The entire door was covered in them from top to

bottom, while the doorknob had one larger eye painted across it, I felt the leer of a hundred little eyes bearing down on me.

Once again my emotional spectrum shifted; it was fears turn to have its icy hand rest on the back of my neck.

I cautiously approached the door of eyes, once again I slowly started to recognize the mastery to which the eyes were painted. Every detail of every eye was crafted with the steady hands of a surgeon.

I took a moment to collect myself, and muster as much calm as possible. Gradually my body stilled itself and my breathing started to cycle itself down to a peaceful rhythm. I reached out and gripped the doorknob. With my eyes sharp and my thoughts firm, I stepped through to confront whatever was awaiting me beyond the door of eyes.

Immediately, I felt like smoke was blown up my nostrils. Similar to taking a smack to the nose, my vision was blinded. And a stinging stream of tears ran down my face.

I fought off the urge to turn back - I lifted my tee-shirt over my nose to try and ventilate the putrid smell.

Like plastic in the campfire.

Gradually my vision started to return, an array of blotches and swollen Grey blurs began to define and form themselves into something visible.

The room was filled with furniture, all decorated with unique blends of satanic artwork. Small smoldering piles of ash filled the room with thick smoke like a disgusting little hotbox. The only window in the room had been boarded up and painted black, along with every inch of wall space. A large round table stood in the center of the room with a single large eye painted across its surface.

I maintained my calm and cautiously approached the center table, still with my nostrils pinched under the thick cotton of my tee-shirt. I realized the upper eyelid was painted as a compressed collection of words, which became more decipherable as I got closer. 'Heart and Vessel to The Erased Man'. My heart rate increased, my calm was quickly diminishing. A hot rush of fear ran the length of my spine and sucked the blood from my legs. *This is not good...*

I didn't know much about the erased man, but I did know he

was very dangerous, an ancient spirit worshiped by blind and selfish followers in search of extended life at the cost of others.

My thoughts then turned to Jessie, and the tragic existence she now faced. My pity for her returned like a strong gust of wind and my fear started to settle.

I knew what I had to do, I thought over the situation and constructed a plan. I gathered my nerves, took a deep breath and headed out of the room towards the kitchen.

First things first. This house is going to burn. Tonight.

CHAPTER 2-

I dreamed a lot as a kid, dreams that were usually completely vivid and clear in their detail. Subsequently, a good deal of my childhood memories feel like dreams I'd had, and sometimes I struggle to differentiate what was real, and what wasn't. Like many dreams, a few of them were recurring. Moments after falling asleep I'd be placed gently back within the same adventures I'd had the night before. Remembering the time I'd spent with Josh Quaid felt more like a recurring dream than a reality. But he was undoubtedly real, and the times I'd shared with him were definitely real too. We were close friends, young friends that shared the mystical binding that only children can seem to share.

Along with Josh, I was close with my mother too, she'd always known how to handle and guide me through the strange and surreal experiences I was exposed to at a young age. Through a lot of these experiences, Josh was by my side. My mother was always so happy that I had someone who could relate to me, as Josh wasn't without oddities of his very own. My mother was also no exception, herself and I were the same, but unfortunately for her she'd developed habits in order to combat them.

At the age of twenty-one her wisdom teeth were removed, and as with most cases—the days following her surgery were discomforting. So in order to deal with the residual pain, she consulted her doctor.

Over the next few years she steadily developed a full-blown addiction to OxyContin and a handful of painkillers alike. She found an unhealthy solace in them, and began to rely on them as a way to ward off the overwhelming experiences she was faced with. The ones that we shared as mother and son.

At the youthful age of thirty-nine, the filthy grip of addiction squeezed its final grasp, and tragically, she lost her life. Her liver was finally brought to its bitter end due to a failed process of extracting the paracetamol from a large quantity of codeine pills. It was without a doubt the worst few weeks of my life so far. It broke my spirit to see someone so close to me drive themselves to death, most frighteningly due to a condition that I myself had.

After she died, I withdrew like a tortoise under heavy distress. I spent a long time keeping to myself and avoiding any form of contact with anybody. Like my mother had done before me, I abused opiates like they were oxygen, and almost destroyed *myself* in the process.

But no matter how deeply I retreated into my destructive shell, there was an emptiness inside me, harboring an ever-tightening knot that would continue to bind my emotions up into an ugly little ball. Guilt and shame consumed me whole, swallowing me as its broken, defeated prisoner. Before I *did* manage to destroy myself, thoughts of my mother grew too much to the point that I was forced to make a firm and final decision: I needed to go back to my roots, retrace the first steps I'd made in life, and face the demons that I'd run from.

I owed it to her, and I owed it to myself. For whatever reason it was that I'd been given my strange abilities, I felt compelled to use them as a tool instead of dying at its hands.

Rehabilitation was horrible and incredibly tedious. Each day seemed to be more difficult than the last. The cold, stone fist of addiction pummeled me to no end, and mercilessly tried to slam me back onto the dangerous tight rope of opiate abuse.

Somehow I resisted the urge, and each day I dragged myself forward a little further, always keeping the image of my mother at the front of my mind.

Slowly but surely, my dreams began to return. I mostly dreamed about my childhood home in Missidnyl, and the young, innocent face of Jessie Quaid. It didn't take me very long to gather an idea that she'd been subjected to something horrific, I also believed that someone was responsible for inviting whatever the terrible force was into her sad life.

The darkest and most disturbing parts of those dreams were the images of Jessie in pain. I would see her screaming in fear, desperately trying to protect herself while curling up into a little ball. Always be at the feet of someone standing tall above her, a man with a blurred out face.

So naturally my first stop was Missidnyl Oregon, my home town. The staple of my childhood, and the birthplace of the first evil in my life.

CHAPTER 3-

It took just one match for the house to accept its fiery end, like a newspaper covered in petrol. The flames danced high, and tangled themselves amongst the white glow of the stars. The intense heat of the fire blew itself outward from the old Quaid house, throwing billows of black smoke in all directions. I inhaled the cool air of the night and watched in thoughtful silence.

Hopefully, burning the house down to ashes would free Jessie's spirit, and destroy the portal that'd bound her soul to the plane of the living. Maybe now she could finally rest, and find her way out from the confines constructed by her sick and misguided Uncle.

Things would get complicated now, in setting fire to the house, I'd thrown myself headfirst into the Rabbit hole. My hunch was that someone associated to Uncle Quaid must've been maintaining the portal for all these years, and whoever that person was is surely going to want my severed head on a platter for destroying it.

I turned my back on the flaming wreckage, and started to head for my old, trusty Ford F-series that sat in the front drive of my old home. I fumbled for the car keys in my back pocket while I half-consciously thought about my next move, but all I could seem to think about was the old Quaid family, and the horrors that'd befallen them. Though before I had a chance to come to any conclusion on where to go, let alone make it to my car, a voice spoke softly from behind me. The hair on the back of my neck shot up, and I froze in place.

"Steven..."

Even without seeing her face, I instantly knew who it was.

"I think I can leave now..."

I turned to face Jessie. Her glow had returned, and she stood like a brightly lit candle in the night. A white aura radiated from her body, and her face was clear like the full moon.

"He's really mad, I can feel it... He wants to make you go away, you need to hide before he finds you."

My face grew hot with fear and my stomach tightened. I'd

known this would be dangerous, and even assumed that enemies would come from it. But now it was completely real, and there was no chance of going back.

"Who wants to make me go away? Your Uncle...?"

"No, the blurry man made Uncle go away, it's the old man."

"The old man...? Where is he?"

"I don't know."

I was profoundly confused; the conversation was making little sense. The blurry man I assumed must be the erased man, but as for the old man, I had no idea at all. The early stages of panic began to rise into my chest, and a steady headache started to drum heavily behind my eyes.

"Jessie, where should I hide? Should I go back home?"

"No he'll know. You need to go and find my big brother, he can make things go away too—he can hide you."

"Where can I find him?"

Jesus wide blue eyes stared at me blankly for a moment.

"You can find anyone you want, your eyes are special. The old man has special eyes too, but he's bad with them. Please don't let him hurt my big brother."

I stood quietly in thought for a while, considering what Jessie had just told me. I knew exactly what she was talking about. *Dreams,* and the second pair of eyes a person wears in the mysterious world of sleep. She wasn't wrong about referring to my eyes as special, but unfortunately that was the true curse in all this. The thought of this evil 'old man' having similar, if not the same abilities that I possessed deeply unnerved me. I began to feel like time was running out.

"Don't worry." I assured Jessie.

"I'll make sure nothing happens to him, I promise."

Jessie smiled weakly before turning her head to look behind her, as if to consider something only visible to the all-knowing, wise eyes of the dead. Her next comment stunned me, and blew all the air from my lungs.

"Your mommy misses you, I can feel her. Stay away from the sky, the car is the only safe way. You need to leave *now*."

I'd always felt a sense of strength when the thought of my mother was close, my rusted old ford was a gift from her that'd always held piece of her spirit, like the lingering essence of an old house.

Throughout my childhood, we spent a lot of time together in that old car. We'd travel all over the state, exploring the winding roads of Oregon. Sometimes we'd move along with no particular destination in mind at all. She'd share stories about her times growing up, and the experiences she'd had as a young woman. I cherished those times, and the memories of them were now a sweet melancholy.

The trip to find Josh would be a long one, and most likely full of danger. But I had to press on with the task that I'd started, and find my oldest friend.

The burning Old Quaid house moaned like a great beast as it quickly began losing its ability to support itself, it warped and distorted like a slowly deflating, enormous wooden ball. Small embers coupled with large pieces of debris spat themselves away from the wreckage as if desperately seeking refuge out from the molten hot confines of the house.

"Time to go..." I thought to myself.

I smiled at Jessie and rose my hand to wave goodbye, she stared at me with her wide blue eyes and returned the gesture before speaking one last time.

"Dream safe..."

Then without warning, a burst of blinding light erupted from behind her, I was blown back on my feet, almost losing my footing. Her body gently drifted back into a bright white void that embraced her like two great hands of light. Her skin lit up so brightly that it was almost unbearable to watch, like staring directly into the sun. Jessie Quaid disappeared within it once and for all, leaving me alone in my old childhood stomping grounds.

I wanted to ponder where she'd gone, and think about my mother, but time was short and it'd have to wait.

For the second time that night, I fumbled for the old car keys in my back-pocket, this time without distraction. The trusty old F-series kicked and rumbled itself to life, and I sat in the driver's seat for a moment contemplating the series of events that'd just unfolded. I recalled what Jessie had said to me.

"You can find anyone you want, your eyes are special..."

Once you learn how to ride a bike, you never really forget, and my hopes for finding Josh were essentially riding on the same principals. A lot of time had passed since I'd overlooked the dreams of another person in the world of sleep, and I was nervous at the prospect of doing it. But I had no choice, the current situation demanded it of me. In order to dream I needed to sleep, but certainly not within my old home. I put the old Ford into reverse and left the old front drive of the house I grew up in, for the final time.

I cruised down the winding roads of Missidnyl and back towards the interstate 84 highway, along the way I saw nobody else, it was just me and the empty streets of my youth. Eventually I made it back onto the interstate, where I was finally met with other late night commuters. I worked the old Ford up to a pleasant cruise, while cracking the window and taking a cigarette from the center console. The knot in my stomach slowly began to loosen, and I gradually relaxed more with each inch that I added between me and the old Quaid house.

Sigmund Freud. The famous neurologist, had his theories on the unconscious mind, and the inner workings of what exactly occurs within the world of dreams. He wrote about 'Wish Fulfillment,' attempts by the unconscious mind to try and resolve a conflict of some nature, whether it was something recent, or something from the past.

I am in no way even close to making psychological theories like a learned neurologist would, at the best of times I even struggle to understand the way my *own* mind works. But through experience, I *have* come to understand the intensity and power that dreams can convey. I've always viewed them as an immaculate painting in motion that depicts the subconscious state of mind, bearing an endless wealth of information and cryptic meaning about the dreamer. But I also view them as a completely private affair, like a hidden diary kept in the secret corners of someone's mind.

The last thing I wanted to do was to reach into Josh's head and stick my face into the pages of *his* secret diary. But times were dire, and my growing concern was this 'old man' reading his diary first.

My thoughts drifted around my brain like a mess of clouds as I drove along the interstate 84 highway. The Columbia River floated by my left side like a great blue serpent, sleeping peacefully underneath the moonlight of the clear night sky. My plan was to head into the town of Endon, a quaint little place located roughly next door to Hood River. Once there, I would find a hotel to briefly unwind, shower, and more importantly, sleep. When I eventually approached the turnoff, a welcome wash of calamity fell over my body, I turned right and off the interstate and down towards Endon.

When I was young, my mother and I would frequently visit the quiet little town of Endon, and just thinking about it made me sigh with a sad nostalgia. My main memory of the place was an early afternoon Saturday, where the last rays of the sun lit up the trees to a shining orange-brown beneath a heavy Grey sky, while a light rain gently showered the wooden houses of the town.

At the time we'd entered Endon in a Ford F-Series, and here I was, countless years later, soon to cruise into Endon in the same fashion. In the way my old car reminded me of her, so did the town of Endon, it felt like a safe decision.

A blur of moonlit pine trees raced passed both my sides as I drove down the turnoff into Endon, they filled the car with a strong, sweet fragrance of nature. It was peaceful, and almost made the earlier events of the night seem like nothing but a disturbing dream I was driving away from.

Old cottage style houses started cropping up on either side of the road, and eventually I came upon a large green sign reading 'Endon.' I had arrived, and it felt good, I had reached my safe haven, a place I could relax and figure out everything which I needed to do. The only thing I needed to do now was to keep my eyes peeled for a hotel.

As I continued making my way down the pine tree road, my intuition suddenly jolted, and a sour feeling began to dilute my calm, my peace of mind quickly jerked itself into an uptight anxiety. My senses sharpened into a mental razor, and knew that something was wrong. Carefully, I brought the Ford down to a slow cruise and braced myself. The old cottage houses continued gliding by either side of the road, but with each house I passed, the more uneasy I found myself. Then in a moment of pure instinct, I stopped the car beside one of the many cottage houses of the pine tree road. There was something different, it felt sinister, and I knew with an almost mystical certainty that it was the source of my sudden anxiety.

I studied the house from the driver's seat window and tried to spot something that stuck out, something that would validate the ominous presence I felt. But nothing was unusual, the house stood as quaint and unassuming as all the others.

Thoughts and logic began to battle my intuition, the rational voice in my head told me to put the car back into drive, proceed with my journey down the pine road, and find a hotel. I was growing more hard pressed for time as the minutes ticked by, I needed to find Josh, and I needed to find him soon.

For a while I sat watching the house with my eyes narrowed, looking out for a sign of any kind, anything that was unusual. But finally, the voice in my head won the battle against my intuition, and I put the old Ford back into drive ready to continue down the pine tree road.

Almost in the exact moment my foot came into contact with the cars accelerator, my peripheral vision picked up movement, and my eyes shot back to the unassuming cottage house. Unlike before, the front door was now ajar, no amount of logic my brain could muster, could convince me to leave now. The battle was reclaimed by my peculiar sense of intuition.

I killed the engine and slowly got out of the car, trying to be as stealthy as I could manage as I made my way up the stone footpath of the front yard while mentally preparing myself for any further sudden movement.

My lungs emptied themselves and my stomach dropped as I halted to an immediate stop. The front door of the house creaked quietly for a split-second just before swinging completely open. Then standing in the doorway, looking no older than the age of five, was a small boy in blue pajamas with a torn and battered plush teddy bear hugged in his arms. His gaze was indirect, his clear little brown eyes seemed to be focusing on nothing at all.

We stood in silence, as the cool breeze of the night carried the scent of pine around us. Though now the smell was unpleasant, it smelt of mold and rot. The air felt colder, it brought goosebumps up all over my body. The boys mouth drooped open slowly, and his eyes suddenly locked focus onto mine. Softly, he began to speak. At first his words were inaudible, like a crackling old radio with the sound turned down almost at mute. But his voice grew louder, and I began to realize he was chanting, and the sound of it was deeply disturbing.

"lupus ad mortem album...
lupus ad mortem album...
lupus ad mortem album."

I had no idea what the boy was saying, but I assumed it wasn't gibberish, just some language I wasn't in any way aware of. My gut also told me it was some kind of omen, but in no way a good one.

After an unsettling stare-down with the chanting boy, his gaze suddenly snapped out of focus and back into a trance, his mouth closed up and his balance started to waver. For a moment I thought he was going to topple over and land face first on the stone pathway, but he steadied himself and remained standing in the doorway like a lifeless little zombie.

I looked back at my car, then back at the boy. I was confused to say the least, but something felt important, as though it was part of the twisted adventure that I'd embarked on ever since setting fire to the old Quaid residence. Hesitantly, I made my way to the young boy's side and stood beside him for a moment, until I worked up the courage to ring the doorbell of the cottage house. The second I pushed the bell, I began preparing myself for the confused and suspicious looks of two parents woken in the middle of the night. After a short while several lights near the door lit up, followed by a rushed patter of footsteps approaching the front door.

An olive tanned woman with long ringlets of auburn hair met with the young boy and I in the doorway. Unrested and haggard she knelt down and picked the boy up and propped him up against her hip. I almost got the idea that it must be a common occurrence for her young son to wander the front drive of her house speaking alien verses of some strange language.

She regarded me with an almost fascinated curiosity while she stood motionless in the doorway, the gentle breeze of the night playing softly with her long ringlets of auburn hair.

"I'm sorry to wake you and everything... I was just driving past your house when I noticed your son was walking around out the front."

Instead of answering right away, the woman stared at me.

After a pause, my discomfort grew to such an extent, that I quickly began to contemplate an immediate mad sprint back to the car—followed by an even madder speeding drive down the pine tree road. But before I had the chance to follow my plan, the woman relaxed, and her laser beam stare faded back down to a mild curiosity.

"My son sleepwalks... You're telling me he was outside of the house...?"

"Yeah, I know it sounds odd, but I just thought I should probably get him inside."

After another uncomfortable silence, the woman's face seemed to relax a little.

"Well, that's the first time he's actually made it all the way outside. Thanks for getting him." She said with a slight smile.

Besides her obvious lack of sleep, and the swollen bags under her eyes, I realized that she was gorgeous.

"Yeah, it's no problem, I'm Steven by the way."

"Olive." She replied.

Before I was about to say my goodbyes and return to the car, her son began to strain his throat, making strange guttural noises. I looked back at Olive worriedly.

"Is he okay...?"

"Don't worry, he's fine. Had a bad infection in his throat when he was born, and the hospital had to operate. He's been mute ever since, he's just saying hello that's all. His names Ryan."

An ice-cold chill ran down the length of my spine.

"Mute...? Pretty sure people who can't talk don't recite weird chants in the early hours of the morning..." I thought to myself.

Lost for words, I gave the most sympathetic smile I could muster.

"Oh, I'm sorry to hear that..."

Olive gave me another one of her slight smiles before rubbing her tired eyes.

"Anyway, sorry I had to wake you. I'd better get moving, nice to meet you Olive." I said as I motioned back towards the car.

"Thanks again Steven." She said before closing the front door behind her.

Once again without company, I stood in the white glow of the moonlight. On my way back to the car, I tried desperately to remember what Ryan had said to me, but unfortunately all I could recall was *'Lupus'*. Oddly Though, there *was* something strangely familiar about it. I felt that no amount of thinking and analyzing would uncover its meaning, but my intuition *did* tell me that at some point, everything would fall into place. I just hoped that it'll end up being something positive.

I got back into the old, rusty ford and took another cigarette from the center console. I sat deep in thought for a while as the thick smoke of the cigarette drifted down the pine tree road with the gentle breeze.

"I'll probably end up with a throat infection of my very own soon if I keep smoking this crap." I thought.

I took one more look over at Olives old cottage house before firing the car back up to continue on my search for a hotel in Endon.

I worked the car back up to speed, the sounds of its old clunking engine rattled noisily along the pine tree road. For a few minutes I was paranoid, and half-expected to fall back into anxiety. But luckily I didn't, it was just me and the town of Endon, reunited for the first time since childhood.

Finally, a bright neon sign reading 'Endon Lodge Hotel' appeared out from behind one of the pines, I turned into the small parking lot out front. The hotel was of the same style and consistency of the cottage houses. It was old, worn and charmingly rustic, nestled between a shroud of tall oak and willow trees. Thankfully, it felt safe. Soon I'd be sound asleep, searching for my oldest friend in the mystical ocean of dreams.

I grabbed my duffel bag from the back seat and approached the front door of the hotel, large dried oak leaves crunched underfoot.

'I hope I know what I'm doing...'

The hotels front doors loudly creaked open, and the soft glow of lamplight spilled outside. As I walked in, the receptionist lazily looked up and smiled with glassy eyes as he yawned and waved a hand. He was an elderly man who almost looked to be a hundred, he had a ragged crown of perfectly white hair that sat high on his head.

"How's it going? Any rooms good to go?"

His smile widened as he slowly shrugged.

'Every room is available..." The old man replied in an aged, crackling voice.

He leaned over and threw me a large green key from the rack to his left, then slumped back down on his desk, dozing off as quickly as he'd woken.

"Alright... Thanks."

The situation was a weird one, but there was no knot in my stomach and no sour feeling about it. Thankfully I still felt as safe and hidden as I did moments ago. I suppose sometimes, things are just strange.

The large green key read 41. I looked back over towards the old man, expecting some kind of instruction to find my room, or at least to be told the general direction I needed to head, but he continued to lie dozing on his desk, with his forehead rested on the back of his wrinkled hands.

"Ah well... He's old, and it's pretty damn late I guess." I thought to myself.

I walked down the corridor to the right of the reception table, counting along with the numbers on the rooms.

"1... 3... 5... 7..."

Eventually I came to a corner along the corridor, and took a left turn to follow the square shape of the hotel. In the middle of the hotel outside was a large courtyard filled with a mess of colorful flowers surrounding intricate little concrete pathways, all leading to a large round wooden table in the center.

"23... 25... 27... 29..."

Again, I came to another corner in the hotels corridors and continued left on my search for suite 41.

"33... 35... 37... 39..."

Then on the far dead end of the corridor, sat a green door reading the numbers '41' in bright gold. I looked back down at my room key confused.

"Why is only my door green...?"

The general theme of the entire hotel was composed of different shades of Grey. Every door was Grey, the floors were Grey, even the lamps the sat at each corner seemed only to emit shades of Grey. But here was my door, a brilliant shade of forest green and gold. Before sticking the key into the big golden keyhole I listened closely to my feelings. Fortunately, nothing negative rose to mind, no knot in my stomach, and no sour feeling.

I approached the door, stuck the green key into the keyhole, turned my wrist, and warily stepped through.

After fumbling around for the light switch, the room lit up brightly. The moment that my eyes adjusted, my mouth dropped open in awe. The room was luxurious, it had the kind of elegance that I'd imagine appropriate for the wealthiest people the world had to offer. The walls and carpet were a deep ruby color, while the enormous bed in the center of the room was covered in sparkling gold linen. A steaming hot tub sat in the corner of the suite next to a tall set of double doors that led directly out into the hotels courtyard.

In a profoundly strange way, it all felt strongly familiar. Being struck with Deja-vu, I felt like I'd returned to a place that I'd visited long ago. But also in true Deja-vu fashion, the sensation felt more like a distant dream than a reality.

To the right sat the door to the bathroom, taking a long shower was my first priority—I smelt like a mixture of charcoal, cigarettes and sweat, not the most appealing fragrance.

The bathroom was decorated in the same fashion as the bedroom, full of shining gold and deep ruby. It was like something from the Elizabethan era, as if it was directly pulled out from the 1500's and slotted in by some sort of interior decorating time traveler with incredibly expensive taste.

I thought about the old receptionist and the way he'd just thrown me the hotel room key without giving it a second thought. Surely he *must* have made a mistake, I could imagine him at any minute springing awake to the realization that he'd made an error, then rushing down the corridors to find me in hopes of placing me in a down-graded suite.

"Might as well make the most of it..." I thought.

I ran the shower, started to undress as I caught my reflection in the mirror. I looked truly awful, like I'd aged a decade in a day. My light brown hair hung around my shoulders like thick sweaty locks, and the bags under my eyes were big, purple and puffy.

The steam from the showers started to fog up the mirror, and I stood for a moment watching my reflection slowly fade into a blurry silhouette. As I stood and watched myself fade away, the thought of the little boy Ryan crept into my thoughts. The boy was a mute, but he had certainly told *me* something. Even without the slightest fragment of intuition, anyone would assume that what he'd said wasn't good news. I was almost certain that someone was coming for me, and the thought of who it might be gave me an ice-cold shiver down my spine.

The shower was incredible, I felt my bones draw heat from the hot water, while dark dirtied water ran from my feet to the drain-hole. In the way a clean desk makes efficient work, I felt a clean body granted a clear mind. I rested my head against the shower door and tried to rid my head of all thoughts, the task ahead of me needed an empty canvas.

After probably a good twenty minutes, I turned off the water and dried myself, even the towels felt like they had a thousand thread count. I stepped into a clean pair of underwear that I'd kept in my duffel bag and walked back out into the bedroom heading for the bed.

Though the moment my eyes looked into the bedroom, my meditative state was snapped back to full alert and my heart skipped a beat. The large Doors that led to the courtyard stood wide open, and a moonlit silhouette of someone sat at the table in the center of the courtyard.

My eyes darted around the room madly for a moment as I tried desperately to conduct a plan. But before I had any chance to react, the figure in the moonlit courtyard spoke. His booming voice carried the weight of a sledge-hammer—freezing me solid.

"Come and sit down."

Instead of replying, I continued standing frozen in shock, still dripping with water from the shower while wearing nothing but my underwear.

"It's safe, come and sit down."

Motion returned, and as though my body was on auto-pilot, I slowly approached the doors to the courtyard.

"I have protected this place. I assure you, the eyes of Coda will not find you."

I stared at the strange silhouette in the courtyard, confused and lost for words.

"I sit here, as a sane man. Once upon a time I was driven into complete madness, and I am simply what's left... The last shred of sanity.... I have a gift for you, but I must apologize as it truly is an utterly terrible gift..."

In the middle of the courtyards table sat a crown that shone reflectively in the moonlight. Much like the theme and decor of room 41, it looked to be golden, with a large ruby sitting in its crest. For whatever irrational reason, the sight of it completely repulsed me, it's very presence was horrifying. The mysterious man had told me it was a gift, but the thought of actually owning such a thing was the most frightening part of all. When I got closer, I noticed that the strange man's face resembled the same blurry, rubbed out quality that Jessie's had earlier.

I looked up towards the stars in the night sky, and for a second almost began to laugh. Things were getting more ridiculous by the minute. It started with a ghost girl and a burning house, then a strange, chanting mute-boy, followed by an insanely high-class hotel room with a sleepy old receptionist throwing out giant green room keys. Now here I was, about to converse with a ghost in my underwear while a horrible golden crown sat on the table between us.

As I looked into the sky, an overwhelming sensation violently swept through my body. It was a feeling I hadn't felt in a while, and it caught me off-guard, striking me like a mental sword. My craving for opiates rose to the surface of my mind like a giant toxic bubble rising through water. The weight of it instantly threw any idea of laughter straight out of my head. Though along with my cravings, the image of my mother also came to mind. Her weakened, defeated body, laying hopelessly on her hospital bed. Tears began to well behind my eyes, and I instinctively clutched at my head in desperation. I felt like all of my emotions, in all their forms were on the verge of a grand explosion.

The mysterious ghost took a large piece of fabric from his lap and threw it over the crown, while looking up at me worriedly. Thankfully, my emotions slowly began to calm. The white-hot mess of thoughts in my head started to untangle, I looked at the ghost—wide-eyed and shocked.

"What in the hell was all that...? There's no way I'm taking that thing, I hate it."

"As do I. It bears nothing but madness, it has a tendency to split a man's mind into nothing but a butchered mess... But believe it or not, it was once nothing like it is now..."

The ghost shifted uncomfortably in his chair, then considered the crown sitting beneath the fabric for a while, he swallowed hard and continued in a pained voice.

"I once wore this crown proudly, a *very long* time ago. It was made for me, crafted for a purpose that I was chosen to carry out. But unfortunately I was driven to insanity, it broke me like I was nothing but a twig... I sit here as a sane fragment of what I eventually became, while the rest of me sits within this wretched crown."

I stared at the ghost blankly, trying desperately to connect the dots and make some kind of sense out of what he was saying. I was getting frustrated, everything was getting more complicated by the second.

"I don't have any idea what you're saying or what's happening, and why am I in the middle of this? It's insane. I'm not taking this crown."

The ghost's eyes burned red-hot and fierce beneath his blurred out face, and unfortunately his intimidation worked on me. This man had abilities that I surely didn't, and the simple fact was that he'd most likely kill me if I was to refuse his gift. My stomach dropped and my knees grew weak.

"The person who made this crown, was once an incredible man. His spirit was the first within the realm of Coda to be born pure of heart. He was my master, and I failed him. Then in turn, he failed his own master. He faced punishment, and now lives as impure as any other spirit you'd find in Coda."

I looked down at the crown beneath the piece of fabric, then back towards the ghost again.

"Almost everyone is capable of redemption Steven, I have been searching for it for over five hundred years. Even if my search was to become *ten* thousand tears... It would not end... I *crave* my humanity, I miss it with the greatest wealth of grief. And I know, with an intuition much like yours, that my master, or the erased man as you've aptly named him, craves redemption in the same way that I do."

"Well... There it is..." I thought to myself while sighing deeply.

"But why give me the crown...?"

"It is safest with you, and at some point I am certain that it will help you. You're going to have to trust me, because otherwise we'll both end up destroyed."

"Well that's great..." I thought to myself.

"Go and find your friend, I'm sure you understand now that time is limited."

"Just one more thing though." I said curiously.

"Who is this 'old man...?'"

The ghost stared deeply into the cloth covered crown with a scrunched up face, it unnerved me as I couldn't determine whether it was disgust on his face, or fear.

"He is a highly intelligent man, and dangerously capable. But at a price, he is also a man with an endless depth of foolishness. He wants everything, and I mean everything..."

I decided not to press him for more, I was tired, and the last thing I wanted to feel was more fear. I made my way back into the hotel room, leaving the ghost alone in the moonlit courtyard. My thoughts flew around my head like a storm. This whole situation was a complete mess, and I felt the first waves of regret wash over me as I sat on the edge of the enormous golden bed. I feared to suffer the same fate that Jessie had faced, how long would it be before I would be walking the roads of the night chanting verses of some crazy language? I didn't want to think about it.

I focused on Josh, and thought about any memory I could manage to conjure up as I tried to regain my meditative state. In a way, besides the dark circumstances, I was excited to see him. I wondered what he was like now, where he'd been over all these years. I guess it was time to know, especially considering that either way I was going to have to.

I laid on the bed facing the ceiling, with my arms straightened along my sides as I attempted to wipe all of the background noise out of my head. It was difficult, thoughts of Olive kept cropping up into the front of my thoughts. The idea of her and her Emerald green nightgown tightly hugging her figure, showing the curves of her body. I sat up for a moment and shook my head, as if to throw the thoughts and white noise out from my ears.

"Focus... Focus..."

I laid back down and once again closed my eyes, summoning memories of my early memories with Josh. I thought of how I would see him after school, and how we'd play in his old bedroom. I pictured the imagery in my head like it was a roll of film playing behind my eyelids. Simultaneously, I imagined a second roll of film overhanging the first one depicting the early years of Josh and I.

I persisted, and waited for the second roll of film to start. A surge of frustration flared in my stomach. I was growing more impatient as the minutes ticked by, and my focus began to waver, but I resisted the urge to give up.

Then, like a hidden cog resting in the front of my head, I felt something start turning. A red light sparked, and washed over the second roll of film.

"There it is..."

I kept my body as still as possible and after a while began to feel my muscles fall into a deep sleep. Everything was instinct now, I let the red light of the second roll of film wash completely over me, my mind was sucked into it like it was a vacuum. For a short while, my vision flew and blurred around me, surrounded by a dazzling display of deep red. Eventually, my eyes began to adjust, along with my body, and I stared out through the endless red void.

"Time to find Josh."

When I was young, the red void would commonly be the main catalyst for the most disturbing nightmares I'd had.
Not knowing what it was, or why it made me feel the way it did, caused me to fear and hater it. Luckily, my mother was understanding when I told her about it, she taught me how to avoid it, and even how to utilize it.

Since those early times, there had only ever been one other occasion I'd used the red void willingly, and it hadn't gone well. I almost completely lost myself in it, my biggest concern right now was that happening again.

I swam in an endless red ocean, with shadows and blurred shapes floating around me like ink in water. They were dreams, and at any moment I could swim over to one and feel the weight of someone's subconscious, bearing the dark secrets that sat within its depths. But none of them were my business, nor would they ever be. I kept the thought of Josh prominent, and felt a pulling motion like I were a magnet. Somewhere in the red void, he was floating the same as all others, and I was on track.

I ducked and weaved accordingly, while making sure not to lose the pull that was directing me. My mother had taught me everything that I'd ever need to know when it came to navigating the red void, though it had always come natural anyway. Far in the distance, I noticed a shape that wasn't quite like the others. it *looked* identical to all the others, and it *moved* the same as all the others, but my intuition spoke up and told me otherwise. It was Josh, without question. I locked my sight him and picked up my pace, the blurry shadows flew past both sides of my peripheral vision, just like the trees of Endon's the pine tree road. I slowly closed in on the target and braced myself to feel the weight of Josh's subconscious.

"Here we go..."

It hit me hard, I was sucked under a turbulent tide that crashed at me with an incredible force. Strong emotions and dark thoughts thrashed me about like a kite broken from its string. I could never fully explain the way it feels in the event of being overcome by someone's subconscious, it's an overwhelming sensation that seizes the heart with iron fingers. All that mattered was that within milliseconds, I knew that Josh was living in New York City. Though unfortunately, he was far closer to danger than I was. I could never receive an entire detailed biography from someone's subconscious, in fact it usually didn't grant much at all. Thankfully though, I had learned exactly what I'd needed to know.

CHAPTER 4-

'Nostalgia,' by definition, is considered to be a sentimental longing or wistful affection for a period in the past. Josh Quaid spent very little time longing for the past, to him the past was a bleak road littered with fear and confusion. It wasn't often at all that he'd reminisce about anything before he'd turned his back and ran from those dark times. According to Josh, the greatest decision he'd ever made was to get as far away from Portland as possible. But there were rare moments when he'd remember little pieces of memories that showed him the unbroken home he'd lived in before things went bad. His Uncle had taken in him and his little sister after his parents had gone off the rails. Josh didn't know the full story of his parents, and he didn't really have any interest in ever knowing. As Josh would commonly put it, *'the past is past, who cares...?'*

These days he lived in a small one-bedroom apartment right in the heart and center of New York city, throughout the day the people of his neighborhood would cram themselves into their means of transport like an ever-flowing school of suited up fish. Life around him was always busy, and so long as he was surrounded by a busy atmosphere, the flow of thoughts in his head would also remain busy, and it suited Josh perfectly.

In recent years gone by, Josh had worked several short-lived jobs. There was the four-month stint at a local gas station, then for about half a year he worked at an ice-cream parlor, and then there was the bookstore. The bookstore was a disturbing memory that stuck out like a thorn. Josh knew a thing or two about literature, and as with most things, he was content with his limited knowledge on certain subjects. But what didn't sit well was when Jeremy Harmond (owner of Harmond's bookshop and subsequent employer of Joshua Quaid), pointed out his limited knowledge on the said subject.

It could have been the rain-soaked shirt sticking to his back, or the single fingernail on his left hand he'd forgotten to clip the previous night, but Josh was irritated, his mood was on the sour side of the spectrum that morning - steadily declining with each pulse of blood that ran through his angry head.

"Just one more thing Jeremy... Just one more goddamn thing..."

Jeremy's tortoise shell glasses sat low on his wrinkled nose beneath his two beady little blue eyes, one of his eyebrows raised slightly more than the other. Josh could feel his judgmental eyes piercing into the side of his head, h could hear the quiet and steady rasp of Jeremy's breath. He was at the end of the tether, ready to explode at the drop of a hat. Then, Jeremy opened his mouth and began to speak.

Things went dark for a while at that point, Josh remembers losing control of himself in a fit of animalistic rage. The way his fists felt like rolling pins against a clump of dough...

"This is what you get... This is what happens..."

Things got tricky for a while after that. There weren't many times that Josh was pressured to call upon connections and resources from his past, but this was one of those moments. From time to time Josh would seek the help of Hans Varlyn, he and Josh shared an interesting relationship that rooted back to his early years in Portland. They'd first met during the bad times, at a time when his Uncle was going off the rails not dissimilar to his 'good-for-nothing' parents.

"Have another Bottle your pathetic booze-hound, it's the only thing you seem to do properly around here..." Josh remembered saying towards the end. Though this wasn't entirely true, because as of his later years Uncle Quaid had become quite an avid painter, but this was all thanks to Hans. Hans taught him the fine art of the brush and the necessary patience and discipline that came along with it. But as each day passed, Uncle Quad's steady hand was slowly lost at the bottom of an empty bottle of straight whiskey, until he passed almost every hour at a chair beside the window, staring out at the streets with his blood red, glassy eyes.

Hans had also taught Josh to paint, and to Uncle Quaid's displeasure, Josh had formidable talent from the very beginning. He quickly adapted to the artistic medium and demonstrated an impressive natural ability to work the brush with the concentrated hands of a surgeon. He loved it, Josh would feel a sense of elation, a passionate buzz that would grant him a warm sense of achievement. He took great pride in his art, and would more than anything crave the peaceful meditation that it offered. It'd help Josh forget about everything awful, even if it was just for a little while.

During the worst week of Josh's life, his younger sister Jessie, was stricken and tragically met her end due to a strange and mysterious virus. Josh can remember overhearing a nurse comment to his Uncle.

"It's almost as though the life is getting sucked right out of her, but I assure you that we're doing everything we can manage".

Unfortunately, nothing had worked, Jessie died, and had that nurse promised her survival, it would have been a promise badly broken. Josh was never the same after those times, he struggled to think back to a time where sleep came natural. He'd sometimes dream of Jessie, and the early times that he'd shared with her. But the dreams would always darken, the mood would change to a terrifying scene involving being chased by someone, or something—darting and weaving hopelessly through the broken and cluttered confines of his old Portland house, only to grow too afraid and paralyzed with dread to help Jessie after all. *Curled up into a little ball...*

Josh would wake covered in sweat, flailing his arms about, desperately trying to fight his way back to the world of reality.

He would have other dreams too, mostly just snippets of fuzzy imagery like a grainy VHS tape, not really seeming to convey any kind of message at all. They were usually about girls, and women of his past that he'd never had the courage to approach. In fact, because of his past, Josh had always had trouble approaching anybody. His life was lonely, like a wounded Wolf limping about, never seeming to find a pack of its own to run with. But despite his isolation, he would soon be running with a fellow Wolf with a limp, because a very old friend of his was searching for him, someone who hadn't crossed his mind for a very long time.

As of recent times, every day in Josh's life seemed to rattle along and then just fade into the next. Mostly, things would always play out in the same old monotonous way. But then on one particular morning Josh woke suddenly, and within seconds determined that something definitely didn't feel right. His eyes slowly adjusted to his small, dainty bedroom while he waited for the odd feeling he'd woken with to settle. But it wouldn't.

Even his bedroom seemed off, as if someone had broken in during the night, and sabotaged everything to be slightly askew. Leaning over, Josh clicked the kettle that sat within reach of his bed before grabbing the jar of coffee that sat next to it. There were old, unwashed dishes scattered across the bedroom floor, most of them covered surrounded by ants. Looking around half-asleep, he grabbed what he guessed was the most recent coffee mug. The kettle clicked while Josh poured a more than ample amount of coffee into his dirty mug, followed by a shot glass worth of boiling water. He took a cigarette from the packet on the bedside dresser and walked naked over towards his one and only small bedroom window.

Rain was falling hard, and the weather was unusually violent. Aside from Josh and his bedroom, it seemed the entire city of New York was off today. It was as though the weather was his own personal mood ring, reflecting the harsh tumbling emotions that were bashing around in his head.

"What in the hell was I dreaming about...?"

The odd feeling wasn't leaving, if anything it was getting worse. Josh sensed that he was only a hair away from discovering what was causing it.

"Think... C'mon Josh think..."

The rain continued to crash into the outside of the window, filling the room with a speck, Grey overtone. The sound of distant car horns blared from the busy roads of New York. Josh placed his hand on the window and felt the freezing cold temperature of the day travel up his arm.

Then Josh twitched, *something* about his hand caught him off-guard. He examined it closely, then closed his eyes in deep thought.

"Something about a hand...? Or, something about my hand...?"

Just before he gave up, letting the memory of his dream recede back into his brains trashcan, a disturbing visual image rushed back without warning. The sensation shocked Josh so much that his coffee slipped from his grasp, smashing into a glassy mess beneath him. It was an image of translucent hand, forcing its way into Josh head and digging around like a shovel. Josh shuddered hard, it was an awful visual. Most horrible though, it didn't feel like it was a dream at all. Even though Josh was naked as the day he was born, the idea of some weird hand digging around inside his head brought on feelings of a *true* nakedness. He felt exposed, and rendered to a state of complete and utter vulnerability.

Momentarily, Josh staggered back across the room, the effects of vodka were still hanging around, throwing his sense of balance off. The sound of glass and cutlery clinked, and Josh began to feel too cramped to move. Everything about the room seemed so much smaller now.

"I have to leave, screw this place..."

Dishes were strewn everywhere on his apartment floor, but more than anything were the empty bottles of straight alcohol. Every night Josh would drink himself into a state of complete drunkenness, but no matter what, he could never block out the bad thoughts that stirred around his head. There was always a level of consciousness that remained, and that shred of consciousness was always deeply fearful, when he was in those drunken states—his fear wanted out. Josh would fix his eyes on the dim light-source of the window and prey for his sobriety to return--and prey to feel in control again.

'This is the last time... This is it...'

Then when sobriety did eventually return, he'd quickly realize why he'd left in the first place. It was Josh's vicious cycle, his dark and dangerous ritual. It was a like slow-burning self-destruction.

The inheritance he'd received from his parents was a big one, though no doubt dinted heavily due to the copious amounts of alcohol he'd bought over the years. In a way, Josh was a slave to his inheritance, utterly under its spell. It was a large sum of money that hung over his head like an enormous swollen raincloud.

Clothes littered the floor just like all the other mess, the apartment was an unhygienic disaster and so was Josh. But on this morning, Josh felt particularly unclean. Not from the smell of old sweat that hung around, or his long oily mop of blond hair that fell around his head, it was the sense of violation that the dream had conveyed.

Josh shivered as he tried to gather the cleanest set of clothes he could find. It was time to leave and find somewhere better to live. His half-baked plan was to board a train, clear his mind, and wait until it felt right to get off. Wherever that place was, would be his new home, and it would certainly be better than this.

After throwing on some old clothes and finishing his coffee, Josh packed a small suitcase full of all the alcohol he could find, some more dirty clothes and his wallet. Anything he'd need could be bought, and chances were that aside from food, he probably wouldn't need anything else. Josh looked around the apartment he'd been living in for the past couple of years for the final time, it was like seeing an accurate visual image of Josh's own mind. A clean environment that inevitably relapses into a complete clattering mess.

Get frustrated, move away, get frustrated, move away. Etc... Etc... Rinse and repeat.

But time around, things would be different. For one, he would finally kick his alcohol habit. Secondly, he'd fulfill his dream of being a famous painter. It was all waiting for him in the next location--*the final location*. It was time to leave this mess behind him, and start life again with a fresh head space. Like the early bird workers of the morning, Josh rushed his way through the apartment complex with a busy determination. With his suitcase tucked under his arm he quickly descended the flights of stairs on the way down to the street.

Outside, the rain pelted down from the heavy Grey sky above, and Josh welcomed it. He let the water cleanse him, and run down the length of his body. Like nature's own shower, he let it purify the darkness he'd felt since waking that morning.

CHAPTER 5-

Morning had arrived. I sat drinking a cup of coffee on the edge of the hotel bed rubbing my muscles, feeling as though I'd only slept half an hour. It was like my body had rested, but my mind hadn't at all.

My journey through the red void had been intense, and my brush with Josh had almost totaled me—like an insane roller coaster without a harness. His suffering had hit me hard, and the depressive cloud that swarmed in his head had stung me like a giant wasp. It wasn't as if he was out of his mind, crazy or anything, but he *had* unfortunately become a delusional person. I felt pity for him, and wished he didn't feel the way that he did, but there's nothing I could do, or at least until I found him in New York that was.

The morning began to unfold in the exact manner that I had predicted, ridiculously. The first thing I'd noticed was that there was in fact *no* courtyard that sat in the center of the hotel. The large set of double doors that'd led outside was now nothing more than another wall within my hotel suite. Secondly, and worst of all, the conversation that I'd had with the courtyard ghost had certainly been real. The proof was the terrible gift that sat wrapped in cloth beside my belongings. I didn't want to have anything to do with that damn crown, but I had the idea that it wasn't my decision to make.

I sipped the rest of my coffee and grabbed some clothes from my duffel bag, a black t-shirt and a pair of jeans. Same as yesterday. As I got dressed, I tried to think back to a time when I'd worn a different outfit, but couldn't remember for the life of me. Mid-thought, the cloth covered crown caught my eye, I stared at it pensively.

"What if I just leave it here…? Maybe this whole thing is just a lie…"

I approached the crown and thought about it harder, my gut told me that to leave it behind would be disastrous.

"Damn it."

Like quickly ripping off a band-aid, I picked it up and threw it into my duffel bag in one fast motion. I hated everything about it. Aside from fearing the crown itself, my true fear was the thought of someone actually *wanting* it. If the old man did somehow manage to get it from me... I shivered at the thought.

"Time to go..."

In the hallway, I noticed there were no windows to the right revealing a courtyard, just more hotel rooms. I looked down the length of the hallway to the corner at the end. Something else was different, but I couldn't place it.

A sensation of vertigo suddenly struck me, and it seemed like the floor was tilting me forward, tipping me over. For a moment I just stood off balance and confused, then just before I could collect my thoughts, things got really bizarre.

An invisible force thrusted me forward, throwing me into an all-out sprint. My feet pumped along like pistons in an engine as the hotel doors flew past me down the corridor. I looked down, and immediately started to panic. The floor had indeed begun to tilt, the entire hotel was warping and shifting into some kind of crazy downhill deathtrap—leading me down towards the corner at the end of the hallway like a bullet.

My feet managed to tangle themselves underneath me. Then screaming, I buckled down-wards and was sent rolling violently along the distorted corridor--bashing against the walls and the floor like a human pinball. My eyesight was blurred, failing to lock onto anything, my limbs slammed hard against the floor with each tumbling motion.

My last shred of rational thought finally kicked in, and I instinctively drew my knees against my chest, holding myself tightly. I was heading for the end of the hall, and the last thing I wanted was broken bones. I felt my body crash into the wall, and my bowling ball grip gave out. I shut my eyes as tight as possible, waiting for searing agony to overcome me as I sprawled around helplessly. Curiously, pain didn't come, but what did come what did come was far worse.

When I slowly opened my eyes, I saw nothing--literally nothing. I'd crashed through the wall and into some kind of black space, I span and tumbled around with the same speed I'd had in the hallway. In the red void, I had the ability to maneuver myself around like in a swimming pool. Unfortunately, though, within this black void all I could do was fall aimlessly.

I'd seen plenty of sci-fi movies about space before, and in some of them astronauts were occasionally thrust out of the ships airlocks; and doomed to float along the great vacuum of space alone, while maintaining original inertia. Maybe I had somehow suffered the same fate, doomed to fall helplessly through dead space but without an astronaut suit.

A dreadful fear gripped me, and it grew with every spinning motion.

"Help...! Someone...!" I screamed desperately.

"What the hell is this...?"

I craned my head in all directions, trying to spot something, any sort of exit I could writhe around towards. But all I could see was more black space, an endless vacuum of nothing. My heart was beating out of my chest.

"Please...!! Help.!"

...I closed my eyes and tried to calm myself.

"No use in panicking... There has to be a way..."

I thought hard, trying to come up with a plan.

If I was thrown inside this place, surely I must be able to somehow climb back out of it.

Then, an idea came to me.

"If there's nowhere to go within this black void... Maybe I'll try my luck in the red one..."

I didn't know if it was even possible to get there under these circumstances, but the only option I had was to try.

CHAPTER 6-

The old man stared at the great pile of wreckage.

The Endon hotel had been reduced to nothing but a large pile of twisted, broken debris. This made him happy, he smiled with satisfaction while slowly nodding his head. The erased man on his side, standing tall and still. His blurred face staring expressionless at what he'd done.

"The boy is gone then?"

The erased man replied in his ancient, rasping voice that sat almost two octaves below someone's usual tone of voice.

"He is nowhere."

"Good, and everyone in this town will remember what?"

The erased man turned his head towards the old man, maintaining his expressionless glare--as if he'd taken offense to the question. The old man looked away.

"Right, good then."

The old man approached the wreckage, studying and assessing it with his eyes. His *special eyes*. He'd be long dead before someone else; especially some little prick kid, was going to share the same eyes as him. But fortunately, the boy had suffered a fate worse than death, now it was just the old man. The way it *should* be, his smile widened as he thought about the future. There were good times ahead indeed, and *he* would be the one to bring these good times to fruition. Who else had the talent and ability to juggle the power he would soon obtain...? Nobody...

Though a time would come, he thought, when the erased man would need to be dealt with. He'd need to be put down like the rabid pet he was. Ultimately, there could only be one throne. And the old man wasn't exactly the type who enjoyed sharing. He looked back towards the erased man for a moment and considered the damage that he'd brought upon the hotel.

He hated the erased man for what he was. Not due to the horribly immoral acts he'd committed, but because of the raw power that he possessed. He was undeserving, *unworthy*.

The old man's thoughts returned to Steven. He wondered how much the boy had known, he wondered if he'd even realized what he'd destroyed along with the Quaid house. The little girls spirit was an absolute gem, her sacrifice had granted the old man at least another ten years. Then this little prick had come along and wrecked it, he'd destroyed a magnificent portal that had taken years upon years too perfect.

But then again, none of this mattered. Because soon enough he would be walking through the realm of coda himself. First he would find and restore the crown, then assume his position as the one and only true king of coda. His power would know no bounds.

"Good times ahead..."

The old man took off his glasses and wiped them with the cotton of his shirt. As special as his eyes were they still didn't manage to grant him 20/20 vision, even still he was anything but powerless. His most dangerous asset stood tall beside him, staring deeply at his master. Their relationship didn't have one shred of trust, the old man simply possessed the ability to summon him-- and that was the one and only reason he did his bidding. It was the natural law of coda.

Amongst the wreckage of the hotel, a white tuft of hair jutted out from between to sheets of wood. The hair was attached to a badly wounded old man desperately trying to find a last ounce of strength to pry himself out of his wooden grave. His legs were surely broken, and he wasn't even certain if his arms were connected to his torso anymore. The only act he could find the strength for was to yell. The old man heard his muffled cry and spotted his crown of white hair in the debris.

"So the hero lives!" He proclaimed as he wandered towards the beaten body of the Endon hotels elderly receptionist.

"You sir have played a very crucial role here! Your sweet old eyes saw someone that we very much needed to see. And as a result, we found him!"

The receptionist moaned in agony as the old man continued his speech while stepping onto one of the wooden sheets.

"Do not worry though my friend, rest assured with the knowledge that you have been a very important stepping stone for me."

Despite the blinding agony the old receptionist felt, he still had enough lucidity to realize the lunacy in what he was hearing. 'That boy,' he thought, must be the person he was referring to.

And what kind of trouble could he have possibly gotten himself into to bring forth the destruction of an entire hotel?

"You see, I have a calling... Quite a grand calling it is too. I am the man destined to wear the crown of coda and sit high upon the throne."

The wooden board underfoot continued to pin against the receptionist, and the pain grew unbearable. He prepared to exert one last ounce of strength, he gathered as much energy as possible and spoke what would be his very last word. Though it was in a tone of defeat, muffled by broken debris.

"Help..."

The old man tilted his head down and regarded the man with the white crown of hair.

"Hmm... I am truly sorry my friend but time is of the essence. I'm afraid I must be on my way. Besides, I am just an elderly man, much like yourself. I doubt I'd be much help in lifting those wooden boards, you see I don't quite harbor the strength that I used to."

The old man stepped off from the debris and headed back towards his associate, still wearing a sick smile proudly on his wrinkled face.

"Much to do. Say goodbye to Endon." He said as he passed the erased man on his way towards the parking lot.

By natural law, the erased man was under obligation to show obedience to the old man. However, that didn't mean he had to share everything with him. The elderly man with the white crown of hair most likely *had* seen the boy when he'd checked in, but that wasn't what'd given up his location. It was something else, something that'd taken place not a ten-minute drive away.

There was an old chant, that the erased man hadn't heard for an age, and someone nearby had recited it. He himself had recited it, long ago during his darkest days that'd followed his final punishment. He hadn't felt a scrap of intuition since his heart was pure, but for whatever strange reason--he felt it about this. It was like a tiny fragment of his long-lost humanity. He clung to it desperately.

CHAPTER 7-

I awoke dazed out of my mind on a cold patch of wet grass, with mud smeared all over my aching body. Before I even knew where I was or what'd happened, my first move was ripping the wretched crown from my head, then throwing it away from me. I felt like I'd woken with the most unforgiving hangover of all time, a razor-sharp ache was erupting all throughout my head. The first sign of good news was that I was no longer in the midst of an endless black void, I had managed to escape. No matter how badly my head throbbed, or how cold and wet I was. The current situation was much, much better than a floating pitch black prison.

The second good sign of news was that the effects of the crown were subsiding. Slowly, but surely. I had indeed made it into the red void, and were it not for the horrid crown--I doubt it would've been possible. For the majority of my twisting, agonizing and ungraceful escape I would have easily welcomed death. One more moment wearing that crown would've pushed me over the edge. It had allowed me to travel into the ocean of dreams while being in a completely lucid state.

I sat up in the grass and felt the blaring sunlight hitting my eyelids, the sky was bright, but the air was bitterly cold.

"Where in the hell did that thing take me...?"

I sat for a while rubbing my temples, trying to ease the throbbing pain in my head. I thought back to the morning in the hotel, something obviously went incredibly wrong. But what? Had someone consciously thrown me into that void? It couldn't be the old man or the erased man surely... That ghost had assured me that I was safe.

"But why trust him?"

"What reason would he have to lie?"

"There's probably a whole bunch of stuff you don't understand..."

"What do you mean...? What things?"

"How should I know? Answer your own questions."

"Okay... Whatever..."

"You should probably open your eyes, your acting like a

crazy person."

My eyes shot open and my chest tightened. There had undoubtedly been times in my life when I'd spoken to myself, and I'd never thought of it to be an uncommon thing. But there was something so *real* about what'd just happened, it truly was as though I was two different people, like I'd been split in two.

I looked around suspiciously, surveying the scenery.

"Where the hell am I...?"

"You aren't from 'round here are you Steven?"

This time, I shot to my feet in a panic. There was no question I'd heard a perfectly audible voice in my head. Maybe I was finally losing my mind...

My eyes continued darting around the area, a huge cluster of tall trees stood in front of me. I was outside of a forest, and by the looks of it, it was enormous. I didn't have a particularly good grasp on plants and agriculture, but I knew enough to realize that I wasn't seeing any normal trees. Wherever I was, it seemed more like a completely different planet than Earth.

I was standing on the summit of a steep incline, where a cliff of grass rolled all the way down to the bank of a horribly murky ocean of crimson red water.

"Am I dreaming...? Surely I'm dreaming this."

I watched waves of red liquid gently roll into the shoreline, mesmerized by the sight of it. An ice-cold thought rose to the surface of my mind: Was it blood....? Could it be...? No... There couldn't even be enough people in the world to fill an ocean of that size. Either way, the thought of it made my stomach turn.

"What is this place...? Hell...? Did that crown bring me to hell...?"

"I saved you ya know."

I turned back to the dense mess of alien trees and watched carefully. Someone had spoken to me, and this time it was *outside* of my thoughts. The trees were almost the height of skyscrapers. The foliage at the treetops were colored with deep yellow and purple tones. Their trunks were virtually covered in a flowered kind of moss, out of it sprouting hundreds of little rainbow colored petals.

Suddenly, my eyes caught movement. Subtle movement, but movement nonetheless.

"Ha! Yup! Now you see me huh?"

A small boy slowly started descending down one of the great skyscraper trees. In a bear-hug lock, he wriggled down with one fluid movement at a time. All the while he stared directly at me with a great smile that stretched across his little face. Towards the base of the tree he hopped off and made his way towards me.

"I saved you ya know?" He repeated.

All I could do was stare back at him, stunned and motionless. What in the world was going on? I thought yesterday was weird, but it literally *paled* in comparison to what was happening now...

"I saw ya washin' 'round in shores of the dream sea so I decided to help ya... So, I guess you owe me huh?"

'The dream sea...? could it be the red void?' I wondered.

Without warning, the little boy's eyes shut closed. The skin on his forehead ripped open, revealing a little red eye that darted around crazily, moving around wildly in all directions. Despite the constant barrage of strange experiences my life had so far exposed me to, this one especially shocked me. The sight of it blew the air out of my lungs and I staggered back almost falling to the ground ass-first.

"What in the world was that.?" I asked.

The skin on the little boy's forehead folded back over and he re-opened his eyes. Instead of answering he just continued to stare at me laughing. But it wasn't maniacal or evil laughter, it was the laughter of a fun-loving child. Though somehow, it was far more unsettling that way.

"My name's Pito, the most dangerous spirit in the universe!" He raised an eyebrow, cocked up his head, and flexed his arms all in a childish manner. He was no taller than three feet, his skin was as dark as the night, and he was wearing nothing but a make-shift pair of underwear from the purple foliage that sprouted from the great treetops.

All I could do was stare in disbelief, what the hell kind of kid was this? And more importantly, what was a third eye doing, ripping out from his forehead? With each second that passed, my idea of being on a different planet continued to grow. And I still needed to find Josh. Soon. Pito continued.

"So... How'd ya get here anyway? Boat? Are ya one of those slave guys from Zugai? How'd ya get away?"

I considered him blankly for moment, feeling a profound confusion. I didn't even know where to start.

"I have no idea what you're talking about, all I know is that I was in a hotel in Oregon one minute, and then things went completely insane for a while, and now I'm dripping wet freezing talking to you. Where is this? What's going on?"

The boy's eyes thinned out into a wary glare as he began to back away, deeply disturbed by my response. His regard for me became suspicious, and he didn't seem so friendly anymore. If anything, he now seemed afraid.

"Oregon...?" He asked quietly while slowly raising his hands, still slowly moving backwards.

I kept my eyes locked on his, and kept my stance firm.

"Yes... That's right. Oregon. So... Are you going to tell me what's going on now? Or are you going to just confuse me more?"

"So that crown ya had on... That was the real one wasn't it?"

The boy suddenly dropped to his knees and bowed his head. His hands remained up for a moment before he slowly lowered them to the ground, trembling with fear.

"I swear I didn't know it was you... I j-just thought ya were a Zugai follower... Please don't kill me. I swear I didn't know..."

Still--if not *more* confused than I was before, I watched the young boy shaking in terror, his head bowed down in fear. I very slowly stepped towards him, with a baffled sense of guilt in my stomach.

"Pito... I'm not going to hurt you. Who do you think I am...?"

He raised his head and seemed to calm a little, but his tone of voice still carried the paralyzed fear of a child.

"Solus...?"

Understanding hit me like a bolt of lightning, and I knew exactly who it was Pito was referring to. Yesterday, moments before the spirit of Jessie Quaid had crossed over to wherever she had gone, she had told me that I wasn't the only person with special eyes. The 'old man,' shared them too. If the great red ocean behind me *was* the red void, it could have just as easily been *him* emerging from its depths and not myself. It was the crown. The crown was the key, and I had unknowingly unlocked the door, and stepped right through it, and this alien place must be Coda itself.

My mother had taught me a lot of what I'd come to know

about Coda, and the dreams I'd had throughout my life had taught me somewhat as well. Little fragments and pockets of information all leading up to this moment; finding myself within the realm of Coda. And What's-more, my enemy, the 'old man,' had a name just like anybody else: *Solus... Old, Ancient, Solus...*

I moved closer to the boy and spoke as calmly as I could.

"Pito listen. I'm not Solus, I'm *nothing* like that man. My name is Steven, and I'm a friend okay? I promise I won't hurt you."

Pito slowly looked up and met my eyes, he began to calm, and his trembling fear started to soothe into a mild curiosity.

"You're a friend...?"

"Yes Pito, I am a friend. I promise."

"But things don't work like that here, spirits don't have friends, none of us do that. I don't know what that'll mean..."

"Well it just means we're friends, that's all. So I guess your different aren't you Pito?"

I hesitantly extended my hand out to shake his, and for a while he just stared at it silently, but then slowly began extending his own. He suddenly grabbed my hand and shook it madly with a huge grin on his face.

"Friends!" He yelled.

It moved me, as he was in my mind, just a child. A child who was in the company of someone he could call a friend for quite possibly the first time. Regardless of being spirit or human he struck me as lonely, and it felt good to make him smile. When his energy finally flattened, I looked back at his forehead, thinking about the strange third eye that had appeared there. Darting around crazily.

"So Pito. What was that third eye on your forehead about anyway?"

He regarded me with a smile, and for the second time raised an eyebrow, cocked up his head, and flexed his arms.

"Right... I forgot, you're the most dangerous spirit in the universe?" I said smiling.

Pito slowly nodded, and for a moment we stood in silence. Then something magical happened; I laughed, and so did Pito. We laughed hard, and the feeling was nothing short of a miracle. I couldn't remember the last time I'd laughed in the company of someone else, and I could feel all the stress weighing me down gently lift. I cherished it, and for the first time in a while, things didn't feel so bad.

"I suppose the heart can heal even in wildest of situations."

***

During my years in high school, I was never much of a standout student. I wasn't by any means *far* below average, but I certainly wasn't one to be consistently pulling out an A+ average. But if there was one class I was particularly fond of, it was Japanese studies. The language itself had interested me from the very beginning, and it'd always been a silent ambition of mine to reach fluency, and learn to speak the language in the way that an actual Japanese person would.

I went far with my Japanese studies, and managed to pass all of my classes all the way up until my high school graduation. After-wards though, I was quickly disheartened when I found myself attempting to converse with someone who was born and raised in Japan. I was disappointed to find that I lacked natural fluency, the Japanese man I spoke to was left confused and lost by my lack of ability, and natural grasp of the language.

My teachers would often say. *"You've achieved just one step, you need to expose yourself to the culture for a matter of years in order to attain mastery of its intricate language."*

Suffice to say, the wind was quickly blown from my sails, and the teacher was right.

Like Japan, Coda had been another one of my silent studies over the years, and I believed that I'd had learned a good deal about it. But I was wrong... Everything about it shocked and frightened me, it was completely unknown to me.

Pito, had over the years developed *his* understanding of language by watching over and studying the souls drifting around within the red void. Or the *Dream Sea* as it was apparently known as here. Although he wouldn't watch the red void with his two normal eyes, but with his *third* eye. Being as lonely as he was, it was his way of feeling the company of other people. Even if they were just little snippets of a completely random persons subconscious.

Sometimes, he'd be disturbed by what he'd see, then other times he'd be elated and joyed by what he'd find. The curse *was* though, that the passage of time within Pito's forest moved far slower than it did back on my realm. So he could never experience the company of someone's life in motion. That is at least, until now.

In the beginning of my time in Coda, Pito showed me his home.

It was far, far different to any home I was accustomed to. It was an enormous hollowed out tree that stood in the center of a large clearing within the forest. Over the years *(or possibly centuries),* Pito had furnished it out with all sorts of strange artifacts that he'd acquired from the forest. Pito's tree-home had four levels in total that were separated by a dense mess of branches and leaves to act as both a floor and a roof. Outside of his tree-home, the forest itself was unbelievable. Never in my life had I witnessed nature of such a lively deep green.

Coda, by the sounds of it, was infinitely big. We'd spend the nights in Pito's tree-home eating fruits we'd collected during the day (which tasted a lot like mangoes covered in sugar) while he'd tell me stories about some of the faraway places of Coda.

Freezing ice tundras, long blistering deserts, and great mountain ranges that stood the size of giants upon giants. All of which housed colonies upon colonies of spirits that appeared in a variety of different shapes and sizes. Some of them incredibly powerful and dangerous, and some simply *wanting* to be incredibly powerful and dangerous.

As it turned out there were very few other spirits that ever bothered to set foot in Pito's lonely forest. At one point while talking in his enormous tree-home over a fruit dinner he'd told me.

"Every spirit in Coda wants to be better and stronger than everyone else, and there's nothin' they're gonna find in this forest that's gonna help 'em with that. Besides, most spirits that leave their home will die, just the way it is."

But Pito did tell me a story one night about a spirit that *had* entered his forest. His tale frightened me, it resonated with me in a bad way.

"A real long time ago, a spirit walked into this forest lookin' like he was on his last legs, he was bleedin' all over the place and the trees and everything around him were dyin' when he walked passed 'em. I don't know what he'd done to make the king punish him so bad. But he screamed like a maniac for days and days while his soul got completely ripped apart. I saw the whole thing from a tree a couple of miles away. He was the most powerful thing I've ever seen, he was real dangerous Steven... Real, real strong... Besides the king I spose."

For whatever reason I kept my suspicions about Pito's story and the monstrous spirit he spoke of to myself, it wasn't by any means an intuitive decision--I simply just didn't speak up about it.

Then again at any moment Pito could have just fished it out from my mind with his third eye. But we'd developed a friendship, and I felt he wasn't going to use his eye on me anymore out of respect. And there was no question that our respect went both ways. He was undoubtedly one of the most colorful and interesting people I'd ever had the pleasure to meet. After all, he'd saved my life.

Coda's sunlight didn't reflect off the surface of the dream sea, no glare bounced back into my eyes like the way it would on a sparkling body of water. Then again, it wasn't water at all, it was a vast ocean of consciousness... *The red void.*

My last few days were like something taken directly from a fairytale, it was incredible to imagine that I'd met someone from a different realm. They were memories I'd never forget, and a big part of me didn't want to leave it behind. It was lucky to have emerged in a place like this, I thought. Considering some of the places that Pito had told me about, things could have gone so much worse. I shuddered at the idea of tumbling into Coda, only to find myself on the shore of a giant spirit cave full of giant spirit huntsman's—Or an endless desert full of massive sand creatures or something... But something *that* unfortunate just wasn't meant to be, maybe arriving here was in fact no coincidence at all.

I'd woken early that morning with a newfound sense of urgency. Despite the passage of time here an incredible deal slower here than where I'd come from, all holidays had to come to an end at some point. I knew in my heart that it was time to finish what I'd started, get back to my own realm and find Josh.

A little while after I'd arrived, Pito and I had retrieved the crown from where I'd thrown it in my panicked state and stowed it away in a secret little apartment towards the top of his tree-home. Thankfully all wrapped up in the cloth that'd originally come with it. Soon I'd have to wear the wretched thing again in order to leave.

"Goddamn that crown... Ah well, time to go."

When I turned back towards the forest, I noticed Pito sitting glumly besides one of the great trees with his head bowed down in silence, absentmindedly ripping little bits of foliage from the trees. Without meeting my eyes, he began to speak.

"Your gonna leave... Aren't ya...?"

A sick guilt flooded my stomach. I didn't see Pito as some kind of evil or dangerous spirit, to me he was simply just a boy. And a lonely one at that.

"Pito... I'm really sorry. But there's someone who needs help, and I need his help too, probably more than he needs mine..."

"Please don't leave me alone here, you don't understand..."

He plucked another piece of foliage from the tree and solemnly continued to rip it into little pieces before sprinkling them onto the ground in front.

"Pito listen. We're friends, and we'll always be friends okay? I promise I'll come back as soon as I can."

Pito didn't budge, he continued to stare unfocused towards the ground at his feet. Breathing deeply, he slowly cupped his head in his hands, and began to cry.

His muffled tears ripped into me like knives, and I was reminded of Jessie, and how she must have felt for all those years being alone.

I slowly knelt down besides Pito and placed my hand on his little shoulder. "Pito.... Do you know what a *surname* is?"

He continued to cry with his face buried in his hands.
But very subtly, he nodded his head.

"And Pito, do the spirits of Coda have surnames?"

This time, he subtly shook his head.

"Well *my* surname, is Marron. So my name is Steven Marron.

And your name is Pito. But, from here on out you aren't going to be just Pito anymore. From now on you're Pito Marron, not just my friend, but my Family too..."

Slowly, Pito raised his head and looked at me in the eyes

while a slight smile spread across his little face.

"Really...? And you promise you'll come back?"

"I promise."

With that, I raised an eyebrow, cocked up my head and flexed my arms.

"I am Steven Marron! Brother of Pito Marron! The most powerful family in all of the universe!"

I chose to stay a while longer, to spend the remainder of the day with Pito, I decided that I'd leave at the first sign of sundown. The sunlight was pleasant as we basked on the grass while we ate the sweet fruits of Pito's forest. The fruit was delicious, not even the freshest fruit from a fruit market compared to it. Neither one of us wanted the sun of that final day to go to rest, so we made the most of it and cherished each and every minute that passed. But every chapter needs to close in order for a new one to open, and there *was* much to do.

He told me more stories about Coda, and I told him a few tales of my own. I told him about my loving mother, and even a little about the father that I never knew.

The day slowly progressed until finally, the time came. Together we walked back into Pito's tree-home clearing while he retrieved the crown from his secret compartment. I sat waiting anxiously amongst the trees, trying to clear my head for what was about to come.

Pito emerged from his home carrying the crown, still wrapped in its cloth. He sat beside me and passed me the horrid crown of Coda. I stared at it deeply for a moment, already starting to feeling the violent, hurricane of emotions that it brings forth.

"I hate this damn thing Pito, god how I hate it... I wish I didn't need to use it. But it's the only way."

Pito looked at the crown himself and nodded as if to agree. Curiously though, he was smiling.

"Don't worry Steven, just put it on. Trust me okay?"

Intuitively I knew that he wasn't talking with the naivety of a child, I completely trusted him. So on my head, went the crown.

I thought of the red void and instinctively fired up my abnormal techniques, and for the second time did so without the need for sleep. *Also* for the second time, I was blasted by an immeasurable force of crashing emotions. Every negative memory of my life, span out from the depths of my subconscious and shot at me mercilessly like a Gatling gun. I reeled back and forth, exploding in searing hot emotional agony. Then just like last time, a strong and prominent thought surfaced into my mind: I would rather be dead than feel the brunt of this. I want to die but I can't move.

True and pure panic seized me, a cloud of toxic fear. *Worse than last time...*

"I can't do this. Oh god please end this. I CAN'T DO THIS!"

Before my mind was shattered into a million pieces, events thankfully took a different turn. For a split millisecond I caught a foggy glimpse of Pito and his little red third eye darting around crazily. Then by complete miracle, my emotions started to settle.

Pito had a Gatling gun of his very own, and he launched a barrage of thoughts into my head, all pleasant and comforting images that fought my dark emotions like little soldiers of the mind. The terrible force of the crown was slowly replaced with something much, much better. *Good memories... My fondest of memories... My mother. Christmas mornings. Early years with Josh. Girls from my high school days. Driving for the first time...*

And amongst these memories were Pito and I, sitting and laughing together on the deep green grass beside his forest. For whatever reason, it was this thought that I held onto the most. I felt myself fade away from Pito's forest, and managed to catch one final glimpse of him sitting beside me.

"I'll come back soon."

I gently drifted into the red void, and was pulled through its murky depths like a magnet smoothly running its predetermined course. Within moments, I'd be back in my own realm. And even though I wasn't sure exactly where, I felt safe.

CHAPTER 8-

Josh Quaid was a complete mess, liquored up to the brim he'd been stumbling through the dimly lit train station in the town of Vickerdon. Until at some point, he'd slumped down ungracefully after finally drinking away his last sense of balance.

A small stray cat had followed him around since his arrival into the town, and appeared to have no apparent intention of leaving Josh's company. Josh's mood was nothing short of rotten, he would yell at it drunkenly, spitting intoxicated slurs which lacked any shred of proper coherency.

"Leave me alone! Piss off! ...For Christ sake.... GO. AWAY!"

Josh would angrily swing his fist at the cat, kick wildly in its direction, and at one point in the night even hurled an empty bottle of vodka at it, which just ended smashing into a mess of glass shards on the train tracks in front of him. But the little black cat wouldn't budge, it would just stare back at him, it's large black pupils watching and following his every movement with a wondrous curiosity.

Josh had always *hated* cats, especially the ones that glared at him with their inquisitive sense of feline superiority, and he hated everything a great deal more when he was drunk. Josh was indeed a big drinker, all though he wouldn't normally drink as 'hell-for-leather' as he was on this night. The day had been a *bad* one, mostly due to the load of crap that'd gone down in the Vickerdon bank earlier. If it wasn't for that, things would be completely fine.

"Listen, I have money in my account. So just give me my money, It's that simple okay? Would you like me to explain that again...? Nice and slow?" Josh had spat at woman in the teller.

"Sir please, stay calm... I'm afraid without the correct indent—"

"NO! You're not listening to me!"

Things just got worse from there. Soon after, he was promptly escorted from the bank by security, and without any money or food, he decided he'd just go ahead and hit the bottle. He *could* have called Hans from a pay-phone, but very quickly he'd shunned the idea. The thought of someone driving out to help *'little, poor, defenseless Josh'* was way worse than the current situation.

The night was cold, and the rain fell against the platforms tin roof above Josh. He'd wrapped himself up in a dirty blanket he'd taken with him from his old New York apartment. Drunkenly, he watched the rainwater trickle down the graffiti covered walls on the opposite station platform. Josh took the last few swigs of his second bottle of liquor for the day, and decided to close his eyes for sleep. Against the cold brick wall of the station, Josh's thoughts slowly drifted off into incoherent white noise. Sinking into a heavy sleep, his body relaxed and drooped into a liquor-soaked mess, all nestled up inside his old dirty blanket. But just a moment before he lost his last ounce lucidity and fell asleep, a loud meow from the little black cat snapped him back to full consciousness.

A jolt of fury ran through Josh. He picked up his second empty bottle of alcohol and threw it hard at the cat, this time not missing--but hitting it square on its front leg. The cat squealed loudly in pain as its eyes widened in fright, it stared at Josh for a moment before limping away slowly, hissing in a shocked and defeated tone.

Immediately, Josh felt terrible. He'd hurt the cat badly, and could have possibly even broken its little leg. Regret washed over him, and he felt nauseated and sick to his stomach. The cat limped around the corner of the station, leaving little specks of blood in its trail.

"...What is wrong with me..."

The thought of everything wrong in Josh's life seemed to fall down in a crashing heap in his mind.

"What am I even doing here... I'm just a delusional idiot... I just threw a bottle at the first living thing that's actually bothered to approach me in years... ...Why am I like this...?"

He held back tears. But then caught sight of the empty vodka bottle just a few feet in front of him, and the little drip of blood just next to it. Josh's face started to scrunch up, and a lump rose in his throat. He tilted his head down to his lap and quietly sobbed his first stream of tears in a long, long time. A while had gone by before Josh felt there were no more tears to cry, and he sat miserably, while contemplating the idea of laying on the train tracks instead of the station platform. He tilted his head back in thought, and unconsciously started to gather the courage to put his pathetic excuse of a life to an end.

But before he had time to think any further, he caught movement on his side. When he looked over, he saw the little black cat limping slowly but hesitantly in his direction. Josh froze, but the cat continued to clumsily stumble in his direction. When the cat finally reached him, it opened its mouth and purred quietly, the sound of it sent a spark down Josh's spine. Josh slowly placed his hand on his lap and patted gently, the cat carefully limped onto Josh and looked up into his face with its big, black, curious pupils.

Cat's obviously can't talk, and certainly don't execute body language in the way that a person would. But when Josh looked into the little cat's face, he could see an expression of need. The cat had returned, and given Josh a second chance, and craziest of all, had potentially saved his life.

Josh didn't end up catching any sleep that night, instead he spent it gently patting his new little companion. And as it turned out there *were* more tears left to cry, but they were good tears. Feeling a long lost connection that he hadn't felt since his earliest childhood, he cried what felt like poison from his bloodshot eyes.

When morning eventually rolled around, Josh soberly stood up holding his new cat firmly against his chest. He walked over to the empty vodka bottle and put it in the stations trashcan, along with every other scrap of alcohol he'd brought along with him from New York. As he walked with his newfound companion towards Vickerdon's main street, he thought about potential names for his new little friend. Oddly though, without much thought at all, one name seemed to just rise into his mind for no rational reason. It wasn't by any means a common name, but somehow, it just seemed to fit. And Josh assumed it must just be a kick of intuition. He looked down into the cat's face.

"I'm sorry about last night little man. I promise I won't ever be that crazy guy who throws bottles ever again alright? From now on I'm gonna call you Marron. Little Marron the black cat."

CHAPTER 9-

The old man Solus drove fast, but his heart raced faster. He pushed the pedal hard, and could barely contain his excitement, everything was rolling along according to plan. With the nuisance boy having been dealt with, he now remained the only person in the world to bear the eyes of Coda. It wasn't as if he was ever afraid of the boy though, there was simply just no room for two, just one.

What made Solus even happier was his brand spankin' new Ford F-Series car, which in fact wasn't exactly *brand new*--it was actually pretty banged up and crappy. He was elated by the idea of Steven suffering a gradual decline into a lonesome, agonizing state of insanity. But taking his last *pathetic,* little sentimental keepsake was the delicious cherry on top. Solus grinned a deeply satisfied grin and sung to himself softly in delight.

"Good times... Definitely good times..."

Nothing would get in his way now, and the crown would soon be his. In a short while he would be aware of its exact location, *very soon.* His glorious, golden destiny would finally become a perfect reality, and he finally wouldn't need the help of his stupid, blurry faced sidekick.

Not long ago, his rabid pet had retreated back into the realm of Coda to rejuvenate his energy, and Solus was more than happy to be in his own company for a while. He dreamily dawdled away the time on the road fantasizing about the immeasurable power he'd soon be juggling effortlessly between his hands, but above anything he loved the thought of finally annihilating that stupid erased man when the time inevitably came. He would be the new, undisputed King of Coda, and every living thing would respect and admire him above all else.

"*Human and spirit, I will rule over all of them....*" He thought, licking his old, cracked lips.

It was a hot day. Vapor danced it's wavy, translucent dance atop the peak of the summit ahead. It had been a long drive, but Solus was thankful for it. It was a good opportunity to reflect, and look back on his long, long life so far. Soon he wouldn't be bound by his poisonous mortality, soon he'd be a god. A perfect, immortal god.

Before his divine ascension, there was just one more thing to take care of, within the hour he'd arrive to meet up with an old friend of his. His old friend was just another pawn in the grand scheme of things, and the king no longer needed the aid of his old and faithful pawn. Though his old friend *had* been a great help to him over the years, it's a dog eat dog world after all.

"old dogs need to be put down when they can no longer fetch the mail."

His old friend had crafted one of the portals for the erased man, but he'd foolishly let the little nuisance burn it to a flaming, useless wreckage.

"Years of work... Down the goddamn toilet..."

Solus believed that Steven must have had *some* ideas about Coda and the world of spirits. But he was however, completely certain that he lacked the ability to summon them. ...But clever old Solus could. Not only did he have the eyes of Coda, he also had the knowledge and grasp of its voice. Like Solus, his old friend was proficient with the ancient art of Coda too. And there were *very* few people who could manage to attain the ability to paint while executing it's old and intricate voice.

The portal of the Quaid house had taken an entire generation to construct. First, the trust and love of the family needed to be cut and broken. Secondly, a room had to be elected to act as the heart of the house. Third, the house needed to be decorated with the ancient voice of Coda through the steady stroke of a brush. Then lastly and most excitingly,

A sacrifice is made in the heart of the house.

Probably could have sucked another twenty years out of her.... Maybe even thirty."

Solus drifted off thoughtfully, and grinned his old sick grin. His mood was as happy as a mood could be—he even decided to crack a window down and smoke one of the cigarettes that he'd found in the Ford's center console. And to make things even better, he would be meeting with his old friend very, very soon. A large sign flew passed the side of the car while he drove into suburbia. *'Now Entering Vickerdon.'*

CHAPTER 10-

"Josh I have to be honest, you don't look so good... Are you sure you're okay?"

Josh stared at the table full of hot breakfast laid out in front of him before happily burying his fork into his scrambled eggs and chipolata sausages. He was starving, and his stomach growled like a beast.

His prominent father-figure Hans had met with him in the town of Vickerdon, and even before his arrival Josh had already guessed the way things would unfold. He knew that he'd have to face the Hans' old, judge mental eyes. But strangely, he was unfazed. In fact, for the first time in a long time, he felt good. With his mouth full of breakfast he replied.

"I'm actually feelin' alright, you didn't have to drive too far to get here did you? Thanks in any case..."

Hans stared at Josh confused, perplexed by his relaxed demeanor. The situation was straight up weird. The Bags under his eyes were the shade of the night, and he couldn't possibly be more dirty, even if he rolled around in a puddle of mud. He looked like a complete and utter mess, but he *did* seem like he was okay. Then there was the cat, the little black cat with the banged up leg nestled beneath his chair. Hans had always been under the impression that Josh *hated* cats with an unfair passion. Hans didn't even know where to start. Josh continued, with a mouth full of breakfast.

"I'm done with New York in case ya were thinking of asking, I think I'm just gonna stay here and focus on my painting and stuff. Try to get a good rhythm going. I want routine, I think that was my problem... A lack of proper routine."

"So you've still been painting?" Hans asked with a delighted surprise.

"Well... Not for a while now, but I really miss it. I miss how it used to make me feel." Josh said as he continued digging violently into his breakfast. Hans leaned forward in curiosity.

"Josh, what feeling is it that you're referring to exactly?"

Josh placed his fork down, looked away from his food and regarded Hans eye to eye, chewing the last of the breakfast in his mouth.

"It's hard to explain... It's like, I dunno... Well, I think it's a mixture of things."

Entranced by his own thoughts, Josh looked blankly past Hans, his eyes slightly narrowed. Even without Josh finishing his explanation, Hans already knew exactly what Josh was talking about, and it turned out to be something that *very* few people had the ability to grasp. Josh spoke softly.

"It's like, there's a tiny little machine in the front of my head, which is controlling me... But I'm operating the machine, with a tiny version of myself, safe inside my head. And, when I really focus on holding the brush and what I'm painting... It's like... I kick the little machine into gear. I know that sounds completely insane, but that's honestly the best way I can explain it..."

Josh's gaze once again drifted off.

"Believe it or not, it sounds like a perfectly reasonable explanation to me." Hans replied.

Josh smiled and looked back down at the table.

"That's good."

Hans was struck heartbroken, in one big blur he considered the disgusting situation that was Josh's childhood. Hans' life was a tangled mess of horrid madness, and a large portion of it was his own fault. He'd been misguided, he'd willingly played part in a game that'd gone so, so terribly wrong. The sight of Josh's broken smile on his tired face crushed him. *"For the love of god, it's a wonder that this poor boy still lives,"* thought Hans.

"Do you remember how we used to paint together Josh? Back in Missidnyl?"

Josh dug back into his breakfast.

"Of course, you taught me."

"Yeah I suppose I did. I'm glad you have those memories Josh, they were good times."

Josh's face stayed fixated on his breakfast, but Hans could tell it wasn't the same broken expression that he'd adopted since the horrific death of his sister, it was brighter, a radiance invisible to everyone but Hans. Something in him was beginning to heal, like an old dismantled engine slowly being put back together.

Hans again noticed the little black cat nestled up beneath Josh's chair.

"So I thought you always hated cats, what's with him?"

Josh reached under his chair and gave Marron a scratch on his head, the cat purred and lazily rubbed its head against Josh's hand.

"Well, I do hate still them. I just like this one."

"You name him something yet?"

"Yeah, his name is Marron."

Hans frowned with a mild suspicion and leaned forward.

"Marron? What made you think to call him Marron?"

"I don't know, it's just a name I came up with for him."

Hans leaned back in his seat and fished two cigarettes from his shirt's front pocket, one for Josh and the other for himself.

"Josh, how well do you remember Missidnyl? I'm not talking about the bad times, I mean before that, when things were still okay."

Growing curious, Josh lit his cigarette and slumped in his chair thoughtfully. Watching Hans strike a match.

"I guess pretty well, I remember Jessie plenty if that's what you mean. Why though? What about Missidnyl?"

After a pause, Hans exhaled a thick plume smoke from his cigarette, and spoke with a cold seriousness.

"Steven...? Steven Marron?"

Josh narrowed his eyes at Hans and twitched uncomfortably. The feeling of the ghost hand digging around the inside of his head returned for a horrifying split second, and his thoughts were thrown back to his last moments in his New York apartment, scrambling around the cluttered room like a wounded animal searching for safety. A domino then suddenly fell in Josh's mind, followed by another. A long ago dream returned to him like a flood of the mind.

"...Steven... Steven *Marron*. Yeah... I remember him now. How the hell could I have forgotten...?"

Hans nodded slowly, drawing in another deep drag of his cigarette.

"I know it feels like it didn't happen, but you need to understand that those times were completely real. I understand that this all sounds utterly ludicrous, but you need to find him Josh, and you need to find him more sooner than later."

"Hans, what are you talking about? Why is this so

important...?"

Fear spread across Han's face, making Josh deeply anxious.

"Hans? What is it...? Man you're freaking me out."

"Josh I'm so sorry..." Hans said quietly.

"Sorry about what?"

"Everything."

Before Hans was given the opportunity to explain everything he wanted to explain, an old rusted Ford F-series had pulled up on the other side of the road. Sadly, Hans didn't manage to notice the driver until he'd walked up to their table.

CHAPTER 11-

'Voyage of the planet crusaders' was a book I read when I was in the fifth grade, I would cite it as the first book that moved me, causing me to feel heavy emotion through the art of words. The book had begun with 'Bert' and 'Kel,' two famous voyagers who explored the universe. They would land on alien planets and overcome the dangers of the evil and terrifying alien races that inhabited them. In chapter one, they'd landed on an enormous planet called 'Sebez' where they fought a gigantic horde of over-sized wasps. They went at them head on with laser pistols, plasma shooting--Gatling cannons, and a whole arsenal of other futuristic weapons. Unfortunately, they were no match for the giant insects. So quickly, Bert and Kel realized that they were in over their heads, and didn't stand a chance against the hideous horde of wasps. They needed to retreat to their space ship pronto.

But during their mad sprint back to the space ship, Bert fell, and instead of being helped up by his trusty fellow voyager Kel, Kel instead ran straight over him, even planting a foot on Bert's back, squashing him further into the mud. Kel made it the ship, fired it up and left the planet Sebez in a hurried frenzy of panic.

'Voyage of the planet crusaders' was also a picture book, and I'll *never* in my life forget the final two illustrations at the end of the book. The first, was Bert looking up from the mud, tears running down his face, the over-sized horde of wasps just a matter of feet away from him. The second was of Kel, also crying, sitting inside his ship in the orbit of planet Serbs. *Betrayal, and shame.*

The book had ended with tears running down the faces of both of the voyagers. It made me badly upset, I would curse Kel for being such a traitor every time I made it to the book's end. My mother had assured me that Bert had befriended one of the gigantic wasps, then ridden it back to earth. But I didn't believe her. Although in time, it didn't matter, because I had soon come to appreciate the message that the simple children's book had conveyed at the end.

'The man who lived, suffered a fate worse than the other.'

Or at least, that's how I came to interpret it. Either way it didn't matter, because It gave me one of my first harsh perspectives in life.

Missidnyl west primary school held a great deal of my most prized and cherished memories. Some stood out with a complete visual accuracy, while some of them just a simple blur in my mind's eye upon reflection. So many mornings, I would brew a coffee, light a cigarette and just bask in these old memories. And commonly, when I find myself thinking of these early times in primary school, I'd think hard enough to see the thousands of little threads that run from my youngest days, all the way up to the young man that now was. I hold onto my childhood as though it's a life support system, and never, ever, will I lose the firm grip I have on it. I've always thought that if I *was* to lose my grip, I would lose the biggest spark I have.

The old man, I'm *assuming*, wouldn't commonly reflect on his past. Instead he steals life, and lives out his extra, unnatural time while looking for the next sacrifice in order to attain even more years. I am, (like everybody else) saddened to the core to learn of the death of a child. Jessie Quad's life had ended, and not by any accident. The old man had stolen it from her, and he now lives and breathes the years that'd originally belonged to her. She will never have the opportunity to look back, and bask in the warmth of long gone childhood memories. And for that, I will risk my life if it means putting a stop to such things. In fact, I'd happily die for it.

It only took around three seconds to realize where the crown had taken me, I certainly wasn't in Coda anymore. It took even less than three seconds to rip the crown from my head, and throw it across the room.

"Not nearly as bad as last time... Thank Christ for Pito."

The bad news though, was that I didn't end up in a place I had much interest in being. I'd been here before, years and years ago during a time where my life had lacked any sense of stability, horribly reckless times, hopelessly lost and hateful. A time when again and again I'd almost kill myself on a daily routine.

There was almost no wall space that wasn't covered in graffiti, the building couldn't possibly be more run down and broken, even if a bomb was dropped on it. It was an old abandoned factory, used however long ago for whatever other purpose. But its purpose now, was to act as a place to get together and take copious amounts of drugs. And in this very factory, I had taken a stupid of them. I walked through the dusty, eroded floors on my way towards the exit while keeping my head down. I didn't have much interest in sticking around and taking a trip down bad memory lane. Bits of broken brick crunched underfoot with each and every step, and the old rusted smell found my nose giving me a sour nostalgia.

"Man, glad I made it outta this place back in the day," I thought to myself, while making my way around a corner to my left. Sunshine spilled in from outside, lighting up the factories doorway. I briefly wondered to myself if the crown had a personality of its own, or if it was just some sort of amplified reflection of myself. Then again, maybe it was neither, maybe it was some kind of fate. Then it occurred to me that the crown was still where I'd left it, after I'd instinctively thrown it away.

I was about to turn back when suddenly, I heard an old voice from behind. A voice I had absolutely *zero* interest in hearing, though curiously, I wasn't at all startled by it.

"God damn man. Long time no see."

I knew exactly who it was the moment the voice had spoken, and the only thing I felt was pity. Pity for an old acquaintance that'd never made it out of the decadent drug nest of the lost people. I turned around, mustering up a smile.

"Shaun. Jesus man it *has* been ages. What's going' on?"

A terribly scrawny man lifted himself from the concrete floor and hobbled his way over towards me. Like an old man, he struggled as he mixed up one foot with the other. Back when I'd known Shaun, he was still somewhat the same hope filled guy I'd known from high school. But now, he was a banged up, bruised skeleton, completely dismantled from what looked like an insane onslaught of never-ending drug abuse. Pity continued ripping at me as I reached out my hand to shake his.

"What's been happening Shaun? How is everyone?"

His hand felt like a loose pile of chicken bones that could crumble under the slightest stress.

"The same old stuff man, everyone's cool. What happened to ya back in the day anyway? And how come ya here? You got anything on ya?"

I just wanted to turn around and leave, and to not look at Shaun for one more second. He'd pressured me into making bad decisions in the past, and had said some disgusting things to me. Though now, all I wanted was for the past to stay the past. I needed to leave.

"Man it's a long story, things have been crazy. I'll fill you in another time though, I'm so sorry dude, but I really got to go."

After saying that, I'd probably made it one single step towards the exit before the old familiar Shaun I'd known came raging out of his shell. His voice rasping in a wheezy croak, he spat words at me with the heat of an angry fire.

"Fine asshole, piss on you and ya dead mom. Ya know she probably did herself in coz you're such a dick."

My blood felt like it'd immediately hit boiling temperature, and a spark of rage light up the inside of my head. The better thing to do would've been to just continue forward and leave the old rotted factory behind me, but like most instances involving anger, I bit back like a dog taking bait and turned back to face Shaun.

"If you say one more thing like that, I'll rip your junkie arms off your body. I swear Shaun, don't push me."

Shaun was completely unfazed, with his skeletal arms raised up like a drunken boxer with brown teeth, he just continued to stare at me like he was ready to start swinging wildly at any second. Like a starved dog, he waited hungrily for more, and I was right about to give to him if he hadn't have spoken first.

"None of us even liked ya here man, we all just felt bad coz of your dead mom and all that. You were a loser in school, and you were a loser in here. The only reason we let ya hang around with us and take our drugs is coz you'd buy 'em for us... Ya know... I always wanted to punch you in the head, right in ya damn face."

Staring at back at Shaun, I started to realize something.
He honestly thought he could knock me down, and his inflated sense of confidence was completely delusional. To the point that he probably didn't even realize the condition that he was in. He'd always been the guy who'd call all the shots in this place, and at a point in my life when I was at my most venerable, I would've done almost anything to appease anyone, just to feel *some* sense of belonging. I had friends, but I *was* an outcast in school, and had most likely come off a little weird to most people. But I'd taken

some heavy hits in my life, and some big things had happened to me. But Shaun on the other hand, I doubted had ever felt even slightly threatened. And right now, all I wanted to do was change that.

He didn't at all back up when I approached him, instead he just widened his snarling grin to show more of his decaying, brown teeth.

"Okay Shaun, now's your chance man. You wanna give me a smack in the face? Well you go for it, give me a good one."

Without a second thought, Shaun swung his skinny little purple arm at me in a fast hook. Not only did he miss me, but he also fell to the floor, winding himself on the concrete. The air in his lungs blew out of his mouth as his face immediately turned bright red. I'd never seen someone with so much anger on their face before.

He sluggishly rose to his feet and went to punch me again, but this time in the stomach. Surprisingly, there was some force to it, but I didn't budge. Instead I just continued staring into his raging, bloodshot, beady little blue eyes.

I didn't throw a punch of my own, instead I stepped forward to him and pushed him with every ounce of strength I had.

Then Shaun, the guy who used to threaten to stab people for money, cut the tails off Rats to use as necklaces, and rape girls with drugs, was sent flying across the old factory like a weightless rag doll. He slammed and rolled along the floor letting out grunting sounds like a popped, deflating ball, before finally coming to an ungraceful stop amongst a pile of smashed brick. huffing in pain, he looked in my direction, with bloodshot eyes no longer full of fury, but of fear and confusion.

I kept staring at him, waiting for another smart-ass retort. But none came. There was no further talk of my mother, my high school reputation or of anything. Shaun was done, and the swelling in his eyes confirmed it. His rotting mouth hung open as he mouthed something inaudible. I approached him slowly, and started to feel my pity for him return. I didn't in any way regret what I'd done, in fact it needed to be done, I was sick and tired of people like him. But my pity for him still dug into me, and decided that as horrible as he was, the only things he had was a decaying old factory and a limited number of brown teeth. When I reached him I finally heard his voice.

"Steven, I'm sorry."

My mind went blank for a moment, distracted by his sudden change of attitude.

"I don't know why I said that stuff. But I guess your right man, I'm just a junkie." He said.

He continued wheezing and rasping while he lay on the floor, it was a sad and awful sight. The worst thought though, was of how close I came to being what he is now. I spent a lot of time here in the past, and it was *certainly* now time to leave it behind me forever.

A moment before I turned around, Shaun shakily reached out his hand. And I shook it for the last time before helping him up to his feet.

I've always thought the best approach in life, was to try and see the best in people. I've never believed that anyone can be entirely devoid of good. Unfortunately, when I think in this way my guard is at its lowest. I should have just left Shaun amongst the bricks and never looked back. He'd been concealing a small rabbit knife in his back pocket, and as soon as I'd finished helping him to his feet he drove it deep into my stomach.

At first, I felt no pain. I mightn't have even noticed if it weren't for all the blood. I dropped onto my knees while immediately grabbing at the wound as Shaun stood over me laughing, I could even feel small droplets of spit shoot from his mouth while he excitedly relished in what he'd done.

I started to feel a dull throb, and my instincts told me that panic was well and truly just around the corner. With an excruciating strain of effort, I somehow managed to find my way onto my feet, then began to slowly shuffle my way forward. The throbbing I felt began to evolve into the early stages of complete and utter agony. All of my senses started to dull and wave around like a blurry, trip on some bad mushrooms.

Then I saw it, the words written just next to the factory's door, in a huge spray-painted, bubble font. 'CODA IS KING.'

And in my last lucid moment, just before I was entirely seized by panic I briefly thought of it.

"Why is that here? What is all this?"

Then finally everything started to go dark, and the world

around me faded, I could barely even hear the sound of my own voice, let alone even control what I was saying. A hazy string of images started running through my head, Olive from Endon, standing in her doorway, the night's breeze playing with her long ringlets of hair. The pine trees flying past the sides of the car windows in the dead of night, and the sleepy receptionist throwing me my hotel room key.

Once upon a time I came close to dying in this very place, and curiously just like last time, my final thoughts were of my mother. I saw the sunlight from outside slowly approaching me, and just as my feet tangled up, I fell outside bleeding like a pig. The only thing my voice could manage to utter was my mother's name, followed by something else I'd never remember. Then darkness.

"Ruby... Why did you have to die...May the Wolves of Coda carry you somewhere nice... Somewhere far away from here..."

CHAPTER 12-

'A surveillance camera has recorded the horrifying moment of a man being shot dead at point-blank range, while sitting down at breakfast with an unidentified individual at a cafe, in the town of Vickerdon, Utah.

The recorded footage shows an unidentified, elderly aged gunman approach the cafe, walk up beside the breakfast table before pointing a small handgun at his victim's head and firing.
The unidentified individual, (looking to be around approximately his mid-thirties) immediately flees the scene as the cold-blooded killer unloads one more shot into his victim's torso before leaving the scene and leaving range of the cafes' surveillance camera.
The victim was identified as eighty-seven-year-old Hans Varlyn.
Police are still searching to find the whereabouts of the elderly gunman and the individual to flee the scene.'

No pictures...

Josh placed the newspaper down a moment, and took a large sip from his coffee. It was nothing compared to the alcohol that he so badly craved, but at least it was something. He thought back to the events that'd occurred at his breakfast with Hans, and grimaced with an expression of shock and confusion. Moments before the crazy old guy had walked up to their table, Hans had said a whole bunch of things in a speeding panic. Josh was slowly recalling everything that he'd said, except for one thing that Hans had made abundantly clear.

"Get out of here, there is nothing you can do. Just leave now!"

Josh looked back down at the news article, and stared directly at the words 'elderly aged gunman' for a good five minutes while periodically sipping on his coffee. He spoke to himself while he did so.

"I am going to kill that rotten bastard, and goddamn is he gonna suffer. I am gonna bleed you dry, you sick filth…"

Little Marron, had somehow found him after his flee from the cafe, and rubbed his little face against Josh's leg, snapping him out of his vengeful haze of thoughts. Josh watched the little black

Cat for a while as it affectionately walked around his ankles, then something began to surface, 'Marron...' The name Marron reminded Josh of something else that Hans had said moments before Josh had left.

"Find Steven, as soon as humanly possible..."

Josh sat back on his chair, still reeling with shock, and thought to himself. *"What in the hell is happening..."*

What had happened at the cafe was insane, but what happened afterwards was possibly even more ridiculous. After Josh had fled the scene, everything had become flight-or-fight, a panicking sprint driven by pure adrenaline. All he could remember from his mad scramble was what Hans had said just moments before it, it rang through his head like a high-pitched alarm clock. He ran aimlessly, before throwing himself directly into an open door of a house without even thinking about it.

The house was incredible, full of bright gold, and dark red furniture. It was like something from the age of kings and queens. Soon after, at some point after launching himself into the house and semi-lucidly surveying his surroundings, Josh had passed out.

Then not long ago this morning, Josh had awoken on an enormous bed of gold linen, and soon realized that it was all real. It hadn't been a dream, or a *nightmare,* which was probably more fitting.

Though stranger than anything, was the overly accommodating resident of the house. He spoke in weird riddles that Josh could barely understand, and all he would seem to do would be to just think to himself quietly, before moving into another position only to continue doing the exact same thing. Josh spent the morning questioning him about everything he could think of, but all the man did was stare back at him with what appeared to be a face devoid of all expression.

Josh eventually decided to resign to the notion that he was just some senile old guy, who had no problem with Josh hanging around. Thankfully such an arrangement suited Josh perfectly fine, no point in throwing away a good situation.

But then again, the situation wasn't good in the slightest. In fact, it was nothing short of terrible, Hans had been shot point blank and Josh didn't even know how to process it yet. Everything about it was just so surreal, like a gruesome, sick dream. Josh's thoughts once again turned to the old gunman, a well postured man who couldn't have seemed more sure of himself. Despite the immense wealth of hatred that Josh had for him, he was still intimidated by the thought of him. The old man, the infinitely evil, old man with the handgun. And why wasn't he found? How could it possibly be that this man could've escaped without a trace after literally shooting another man in a public area?

Josh looked around, and wondered to himself.

"Maybe he found a weird hiding place in the same way I did."

As though the resident was reading Josh's thoughts, he floated into the room like a ghost and sat on one of the golden armchairs. He continued to sit in his odd, pensive silence. Josh approached him.

"Ok man, what's happening here? What do you know that I don't?"

The man stared back, and Josh felt an airpark of frustration.

"Seriously, what's happening??"

Josh's eyes locked onto the elderly mans, while a small yet familiar bubble of anger started to rise.

"This is nuts; can you answer me please…?

Nothing.

"For Christ sake... Do you have dementia? You're touched in the head? Not quite all there??" Josh moved closer to the old man, who just kept staring.

"Look, I'm real thankful and everything. But I was in the paper. I was the guy who fled the cafe shooting. You're not worried about who you let in your house?"

Josh averted his gaze for a moment, and grew paranoid. Maybe this man was an accomplice of the gunman, maybe Josh fell prey to a trap of some kind. And just maybe, a gun would soon shoot a bullet through his own head. He looked back at the man.

"Alright. No more games! Who are you man? Are you with the gunman?? That's it isn't it?? You're an enemy! Well I'll kill you before you even think to move!"

Josh ran at the man with his arms raised and ready, he wound up his right arm to hook him with a punch to the face. As his fist flew into the man's face, all Josh felt contact with was the golden silk of the armchair. Then in a horrifying moment his arm was literally inside the man's head, like he was a hologram being projected onto the armchair. Josh jumped back in fright and confusion.

"What?? Man what are you?? ...H-how?"

Finally, after an excruciating silence, the man spoke to Josh, and his voice echoed in his mind as if he was somehow communicating directly into his head.

"Your part of an ugly web Josh, and I'm afraid that you're going to suffer greatly for it."

Josh's eyes widened in fear, unable to speak.

"The old man will almost certainly find you, and when he does, you'll wish that the bullet had passed through *your* head."

After more silence, Josh found his words.

"What web? What's gonna happen...?"

The man rose from his chair, and stared out the window into the sun-lit brick of the house next door, lost in thought as he was before.

"The nightshade is a cruel pocket of space, utterly devoid of anything. Once a soul occupies it, one doesn't age, nor can be harmed. There is absolutely no way out it, it is a realm that lacks an ending. It is demonic, pure doom. And he wishes that this be your fate."

Josh felt the sting of hot panic, the feeling he had while running from the cafe returned, he grew frantic.

"I don't believe you, that can't be. How do you know all this?"

The man looked back at Josh, and his face began to change. Delusion became reality. Josh had seen a face like this before, but only in sleep, only in his most disturbing nightmares.

"You've had dreams about him. Your days in Missidnyl, were wrecked by a man who wears a face like this. Simply put, he is the worst person to ever find yourself involved with. Your old friend failed, and soon you will join him in the nightshade."

Josh's memory of his final conversation with Hans twigged at this, and a portion of it spilled back into his memory. He shot his gaze back towards the man, and stared into the fierce eyes beneath the hazed blur that covered his face.

"Your wrong, Steven didn't fail. Hans told me that, right before I ran from the cafe. He's still around."

"Impossible."

"No asshole, possible. Hans told me, and I trust him. But better yet... I'll prove it... Get me some paint and paper. You'll see."

The blurry faced ghost gave Josh a curious expression, and slowly, his face returned to its former state. He was baffled.

"...Paint...?" The ghost asked.

"Yes. Paint. Or are you so senile that ya don't even remember what that is anymore? Sticky colorful stuff that you make arty crap with?"

After another discomforting staring contest, the man leaned in towards Josh and regarded him with a sense of close curiosity. Or horror, Josh couldn't quite tell.

"Okay... Go ahead, paint."

Josh looked around blankly.

"Usually you need paint if someone's gonna to paint..."

"It's on the table, get started."

Josh hesitantly crossed the room, and was stunned to find a large array of oil paints strewn across the table. They were all perfectly arranged by their tones of color, all of which lay on top of an enormous stack of paper. A varied collection of brushes sat at the front of the table, next too old fashioned, gold jars of water. Basically every essential a painter would need. It was incredible, Josh's breath locked up in his throat.

"...Whoah..."

Josh studied the set of painting equipment as he spoke.

"Who are you?" Asked Josh.

The painting equipment looked like something from the past, it was nothing like what Josh was used to. Usually he'd Just use the cheapest acrylic paints he could find at 99c stores. But not this, this was magnificent.

"How did you do this...?"

Without a reply he slowly turned his attention back to the bizarre, ghost-like resident behind him. But he was gone, had disappeared without a single sound. Josh felt unnerved, and suddenly felt awfully venerable.

"You prove your case first, then we talk."

Josh's eyes darted around the room, trying to lock onto the source of his voice, but there was nobody to lock sight onto.

"Where are you?"

"Paint... And then we'll talk."

"What is this?" Thought Josh.

He looked back at the paints, and after a while just shrugged in defeat and sat down. *"No point in wasting time I guess."*

It took a while, but soon enough Josh found his old rhythm. It felt good, like a perfectly safe drug that softly buzzed through Josh's bones, relaxing him into a perfect state of meditation. He thought heavily about Steven, at least everything he could manage to remember. Each stroke of the brush was on key, his wrist moved gracefully without a fault. He concentrated on his passion, and felt a warm rush of nostalgia from his early years in Missidnyl. *The good years.*

Josh had believed in a lot of outlandish things as a child, as most children commonly do. But what was happening now was one outlandish belief that was real, it wasn't make believe. He caught himself wondering how many other things might be real. *After all* he thought, the resident of the house seemed to be more a ghost than a person. So what's next? Mummies and Mermaids? I guess anything's possible at this point.

Gradually an image of Steven started to make itself out. At first, big black blotches started to form into clumps of hair. Then his tired, worn out face. Josh watched it all unfold before him, hardly in control of his own hands. It was surreal, and he regretted straying away from painting for all of the years after Missidnyl. But it didn't matter, because he'd squashed one of his biggest fears. Since his last time painting, he'd worried that he may have lost the ability, like it was an old fairy tale that'd only existed in the depths of his youth. But amazingly, the magic remained intact, and his old feeling of being somewhere else, somewhere infinite, had returned after all these long years.

Unfortunately, things quickly darkened. As the definition in Stevens face grew more decipherable, Josh began to notice it was a painting of a young man in agony. Before long, the painting depicted a mess of blood coming from his torso. Josh felt a sick wave of concern for his old friend, was he shot by the old man in the way Hans was? What had happened?

The background began to emerge, and with every stroke that Josh made with the brush, he tried desperately to guess the scene that the painting was resembling. He instinctively jabbed his brush into one of the water jars, swirled it around before dabbing its tip into some Grey paint. Then within the span of half an hour, Josh could guess that it was some kind of warehouse—or a factory. Then with yet more colors, and more time, Josh saw little tags of graffiti.

"Steven, where are you.?"

Done.

Josh leaned back and drew in a deep breath, and for a short while relished in the last little afterglow of tingling. He was sad for the feeling to fade, but unlike alcohol, he didn't instantly crave more. *'A safe drug.'*

He surveyed his work, grimacing at it. Studying it hard.

Steven was bleeding badly, and things definitely looked grim.

"How am I spose'ta find him with this...?"

Josh tried to spot something of importance, something that would make his brain click into place. But it was just his old friend bleeding badly outside a factory.

"How do I even know if he's in the same damn country?" Josh wondered hopelessly.

Before things became completely desperate, Josh thought of something, *the ghost man, maybe he can help.* Josh looked around.

"Hey! Ghost man! I'm done. He's ali—."

The ghost appeared beside Josh without warning, causing Josh to jump out of his seat in shock.

"...Jesus man."

The ghost was looking intently at the painting, his eyes wide with fascination. Instead of hounding him, Josh just gave him space, and let him study the painting. Maybe he really *could* help.

"Extraordinary..." Said the ghost, staring deeply into Josh's work.

At this, Josh couldn't help but feel a welcome wash of pride. In his life, the one and only other person to speak positively of Josh's work was Hans. It felt nice, that despite everything wrong with Josh, there was something he was good at. Something that he loved.

"So... He's alive right?"

"Yes, it seems that way."

Relief overcame Josh, he may be badly injured but at least he's okay. Somewhere out there, he's alive and breathing.

"Thank god..." Said Josh.

After a while, the ghost turned away from the painting, his expression of fascination remaining in an unsettling manner.

"How did you come to learn to paint in this way?"

Josh gazed at his feet, his head swimming with old memories.

" From Hans, he taught me when I was a kid."

The ghost nodded slowly as if he knew, like it was an obvious statement. With his attention back to the painting, he kept talking.

"You have surprised me Josh, it's very uncommon that someone can paint with such an ancient medium. But it's humbling, it reminds me of an age gone. There is some hope after all, not much—but some." His face scrunched up, and for a moment Josh suspected that he'd start crying. Instead the ghost just drifted away from the painting and looked thoughtfully out the window.

"You promised me we'd talk now... You need to explain all this." Josh said quietly.

"And I will, we talk tonight, and tomorrow we move."

"What do you mean? Move to where?"

"Your friend." Replied the ghost.

Josh joined the man at the window, and stared at the sunlit streets running along the sides of the house. The image of Steven bleeding in pain swarming around his head. *There is hope. Not much, but some...*

"My name is Edmund Golde, I've been around longer than any person would dare to believe. Sit down and get comfortable, it's important that you try to retain every detail."

Edmund, who *was* in some ways a ghost, explained his long story.

Josh didn't manage to retain every piece of it, but he would never in his natural life forget the majority of it. Edmund was old, unnaturally old. He was pushing on five hundred, and with no intention of disappearing any time soon. The crazed gunman, Solus, was almost as old as Edmund was. Some parts of the story crushed Josh, and some parts moved him in a way he could never explain, mostly because so much of the story hit Josh so close to home. As it turned out, Hans was at one point under command of Solus, and had unknowingly invited a horrid force into the old Missidnyl house.

The erased man from Josh's nightmares, was once a great man of purity. Unfortunately, though, Edmund had failed him, in turn causing the erased man to fail his *own* master. His final punishment had caused him to become the blurry faced monster he now was. And there was a crown, originally named, 'the crown of new Coda.' It was extremely dangerous, and had in the end crippled and broken Edmunds mind. Its power was too great, it's purpose too unstable. Solus wanted to harness its power for himself, and his intentions were anything but pure.

Josh turned out to have a rare ability, an ability Edmund had only witnessed twice before. He could meditate and communicate with the old voice of Coda, which was a realm beyond the one he knew, almost like a distorted mirror-image of Earth. Since the beginning, there had always been art, ancient spirits of Coda would use the medium to converse before language had even been thought of.

There were a few things that Edmund didn't know, the first being that he didn't know what Coda was exactly, or *why* it was. And the second was Steven. Edmund knew he had abilities of his own, but never before had someone managed to escape the pitch black confines of the nightshade. It was in Edmund's mind, an inescapable, perfect prison.

Sleep came as easily as shutting one's pair of eyes for Josh that night. He still wasn't ready to grieve for Hans yet, so he pushed the thought of him it as far from his mind as possible. His head was almost completely clear, except for one thought that kept creeping into the front of his thoughts. And playing on an angry loop.

"I'm gonna kill that old man, I'm gonna make him suffer..."

Eventually, his thoughts of Solus were left behind when he drifted into sleep. But what Josh dreamt was worse.

He stood in an alleyway facing an opening which led to the ocean, the walls beside him were covered with graffiti. But what unsettled him was the way the graffiti seemed to move, and dance across the cracked concrete walls in an oddly disturbing way. He moved out of the alleyway and stood on the beach, the late afternoon sunlight warmed his face. Josh was surrounded by palm trees, at least they looked like palm trees, just much, much bigger, and sprouting purple foliage at the top.

Music started to play, which began with the sound of a gospel choir. followed by the beating of an enormous drum. It was beautiful, Josh closed his eyes and let it fill his head. But the gospel slowly started to go out of key, and the drums began to beat faster and faster. When Josh opened his eyes, the ocean had turned a deep red, and he saw millions upon millions of people standing in it, the water reaching the height of their necks. They all sung in unison, but it was now a horrid, detuned mess.

Josh turned and ran back towards the alleyway, which turned out to be the direction of the great beating of the drums. The concrete started to collapse into rubble and quickly, his path was blocked. Worse yet when he looked back towards the crimson red ocean, he saw an endless sea of people walking with expressionless faces up the shores of the beach. Marching to the colossal beat of the drums.

That's when Josh woke, with his arms swinging, and sweat soaking the gold linen of his bed. *"If I didn't know any better, I'd say that was Coda..."* He thought.

Josh caught around another twenty minutes of light sleep after his nightmare, in a semi-lucid state, tossing and turning he eventually got tired of trying and got out of his bed. Edmund was right, Josh *did* need his sleep, and he had been instructed to leave the house only when Edmund deemed it as safe. But Steven was out there, and he needed help. It's all he could think about.

The morning was slow and sluggish, his mind was a wreck, and his mind wouldn't calm itself down no matter how much herbal tea Josh put into his system. He also had no energy left to push Hans from his mind, and the feeling was crushing him. Hans was shot point blank in the head, it was so barbaric. What kind of person could actually do that and leave without a second thought?

Although Josh didn't see Hans a lot, he already missed him. He was his father-figure, a good man who was always there. Josh felt regret for all the times he was nothing but an unpleasant burden with no willingness to change. But what could be done? He was gone, and that was that... Though he still felt somewhat happy in the sense that there last and final get together was warm and friendly, they had enjoyed each other's company.

"Thank god I wasn't a dick like all the other times..."

Without any more time to reflect, he was snapped back to his senses by Marron, who was meowing loudly while nestling around Josh's feet.

"Hey buddy."

Josh knelt down and gave him a scratch behind his ears, he continued meowing, but little Marron began to sound less and less happy. Josh kept on scratching.

"What's wrong with ya? You ok?"

That's when Josh Finally realized, *cats need food.*

"Oh god damn it, Marron I'm sorry, you must be dying. I'll go get some food ok? Just wait in the house, I'll be back."

Josh grabbed some cash from his bag that Hans had given him, and ran out the door. "Has to be a supermarket 'round here somewhere."

Josh hadn't made it two steps out the front door before things started to feel sour, the sense of being watched hit him instantly. But poor little Marron was starving, and it was probably just paranoia playing its old tricks. The sky was Grey and heavy, the air smelt of rain, or an impending storm. The morning sun was only just beginning to rise behind the clouds, dimly lighting the little town of Vickerdon.

Josh made his way downhill towards a cluster of shops and stalls which sat just next to the train station. Strangely, the night he'd spent there not long ago somehow already felt like it had happened years ago, already feeling like an old, bleak memory buried in his past.

Despite everything, being outside felt great. The fresh air sharpened his senses and made him feel stimulated. Like nature's own caffeine, each step he took woke him up into lucidity more and more. It was also the second day for a very long time that Josh wasn't hungover, no splitting headache and no sickening nausea sitting like a sharp rock in the pit of his stomach.

Josh approached the cluster of shops and stepped inside, "Gary's milk bar, surely there has to be some Cat food here."

An old Asian woman stared at Josh from behind the counter, eying his movements and watching intently. Josh had been clean for two days, and had showered for the first time in a while. But still, he looked like he was up to no good. Hans had always told him that he gave off a shady vibe, like he was always planning to do something criminal. Maybe it was his long, unruly blond hair, or his sharp, angular facial structure. Either way he wasn't about to rob the place.

Josh walked up to the counter, staring back at the old woman.

"Hey I need some Cat food, do you have any?"

Without taking her eyes off Josh, she pointed to her left, down an isle behind him. Josh turned around and began to look.

"...Okay, thanks..."

Josh had no idea what kind of food Marron would need, there was too many different brands to choose from, all different flavors and kinds. So he just decided to grab the only packet that had a picture of a black Cat on it. *"Pascies salmon and tuna blend... Close enough."*

He turned back to the old woman and walked towards her at the counter, but things quickly began to seem off. Something about her didn't feel right, Josh's eyes narrowed and he slowed his pace.

"Are, you ok...?"

The woman just continued to stand firmly in place, not even slightly flinching.

"...Mam?"

All she did was reach out and flatten her palm, suspiciously, Josh dug into his pocket to grab some money while they both held their gaze on each other's eyes. His heart started to beat faster, and he felt a nervous prick jab him on the tip of his scalp.

"What's wrong with this woman?"

Something wasn't right and Josh could feel it, this woman seemed like she was scared to death. Aside from how intimidating Josh could come across, it still didn't explain her subdued demeanor. In an instant, Josh just wanted to be out and away from Gary's milk bar. He placed a bunch of cash in her palm and told her to keep the change, but before he could start for the door he heard the old woman whisper something, and Josh's slight nervousness slid into an all-out anxiety.

"Get out of here..."

Josh turned back around to face the old woman.

"I'm sorry?" Replied Josh.

"You need to get out of this town. Now..."

Even though Josh's heart was racing a mile a minute, he was still struck with a strong curiosity.

"What are you talking about? I don't understand."

After a pause the woman continued, losing her cool she went on.

"Forget understanding anything. I'm just telling you. Leave now, and do not come back, this whole town is dying like an old dog and I don't know why... I... I just woke up and knew that it's all wrong... Everything is dead here. For the love of god why are you still standing there...?"

Josh slowly backed away towards the door, not daring to look away from the woman until she was out of view.

"...What...?"

Without replying, all the woman did was slowly shake her head while watching Josh hesitantly back out of her store. And as soon as Josh was out of her view, he sprinted uphill towards Edmund's safe house—with Marron's cat food tightly tucked under his arm.

Josh slammed the door behind him and sunk to the floor in a staggering heap, his chest was pumping fiercely and sweat drenched his clothes. He felt as though he'd unconsciously slipped back into a nightmare. He reflected over what'd just occurred. As soon as Josh had run from Gary's milk bar everything got incredibly weird, very fast. In the dream he'd seen strange graffiti move across the walls like 2-dimensional snakes, and in the most obscure way he could swear he'd just witnessed it again.

Without realizing, Edmund had appeared above Josh, his eyes were red hot in burning anger. For the first time, Josh felt intimidated, Edmund's eyes burned through Josh like lasers, he was furious.

Though the worst part was his silence, Josh kept waiting for a raging onslaught of cursing, but all he did was stare. It wasn't something Josh was used to, never in his life had he witnessed someone say so much without opening their mouth. He didn't dare look up, nor did he move. Even Marron sat like a statue at Josh's side.

Eventually, Josh felt Edmund starting to ease, and his stance relaxed. Josh slowly looked up towards Edmund and opened his mouth to apologize, but Edmund interrupted. His tone smooth, and almost fatherly, like a wind chime if one could speak.

"I instructed you, to leave the house *only* when I deem it as safe. And right now, leaving will invite nothing but danger. Tell me right now, what made you run into the house the way you did?"

Josh flinched, he feared that what he dreamt could somehow be a reality. Like an omen of some kind.

"I know this sounds ridiculous, but. For a second it looked like the walls were moving. Almost like vapor on a hot day but... It wasn't see-through like vapour, it looked real. And some Chick at the milk bar was acting like a crazy person..."

Edmund watched Josh carefully, and narrowed his eyes as if analyzing his words. Josh stared back, growing nervous.

"What...?"

Josh didn't expect what came next, it hit him like a sledgehammer. None of it made sense, and the idea that it was a potential reality made everything so much worse.

"The beating of the great drum, from the broken, black island of Zugai. The shattered spirits of lost souls' march, on a hopeless quest for redemption."

Josh was terrified, over and over all he could think was '*the beating of the great drum...*' He looked away from Edmund and responded solemnly.

"...I had a dream last night, and I could hear a drum, it got so loud it was almost deafening. What docs it mean.?"

"In Coda, each spirit must stick to what they know. And very rarely will one stray from where they began. But when they do, they become broken, it is punishment from Coda itself. Most believe that the spirits of Zugai are broken spirits that exist only to suffer in a constant search for redemption, but I've never been so sure. Even though to say exactly what they are is something I don't have the knowledge to do. But I do know for certain that they are dangerous. One alone not so much, but together they are like a horde of sentient wasps."

Josh thought it over. *The moving walls, the great drum.* He also thought that he'd gotten enough information for the time being, anymore and his head might explode.

"So what do we do now?"

Edmund looked back out of the window, thinking heavily as he always does.

"Stay here, I'm going to locate your friend. While I'm gone, you paint. And don't stop until I return..."

Josh nodded slowly with understanding and met with Edmund at the window, his anxiety finally beginning to subside.

"And feed your Cat, I hope he was worth it."

At that, Josh smiled.

CHAPTER 13-

Pito would spend every morning atop his tree home eating the fruit of Coda while reflecting on what there was to reflect on. *Usually not much.* Then most days he would wander down towards the ocean of dreams to watch and listen. God knows how long Pito had spent doing this, too long probably. Pito missed his big brother Steven. Stevens age wasn't anywhere near what Pito's age was, but he still somehow felt younger. Young Pito Marron.

Pito could recount two major memories, the first was of the immensely powerful spirit that had faced punishment right within his lonely little forest. And the second being of Steven, and the time they had spent together. The first of these two memories had scared Pito, but at the same time he treasured it, because it was *his.* His own memory that he could think about whenever he wanted. Usually he would spend most of the morning reflecting on it, that is until recently when he had something far better to reflect on. *Steven.*

After eating, Pito scaled down his tree and walked towards the red sea. Making his way through the thick foliage, he ducked and weaved seamlessly with the knowledge of the forest's every intricate detail.

Unlike every other morning, each step he took made his stomach drop. It was subtle at first, but soon after he felt an odd sense of dread. As though he was walking directly towards a great beast of some kind. And Pito began to grow nervous, confused by his feelings.

Even if it's in a small way, almost everything in Coda is linked.

When Pito came out to the shores of the red sea he stopped, something is wrong. Something is stirring, Pito could sense it. Instinctively Pito backed away from the shore and towards one of the many trees, and began to climb. When he reached the top he looked out as far as he could manage across the ocean of dreams, trying to spot something out of the ordinary. Something that wasn't right.

An hour or two may have passed before Pito spotted it,

moving like a thick, black swarm. Pito's eyes widened in disbelief.

They were older than Pito, far older. In his time, he'd seen a few, once every couple hundred years or so. But this was different, it looked to be the entire island of Zugai. All crossing the red sea together, and Pito thought to himself. *'This cannot possibly be a good thing.'*

He scaled back down the tree and walked out into the shores of the dream sea and watched, after around fifteen minutes he opened his third eye and tried to listen. At first they were too far away, and Pito struggled to make sense of anything they were thinking. But then he began to pick up on little snippets of information, coming out from a great swelling barrage of fuzzy, incoherent thoughts. They were insane, mislead and fearful, thousands of snakelike black wasps all sharing a common goal.

Pito closed his third eye and tried to think as calmly as possible,

"if I stay here... I won't be safe. But I can't leave... I wish Steven was here..."

He turned his back on the red sea and thought about hiding in his tree home, but quickly dismissed the idea.

"They'll find me, they want no one but themselves to exist here.?"

Pito stared towards the other end of his forest and scrunched up his face, he'd never left his forest, and had never intended to. But if he didn't leave now, the fate he'd suffer would be much, much worse anyway. He stared at the clearing through the forest and toward the broken down concrete alleyway that led to the west valley, a place full of dangerous spirits that roamed in search of something new they didn't already know. It was a cursed, hopeless search. A never-ending goal that would inevitably lead to nothing. Such a wretched place, Pito thought, born into loneliness and suffering, forever doomed to wander alone.

Pito wondered how many other spirits knew of the other realm, were there any others like himself? At least he might find others, who like himself always dream of the day they can be free, and wander the other realm with their future laid out in front, theirs for the molding.

Pito looked back with his third eye and felt the spirits of Zugai gaining on his shore, he didn't want that distance to close anymore. It was time to go, and leave the only place he'd ever known behind him. It was frightening, but also dangerously exiting.

"You're out there somewhere Steven, and I'm gonna find you."

Pito began to walk slowly. Hesitantly, he made his way towards the concrete alley while his fear grew.

"I can do this. I can do this... I'll be fine, I can do this..."

Plants full of razor sharp thorns sat like overgrown, green monsters either side of the west valley alleyway, and Pito slowly placed one foot in front of him at a time. His soft footsteps echoing through the crumbled concrete alley, and for a measure of safety he opened his third eye. If someone was in his company, best he's prepared.

"I can do this, I'll be fine... I'll find you Steven, somehow I will."

The spirits of Zugai were so close now that their swirling thoughts rang through his head as if it was a beehive. They were under enormous distress, someone or something was threatening them. They were mad, thinking thoughts of destruction and devastation. They wanted death, death to every last living thing including themselves.

Pito finally reached the other end of the alley and looked out over the vast valley. It was huge, bigger than anything he'd ever seen during his entire life.

"One more step and I'll have gone further than any spirit would dare. This could be it, this could be my end..."

Pito closed two of his eyes, leaving his third darting around wildly listening for anything. His stomach became a dense mess of knots, then like ripping of a scab, Pito Marron stepped forward and onto the grass of the west valley. He opened his eyes, and looked around happily. Bewildered, he stared back through the alleyway leading his forest. *"I did it, I'm okay... I really did it."*

Pito, for the very first time in his long life tasted his first taste of freedom. And never, would he plan on giving it up. Not for anything.

CHAPTER 14-

I woke to the sound of heavy rain slamming against the windows of an unfamiliar room, Grey specks from outside danced across the dimly lit walls. For a long time, I just thought about the situation, with the same questions running violent cycles through my head.

"Am I dead? Is this where I've ended up? Is this is it?"

I tried to recall what had been happening, everything that had ultimately led to this moment. I went back to the start. First, there was my return to Missidnyl, then the hotel in Endon, followed by the horrid black void. The crown had managed to take me into Coda.

"And Pito... Then there was Pito..."

Then what...? Then this? I thought hard, and even without any energy left in the tank I pushed my mind to recall what I needed to know. It was like trying to remember a dream that constantly tries to snake its way back into the subconscious, but somehow I managed to grip its tail. My eyes sprung wide and alarmed, and my hand shot down to my stomach.

"I was stabbed. Shaun stabbed me in the old factory..."

Bandages were wrapped all over my stomach like I was a mummy, and it obviously must have been one hell of a stab wound. Luckily though, I felt no pain. In fact, I felt great—like I was sitting on a fluffy white cloud in the sky. Drifting along without a care or a worry, feeling the old sweet buzz that I used to chase. Morphine was running the course of my veins, and it was incredible.

"Why on earth did I ever give this stuff up? Is it so bad that I like them? Why should I be denied a pleasure that I enjoy?"

I rolled my head back and closed my eyes, basking in the sweet sensation that it was, cherishing it with a big drooping smile. I had done so much over the last few weeks, and this was simply just a reward. A reward for all my hard work, and tireless efforts.

During my nod, the sound of footsteps approached the hospital room door, a nurse stepped in, flicked on the lights and tended to me. She was a soft featured woman of perhaps her sixties with a round and friendly face.

"It's good to see you awake young man, your very lucky indeed. Someone must be watching over you."

I stared up at the woman and went to speak for the first time since waking, all I could muster was a weak, drooling tone.

"My stomach hurts... really bad..."

The woman stared sympathetically for a while before leaving to retrieve more painkillers, and excitedly, I thought to myself.

"If I'm gonna have a reward, I may as well make the most of it."

I had always enjoyed the rain, I liked the sound of it, the way it bounces off the concrete splitting into tons of tiny little droplets. To me it was soothing, I'd always felt that it promoted a relaxed and meditative state. On this night though, something wasn't quite as soothing about it, almost to the degree that it held a sense of malice. I developed a growing concern that that someone lurked outside, masked by the sound of the rain, using it like an auditory cloak. What scared me most though, was after being hurled into a black void and being stabbed in the stomach. Anything was possible now, I didn't feel safe.

The nurse returned holding a small trey and a small glass of water, two little orange tablets waiting to be swallowed sat in front of me, like to little orange eyes just waiting to be assimilated by my hungry liver. She set them down on my lap and gave me another of her sympathetic smiles, before standing beside my hospital bed. I stared at them some more, they were like heaven embodied in the form of a capsule.

When I reached for them though, the thought of heaven seemed to be the furthest thing from my mind. They were more like forbidden fruits, two deathly little orange tablets that would assure my demise. Guilt rose in my chest, and all I could do was think of what was at stake. How was Josh going to end up if his only hope, was high and doped up on opiates in some hospital? But then again, it was just *two* measly little tablets, surely no more harmful than a couple of beers with dinner. At times like these, I'd usually think of my mother. But instead, I thought of Olive, beautiful Olive from Endon.

I looked at the nurse, and returned a smile.

"You know what? My stomach feels fine, thank you though."

Her eyes narrowed, and she frowned.

"Sir, I'd like you to take them. You've undergone some very serious trauma, so please just pick up the tablets and swallow them."

I narrowed my own eyes and frowned along with her.

"No really, I'm fine. Truly I don't need them, but I'll be sure to let you know if I need anything else okay?"

The nurse grabbed the tablets from the trey and began to pin my arms down on the bed, her face turned red with effort and for a while I struggled against her grip. I started to panic, and couldn't help but yell.

"Get off me! Stop it! Help. Help!"

The woman finally backed off, she rested her hands on her knees and stared at me like a lunatic. Her round face started to bulge, and her eyes looked as though they were going to pop directly out from her face. Every inch of her skin seemed to be rippling like the violent waves of an ocean. Completely stunned and speechless, all I could do was watch in horror.

The top of her head started to split, and a snakelike black fog oozed out from her while her head deflated like a popped soccer ball. Soon after, the black fog revealed two beady little orange eyes of its own. It watched me with seething hatred, cursing me relentlessly with its eyes. Her chest and arms split open and revealed more of the creature, great long black limbs emerged while the woman fell to the floor like a disgusting human-jacket. The creature writhed over towards me and stood tall above my bedside. In a voice sounding like it was a complete two octaves below the normal tone, it boomed.

"Take your medicine little man."

All I could do was scream, and I did. It pierced its way like a knife through to the world of reality, where I woke in excruciating pain and a terrible fever. I rolled my head around shouting and straining my throat, feeling the threat of losing consciousness at any second. Before I slipped back out of reality, all I could retain was the sight of an ambulance, and half a dozen men handling me into the back of it. For now, it turned out I was still alive.

If I was ever asked, what was the most horrible thing you can remember? Until now, it would have always been a tie between two occasions, and the first was obvious: My mother's death. It was hell, true and pure hell manifested and stretched out over an excruciating two-week period. The human liver metabolizes opiates, drugs that aid the process of relieving pain. So naturally without one, she was in constant pain—terrible pain. And I watched it all, the sickest twist of irony that I'd ever witnessed.

And the second choice was something that'd occurred within the very factory I was stabbed in, and funnily enough thanks to very person who'd stabbed me. Around twenty hits worth of LSD was placed in a beer I was drinking one night, and I spent a grueling three days writhing around the concrete floor praying for either the drugs to end, or my own life.

Being stabbed was partly the worst thing that I'd now experienced, but aside from the stabbing, it was the dreams that I was being exposed to. Completely vivid nightmares of a black, snakelike figure that constantly tried to coheres me into using opiates again. During my short stints of lucidity, I determined the dreams to be a battle between life and death. But somehow, god knows how, I fought. And ultimately won. I lived on, but not without scars that ran all the way to my core. Some people throughout my life have told me that scars of all kinds promote growth. But truthfully these were scars I'd prefer not to have.

Irony, being a common thread in my life, once again presented itself when my consciousness returned for good. Rain slammed against the windows of the hospital room, and the room was dimly lit by specks, Grey overtones. Luckily the nurse that was tending to me didn't split open to reveal a grotesque black figure emerging from her body. And when I explained to her my history of drug abuse, she was completely understanding, and prescribed me a handful of benzodiazepines. Which fortunately didn't awaken the great beast of addiction that slept in the shady corners of my ex-junkie mind.

I was in the Vickerdon public hospital, and according to the staff, I was incredibly lucky to still have my life intact. The first day I spent there I felt completely useless, panic and anxiety seized me. I couldn't stop thinking about Josh, out in New York, alone and lost. Then there was the crown, the horrid crown that I had lost to the dingy old factory. Which by now had probably been pawned off by Shaun just so he could score some more drugs. Though I wondered, would he have been affected by it in the way that I had?

Tangles of mysteries surrounded it, and they were mysteries that I needed to uncover. My foremost fear was the old man getting hold of it, Christ in heaven would be a terrible thing.

Oddly, there was no police report. No cops showed up in order to take information on what'd happened to me, but in a way I was grateful for it. The thought of Shaun standing behind bars definitely made me feel a welcome spike of justice, but for the moment all I wanted was to keep to myself. Shaun could be dealt with in time, and before that time came I just wanted to get done what needed to get done. Finding Josh. I needed more than anything to find him, I literally couldn't have been stabbed at a worse time.

"Forgive me Josh... I'll find you soon, I promise."

The next few days drifted by like a heavy cloud threatening a violent storm, and no matter how much I tried to distract myself, I couldn't shake the feeling of impending danger. What depressed me mostly was that I'd forgotten what it was like to feel safe, I wanted to see a light that showed me the end of it, but it eluded me. My dreams were still disturbing too, the good news was that they didn't feature any black snakelike creatures, but what they did present was somehow just as awful. They would be purely auditory, like I was blind and without nerves in my body to feel. I'd be barraged with the sound of a monstrous choir, coming at me loudly from all sides. The most difficult thing to ignore was my intuition, sparking away like a pilot light on the fritz.

On the third day during my stay in the Vickerdon hospital, I shakily walked outside to the courtyard with hopes of scoring a cigarette off someone. But the general demeanor outside was unfriendly and sour, just a sea of Grey and untrustworthy faces. Cigarettes seemed to act like a weird form of currency, a rare commodity only available to the more rotten looking people. And of all the residents, there was one man who won that prize. A big bulky man with maybe three remaining teeth in his decaying mouth, and a huge bald head covered in unnaturally prominent veins. He'd stare at me for every second I was in his presence, with a sickly, childish grin spread across his bulldog face.

Due to his size, he had no trouble bowling down members of the staff to gain access to the files and records behind the front desk. And amazingly, within seconds he had somehow managed to find exactly what he was looking for; my name. Before he was overpowered and sedated he spent a good half an hour following me around the hospital chanting my name through his drooling mouth, again and again and again. If it hadn't been for the staff's reassurance, I would no doubt be under the impression that I'd been placed in a mental institution instead of a hospital. Ironically, the bulky man had been sent to one. But part of me wondered why he was doing what he was doing, and worst of all it made it all the harder for me to ignore my intuition. More than anything, I didn't want more bad times to be waiting for me around the corner. But unfortunately I was already in the middle of something big, something that my oldest friend had been dragged into as well. Despite my condition, tomorrow would be the day I leave—even if I ended up leaving a trail of blood all the way from Utah to New York.

CHAPTER 15-

"So what's the plan? We can't just stay *here* for the rest of our lives."

Josh was frustrated, his mood was at an all-time low. But more than anything he hated the feeling of being useless, things needed to be done but he couldn't do anything. Steven was on his mind, Josh kept imagining him lying dead in some street somewhere, slowly bleeding out every chance of success. It was agonizing, a helpless feeling, and Josh was about ready to throw his last shred of patience into the bin. Outside was dangerous territory, the spirits of Zugai had swarmed into the small town of Vickerdon, and it was a complete miracle that Josh had returned from the supermarket alive and well.

"So... Why did Solus let me leave without a bullet in *my* head?" Josh had asked at some point over a tea with Edmund.

"He most likely wasn't aware of your abilities."

"So if he *had* known, he would have killed me as well.?"

"Without a single moment of hesitation yes."

Josh was afraid, but it wasn't the thought of dying that scared Josh, it was the idea of Solus achieving what he wanted. Chaos frightened Josh, or at least the sense of chaos that Solus wanted to bring forth. Nothing was going to prevent it so long as Josh just continued sitting on his ass in the middle of Utah. It was go time, time to get moving to find Steven to at least try to put a stop to Solus.

"So again, what's the plan? When can we leave?"

It was probably the hundredth time that Josh had asked this, and this time, just like every other time all Edmund did was just stare back for a few seconds before looking the other way, deep in thought. Josh couldn't take it anymore, he needed an answer, some kind of confirmation to put his restless mind at ease.

"Do you even have a plan?? Or are you just ignoring me because your just stumped on it? Edmund...? Damn it!"

After another routine silence, Edmund finally responded, moments before Josh exploded in complete frustration and anger.

"After we get Steven, we need to travel to the east. Solus

resides in that direction, and once we get there I'll build a safe house much like this one. We'll plan from there."

Josh thought about the reply, rubbing his eyes.

"Towards the belly of the beast huh? Good..."

"So, what's stopping us from leaving now? What if the black spirit guys don't let up? What's the point of waiting?"

Edmund replied without delay.

"It could be just *one* Minuit mistake that could destroy everything."

The frustration returned like a heavy splash of molten lava, his face twigged in impatience. Slowly he exhaled, and spoke as calmly as he could.

"Ok... Fine, so if you can build these safe house things, why not just do it while we're walking? Like a mobile safety net kinda thing?"

Edmund shook his head, casting away the idea without even using words. Josh didn't bother retorting, what was the point? Instead he leaned over to pat Marron, his furry little companion.

"There is a deserted old warehouse nearby, and I'm relatively sure that Steven was there. It matches the painting that you made Josh, that's where we need to go."

Josh shot his eyes towards the ghost's, glaring angrily.

"It's been three days, and you decide that now is the time to tell me?? What the hell is it with you and keeping your mouth shut about all this?"

Edmund rose from his seat without taking his eyes of Josh, returning the glare, his face faded back to it's awfully blurry counterpart. And like every other time, it unnerved Josh causing him to look away. It reminded him of Jessie, and the bad times.

"You are hopelessly impatient, and a hair away from being a complete and utter fool. Had you known any earlier, you most likely wouldn't have shut your yapping mouth until we made our move, not that you haven't been anyway. I need to think in peace, and you have the mouth of an unfed dog."

Josh winced at this, it didn't make him feel angry though, or even frustrated. Edmund was right, and that's what caught Josh off guard.

"I'm telling you now because we're going to leave within the hour, the spirits of Zugai are distracted. I have no idea what by, but either way we have a small window of opportunity. So be ready to jump when I say jump, pack your things."

Josh did what he was told, and within five minutes was sitting nervously on one of the satin gold armchairs just next to the front door, with all of his belongings tucked into his bag at his feet. Edmund stood at the window, eyes closed in thought.

Then with no warning, like a gun firing, Edmund's eyes opened and he hurried towards Josh while he eerily faded out of visibility, though his voice remained. It boomed like a sub-woofer.

"Move!"

Josh grabbed his bag and swirled around for the door, his heart racing like a jackhammer he swung open the door and launched himself down the outdoor steps and onto the road.

"Head downhill, and do exactly as I say."

Josh did so, he ran downhill towards the string of shops that filled downtown Vickerdon. Passing Gary's milk bar, he raced along, planting one foot in front at a time, Marron ran beside him taking long strides while staying in profile with Josh.

"Take the next left."

Josh launched up an alley way on his left, growing tired he drew huge breaths. Though he had no intention of resting, he continued pumping his legs along the cracked concrete.

"Keep moving, it's coming up to the right."

For a second Josh thought he'd collapse, it'd been a long time since he'd had any form of exercise and it was killing him. After another four minutes of solid running Josh was finally instructed to stop, they had arrived. A broken down hole of a place stood in front of Josh, exactly the same as his painting. Josh placed his hands on his knees and drew in deep breaths, his lungs were on fire. "Thank god that's over... Damn..."

Edmund once again manifested in visible form and walked into the entrance of the factory, explaining his next course of action as he did so.

"I cannot create safety from the spirits of Zugai during movement, but I can provide safety in a stationary sense. We will stop here for a while, but it'll take a few minutes."

Without having caught his breath yet, Josh queried the ghost.

"So... Why didn't you just come here and make it safe before I came?"

As Edmund spoke, he raised his hands towards the building, assuming an odd meditative stance. Eyes closed.

"There can be only one safe house at a time as there is just one of me. And to someone like you Josh, the spirits of Zugai are especially dangerous."

Josh nodded, *the spirits of Zugai are dangerous.* He hated the idea of them, horrid snakelike things that swarmed in massive groups. It reminded him of certain people from his past, cowards who on their lonesome would prove not to be a threat, but roll in large numbers in order to intimidate. Josh finally started to catch his breath.

"So are the Zugai spirits always in groups?"

"Josh, I need to concentrate."

Once again Josh nodded in understanding. "Right."

What happened next stunned Josh, he witnessed the entire factory begin to glow. It was strange though, it felt oddly dream-like, as though a part of Josh was disconnected from it. A phantom glow, only real to the vivid imagination. Josh had to look away, the sensation was somehow too much for him to bear, but he didn't know how exactly.

When he looked down at Marron, he noticed that even *he* was having the same reaction. Marron's ears were turned back as he made little whimpering sounds, before fearfully seeking refuge under Josh's feet.

"Almost there, another short while and it'll be done."

"Thank god for that..." Josh thought aloud, with his back to the factory. He slowly knelt down and gave Marron a scratch on his back, comforting both the cat and himself.

"It's ok buddy, almost over okay?"

Slowly, the indescribable sensation began to subside, until Edmund finally backed away from the door and motioned for Josh to follow him into the old, broken down hole of a factory.

"Why did that feel so terrible?" Asked Josh.

"It is difficult describe, all I know is that it's instinctive to me. So I really don't know."

"Does it make *you* feel weird?"

"Not really no, but it destroyed me a very long time ago. And I'm hoping that it didn't do the same to your old friend."

Josh shivered, that was a bad thought. *'Oh hey we found*

Steven, but he's brain's all screwed up.' Josh hated the idea, he shook it from his mind and walked inside the factory behind Edmund, Marron running alongside. Into the dark but safe confines of Steven's last place of sighting.

***

"This place is horrible, you couldn't have at least decked it out with some gold furniture with your ghost tricks?"

"That would have taken time that we didn't have, besides all that can be done from the inside."

"Ok well that's good news, do you have a ghost power to make it not smell like piss anymore?"

Edmund turned back to face Josh with a look of agitation on his weathered face, but worst of all it was blurred out.

"Jesus man, don't do that..."

Edmund's face remained blurry and his face agitated, but as Josh stared into his eyes he determined that is was suspicion, something was wrong.

"Edmund, what?"

Edmund looked around like a curious dog with pricked ears, squinting his eyes in concentration.

"We have company, fortunately it doesn't seem like dangerous company though. Just people, they're in the far side of the building."

This time *Josh's* ears pricked up, and an idea came to him. It was a dark idea, but one that he wasn't going to let go of. His face turned blank and he walked down the corridor, through to a large alcove area full of broken glass and brick. Silently, he concentrated hard on what he was hearing, it was faint, but he could just hear them. He headed in the direction he thought led to the source, his fists so tight they were turning red.

It was possible that one of the people in the building may have been responsible for what had happened to Steven, and if they were, they were in trouble. Josh hadn't had a good fight in a while.

He calmed his posture and released the tension within his wrists and continued towards the source of the noise, his fury sitting like a molten rock in the center of his stomach.

"Here we go, just through here."

Josh carefully stepped into a room full of around ten or so

people, all laughing like morons, most likely high on whatever cheap drugs they can get their hands on. He looked around suspiciously while they all slowly turned towards him, returning Josh their own looks of suspicion.

"I'm lookin' for someone, he owes me a ton of money."

They looked around at each other, no one saying a word.

"He told me he'd be good for it, but now I'm gonna have to take his teeth for payment."

All of them sat still, except for one who rose to his feet with the look of a dumb, hungry bulldog. He wore a cast on his left arm and an ugly necklace. Speaking with hostility he answered Josh's question.

"If you try and touch me, I'll still a knife in your neck. I suggest you get out of here before I leave you dead on this floor."

Josh stared at him for a while, he was truly disgusting. A mouth full of brown rotting teeth, and a frame like a skeleton. Josh had a strong feeling, but he needed to be completely sure.

"His name is Steven, we have some serious business. None of you better try and cover for him, where is he?"

The skeletal ringleader of the misfit factory raised an eyebrow and slowly looked around at his fellow junkies. A smirk cropping up on his bony, pale face.

"I knew it! Ha, I knew that he was holding out on me, I knew he'd never get off the drugs. Just like his mom, it's in their genes."

It took every ounce of willpower to resist sprinting across the room and choking every bit of pitiful life out of him, but somehow, Josh refrained. Instead he just casually replied.

"He owes me a lot of money, and I'm tired of him avoiding me. So tell me where he."

"Well your gonna like this, I already took the liberty of dealing with him."

Josh walked over, outstretching his hand to shake his, trying as hard as possible to muster up some kind of smile.

"I'm Josh, what's your's, friend?"

He grinned a disgusting, sick grin and returned the shake.

"Shaun, so Josh what have you got on ya man?"

Josh held fast onto Shaun's hand, every scrap of a smile flushing out of his face. Red hot anger, pure fury swarmed his stomach like deadly little butterflies.

"Yeah alright, get off me dude."

Josh squeezed hard and felt the bones in his hand shift around. He didn't stop until he felt something crunch, Shaun started screaming in pain. At the last moment he pulled Shaun towards him and brought his knee into his stomach as hard as he could manage. All of the air from Shaun's lungs blew out, falling awkwardly to the floor as Josh kept his grip firm on Shaun's bony little hand. None of his friends even tried to help out their leader, instead they just stared in wonder, their eyes bulging from their skinny faces.

Josh brought up his left hand and wound up his fist, he planted it directly into Shaun's cheek. *'Like rolling pins hitting dough... This is what you get, this is how things go for you Shaun.'*

At least four of Shaun's decaying little brown teeth flew out of his mouth followed by a fine spray of blood. Shaun still with the air blown out of his lungs, remained silent, his eyes were as wide as everybody else's.

"Where is Steven? And if you don't feel like answering me, I'll just have to take a few more teeth from your disgusting jawline, then maybe give snap it in half. Sound good? This is fun right?"

Josh let go, watching Shaun flopping to the floor in a sprawling heap, blood running from his mouth. He started gasping like a fish out of water.

"I hate people like you so much."

A girl in the group started whimpering before rising to her feet and running towards the door to the alcove. Josh didn't care, there was only one person here that he had business with, and he was already bleeding on the floor.

"Whoever doesn't want the same treatment, I suggest you leave now, or your teeth are gonna be spread over the floor just like this asshole. Everybody looked around at each other, as if they were mutually saying agreeing to run. Then they did, everybody except Shaun vacated the decadent broken down room, like rats running from a house on fire.

"Well, there go your friends."

Shaun rolled onto his stomach and coughed a spray of phlegm and blood, his eyes red and hateful.

"Speaking of friends, Steven is one of mine. And I'm looking for him, and if I didn't know any better I could have sworn that not long ago I asked you where he was. Do you remember? Remember when I asked you that?"

Shaun stared at Josh without making a sound, instead he just seemed fascinated by what was happening. It enraged Josh, how could someone be this insane?

"Last chance Shaun, where is he?"

Shaun stayed silent, though his look of fascination slowly turned into a smile. And that was it, that was enough to send Josh into one of his fits. Things were about to go blank, he could feel it. A red hot blanket that wrapped over his body and soaked into him, an animalistic rage.

Josh had no idea whether Edmund was there the whole time as he materialized between him and Shaun, his face blurred out with an expression of disapproval, Josh would have none of it.

"Edmund... Don't get in my way, he stabbed Steven and he's gonna pay for it. Get out of my way."

Edmund placed a hand on Josh's shoulder, staring at him thoughtfully.

"This person isn't afraid of your breed of intimidation, but I know what he *is* afraid of."

Shaun blinked vacantly, profoundly confused. Even though he was still smirking, Josh could tell he was unsettled. I guess who wouldn't be, it's not exactly normal for an elderly Elizabethan ghost to manifest from nothing. Maybe Edmund was right, maybe a hardened fist could only get one so far. Josh took one last glance at Shaun, beaten and bleeding on the concrete before looking back at Edmund, subtly nodding his head.

"Ok... Just promise me you'll get it out of him, make him tell us."

"I will, you have my word. Now leave."

Josh turned and left for the alcove, spotting Marron curled up over at the far side of the room, amongst a pile of smashed up drywall. While Josh made his way across the room he heard Shaun speaking, he couldn't make out exactly what it was he was saying, but it was clear he wasn't enjoying Edmunds company. Part of Josh was curious as to what was happening, but after experiencing the feeling that his weird abilities had had on him when he was hiding the factory, he decided that he didn't ever really want to know.

Shaun screamed terrible bloodcurdling screams, they reminded Josh of a child separated from a parent. It wasn't a scream of pain, it was much worse. Deathly fear that pierced through the concrete walls of the building. All Josh could think was of how fortunate he was to not be on the receiving end, he just scratched Marron behind the ears and waited for Edmund to finish whatever it was he was doing. He thought more about Jessie, and the way his life had unfolded after she had died. It was a depressing life, almost completely lacking of good times. At least now he felt a cause, a reason to wake up and move.

"I swear I'll kill that old man myself, I'll make him suffer."

Solus was the living embodiment of all the bad times in Josh's life, and Josh relished in his anger. Feeling a bold surge of justification run the course of his veins. Josh fantasized about his revenge, and thought over what he would say if he got the chance to stand above a defeated and dying Solus.

Ten minutes had passed before Edmund returned to the alcove, with a stone cold expression that read. 'What needed to be done has been done.' Josh didn't say a word, instead he just continued patting Marron, thinking about what might come next.

"I've learned all the information he had, it's not much, but it's a start. He was left bleeding in the factory entrance, then he disappeared."

Josh looked up at Edmund, scrunching his face.

"Ed, that's literally the least helpful bit of information I've ever heard, that *actually* doesn't explain anything. I have a painting that explains it better, and that doesn't even make sense."

"Think about it."

Josh stared at Edmund, with his eyebrows raised.

"Think about what.?"

"Well, your painting did indeed show Steven in a dire condition. But what we know *now,* is that he didn't go anywhere on his own while he was wounded. So, someone must have found him, and taken him somewhere."

"Taken him where?"

"Probably where most people go when injured and in need of medical help."

"You think he's in the hospital?"

Edmund nodded then averted his gaze, going into one of his

common fits of deep thought. Reflecting on whatever it might be within the last five hundred years, and for the first time Josh was curious as to what it might be.

"Things were supposed to be perfect, wheels were set in motion, and I was in the front line. But all that eventually came was destruction. Destruction and madness, just pure devastation."

"What?" Josh asked hesitantly.

"The problem Josh, was me. I lost almost every part of myself, in a great swirling, destructive cycle that I became aware of only when it was too late. I've been conscious for so long now, so unnaturally long... I was a normal person all those years ago, and the biggest fear I have is losing those old memories. It haunts me, the idea of being stripped of the only natural thing I can hold onto."

Josh was completely lost for words, dumbfounded by what Edmund was saying. It scared Josh, he pitied him.

"The erased man was my teacher, not to mention the most pure and wondrous soul that I'd ever come across. But now, he is the undisputed face of chaos, literally an embodiment of madness. He was torn apart, destroyed beyond recognition. And I prey, again and again for him to be restored. I hope with every ounce of my being that there is still some of his old self left."

Josh thought about the erased man, and the impact that he'd had on his *own* life. Part of him just wanted him dead and gone with no chance of redemption, to be punished harshly for what he'd done. But at the end of the day; it was all Solus, the wretched old man who welcomed madness and chaos, with hopes of controlling it and riding its destructive wave to glory. After hearing the pain that Edmund felt due to chaos, it just further fueled his anger towards Solus.

"We'll do the best we can man, when we get Steven we'll plan it all out. All we can do is try. If it makes you feel any better, I have a good feeling about it, the good guys always win anyway."

Despite how stupid Josh thought his words to be, Edmund actually smiled. But sadly, Josh had never seen a smile so utterly broken, and it crushed him.

Josh got to his feet at the sound of commotion, then in the next second Shaun started limping through the alcove, on his way out of the factory. Curiosity got the better of Josh.

"So. What exactly did you do to him anyway?"

Edmund didn't answer, and just as Josh was about to repeat the question he suddenly decided against it. Not because he was afraid of the answer, he simply just felt maybe it was the right thing to do. Instead he asked.

"So when should we make our move?"

Unfortunately, Josh didn't like the answer he was given.

"When the sound of the choir falls silent."

Josh was struck off guard, the nightmare he'd had was no doubt disturbing, and the thought of the great horrible detuned choir being a real thing scared him.

"What is it, what's the choir?" Asked Josh.

"I don't know, and hopefully we won't find out. I'm going to get started on giving this factory a facelift, perhaps you could paint in the meantime."

Josh nodded, exited at the prospect. Like looking forward to a beer after a hard day's work he smiled at the idea.

"Yeah definitely."

Josh couldn't help but continue watching Edmund, hobbling about deep in thought as he always was.

"So, why deck the place out? Aren't we just gonna leave soon anyway?"

"Like I said before Josh, I hold onto my earliest memories with the grip of a vice. It reminds me of my former self, it comforts me."

Josh felt embarrassed, foolish for not realizing that himself.

"Right, of course. Sorry Ed. When you get a spare moment could you ghost up some painting stuff for me?"

"Already waiting for you, all it needs are your two hands."

Josh surveyed elaborate kit of painting supplies sitting in the corner of the alcove, neatly set out to perfection. A little haven of meditation ready to be used.

"You know. We can do this Edmund, we can win this battle. We deserve it, I know that sounds stupid, but I really think it counts for something."

"I think so too. It's time for me to do what I do, so please leave me be."

***

Josh painted like a maniac high on a rainbow of stimulants, his wrists weaved and worked the canvas like snakes in the summer grass. He was feeling the beautiful buzz of focus, and held fast to its welcoming feeling of warmth. He didn't think much at all in this time, or at least didn't think in an active sense. A serene flutter of white noise rested peacefully where his worried thoughts would usually be. The painting slowly began to present itself, and over the course of around two hours, the general body of the artwork sat in front of his eyes. It was the past, a long ago experience that'd occurred during the good times, an experience that would have completely slipped his mind had it not been for the art of painting.

He was in Connecticut with Jessie and his Uncle, playing around as a functioning family in the middle of an enormous field of perfectly green grass. Big broad smiles painted across every face, beaming right out of the canvas to the viewer. He was struck hard with melancholy, it was hard to look at something that was so dead in the past, with no chance of being relived. But at the same time, Josh guessed that it was this feeling that made him feel the most alive, to bask in old memories that were blissfully enjoyed all those years ago at the time. And without even noticing, Josh was praying to himself, praying that at some point in the future, he could offer a similar experience to someone else.

"If there's one thing I could hope for, It'd be this."

Josh finished his painting a little after Edmund had finished the work that he had, and in the time that Edmund waited, he'd brewed two cups of coffee, before them down on a small table between two chairs at the other end of the alcove. The two of them sat and sipped of coffee while Marron dozed on Josh's lap.

"I don't spose you could ghost up some smokes for me?"

"No, nothing in Coda had any use for them."

"So basically, you can only create things that you made back in the day?"

"Essentially, aside from a small number of other things."

"Like coffee? I mean, I'm guessing that the spirits of Coda weren't into caffeine."

"Well actually, that was for me."

"Too bad you weren't a smoker."

"How did your painting go?" Edmund asked, ignoring Josh.

Josh looked over towards his painting spot and thought again about his time in Connecticut as a child.

"Good, it was of my family. We went to Connecticut on a holiday when we were young. And I guess my hands were in the mood to reminisce. It's not a painting of an omen or anything, just a good time I had back in the day."

Edmund looked into his coffee, seeming more absent minded than he had ever been. In a way it just looked like he was enjoying himself, relaxing like an elderly man with a rich life behind him.

"Are they still out there? The Zugai?"

"Yes, and more agitated than usual. Something is stirring them up, and I do not know what."

"Okay well when we have a chance to break for the hospital, let me know."

"Naturally."

CHAPTER 16-

"A goldmine. Black gold, perfect soldiers for important bidding."

Solus had never been to the island of Zugai in person, but soon enough not only would he be there in true physical form, he would have the entire realm of Coda under his command. A new and perfect world, an ideal chaos that would bring forth a new generation. The original house of Coda had fallen, crumbled under the weight of its thoughtless king's ego. Yes, Solus did have an ego, but every aspect of it was justified, he *was* after all, the undisputed ruler that Coda had always needed. A perfect soul in a perfect world, molded in the image of a god.

So very long it had taken to craft the shrine of New Canaan, but it's time of completion had finally arrived. As of now Solus had strings tied to every broken soul from the island of Zugai. They were unguided beings, with no purpose and drive. But being the fantastic person that Solus was, they now had a glorious purpose, they were part of a new order.

Solus watched his faithful followers work, with his special eyes he had a front row seat to witness the restoration of his rightful crown. They danced around it like black smoke, weaving about while being sporadically struck by its power, they were slowly draining the raw force that resided inside it. Its original owner had been driven mad by the crown, tortured into madness. And his insanity had infected it, it sat inside like a horrible virus that stung the mind like a wasp. Solus had lost roughly one hundred spirits to the crown now, they would go insane then quickly fizzle out of existence moments after touching the very thing. But miraculously, Solus had discovered that each time it occurred, a small piece of the crown's insanity would die along with the spirit. They were sacrifices that had to be made, all for the good of the new way.

And just when Solus had thought things couldn't possibly get any better, he'd found out that the little prick Steven Marron had died, stabbed right in the stomach. Boom, dead as a doorknob. There was still the other one, the lowly alcoholic that'd run away like a coward in Vickerdon. But Solus payed no mind, after all, there was no point in being threatened by something that posed no threat. And besides everything, the faithful Zugai followers would make short work of anyone who dared to intervene anyway.

Everything was on track, so Solus just continued sitting in wait for the final deeds to be done. He was in his home, an old townhouse that sat in the center of his hundred-acre property. The desert meets the forest, then meets the home of Solus. Holy ground.

The erased man was currently within Coda resting, recharging his energy for the duties that lay ahead of him. Sacrifices would soon be made in the form of children's futures cut short, Solus needed as many years as he could get.

He rose from his chair and made his way downstairs to the shrine, a room that was covered entirely with the ancient artwork of Coda. His carefully crafted shrine of summoning, two hundred years' worth of tireless work and effort. Solus stepped into the circle of Zugai, closed his eyes and spoke directly to his followers.

"The time draws near my friends, very soon you will all be recognized as my faithful disciples. You will be rewarded, a perfect and endless life awaits you all."

Solus felt a joyful buzz of moral echo through the island of Zugai, they were elated by the prospect of their place within the new order.

"What I say now is of utmost importance, a holy cause that will require every ounce of effort you can muster. I need every one of you to join me in the red sea, we are going to spread word of the new order. Tonight, everyone will dream of the new age."

CHAPTER 17-

My suspicions were confirmed, and what I'd feared had unfortunately turned out to be true. I couldn't leave. But it was so much stranger than that, it wasn't like I was being held captive or anything, it was like being repelled from using the hospitals front door. I couldn't make sense of it, I'd tried everything with no success, some part of me just wouldn't allow my legs to finish the job of walking all the way out of the building. On my fourth day, as soon as I'd woken I had decided it was well and truly time to go, so I wandered down to the front reception. I stared out onto the grey streets of Vickerdon, while telling myself. *'Ok... Go. Move your feet, c'mon walk!'* But nothing... I was terrified, unsettled by the prospect that no matter how hard I tried, I couldn't leave.

I even spoke to the staff, explaining my bizarre situation as calmly as I could. But all they would do was gently usher me back to my room while I just seemed to go along with them like a zombie. And it wasn't until they left, that I would snap back into lucidity and reflect upon it in complete confusion. I spoke to some of the other patients too, quizzing them on how long their stay has been. But what they told me left me even more confused than I was before. One patient in particular had said.

"I'm unwell. All of us need help. Your unwell too, we all need to be helped..."

He said it with such a sure tone, like he was speaking with all the wisdom in the world. I hated hearing it, because soon after I discovered that he was a lunatic, utterly detached from reality. He would walk through the courtyard singing songs out of key while addressing everyone else like we were some sort of high clergy from the medieval era. Then I began to realize that almost every patient in the entire hospital was in *some* way delusional.

Aside from the crazed man who was obsessed with flashing me maniacal smiles, the first few days had been normal. But as time went on, it was like an invisible sheet had lifted from my surroundings, slowly revealing the true and insane nature of the hospital. If these things went on too long, I was pretty sure that I'd become a basket case myself. I had so many things to do, there was the crown that I'd lost, the old man. And Josh, god how I needed to find Josh.

Although, a plan had devised itself over the course of my fifth day. I didn't know if it was a good plan, let alone if it had any possibility of success. But what other option was there? What else could I do? It was either try, or end up a crazy person with a depressing Grey complexion.

The red void. Maybe, just maybe, it was possible to go there, and send a message to someone as opposed to receiving one. Maybe I could find Josh and somehow alert him of my location, and tonight was the night.

The red void had always been a place only accessible when the sun had fallen, it was a place of the night. Most likely because a place of dreams and floating subconscious would only available when people were sleeping. So I waited, to pass time I played with a deck of cards in the common room, I flicked on the radio and even managed to score a cigarette off one of the patients out in the court yard. Then slowly but surely, the day began to fade. And the world of dreams opened itself up to me.

***

Meditating on my hospital bed, I mentally prepared myself for the trip to the red void. I'd decided with my gut feeling, that I would test my new theory on the fly, and attempt the communicate to Josh only when I found myself directly next to his subconscious.

I was nervous, never had I enjoyed time in the red void. Though what unsettled me so much this time, was that I was relying on it as an option for my own safety. It seemed like the only route I had, and I didn't like it at all. Everything started as usual, after closing my eyes I envisioned two separate little screens, the bottom one depicting Josh and the top one ready to spark into life. Thankfully, everything rolled along without too much of a problem, and my mind remained clear, an empty mental canvas.

Like a lighter, red light filled my mind's eye like a struck match, and the familiar little cog began to turn in the front of my head.

"Ok. It's all good, just like every other time."

Slowly, my body drifted away, my psyche floated on its

lonesome, detached from physicality. Then the red light expanded, and I was sucked in, entering the ocean of dreams. I floated for a moment, waiting for my eyes to ease to the atmosphere. The red void was a bright place, almost overwhelming. Moving along using my instinct, I let the magnetic auto-pilot carry me with its gentle hands. But not after long, my nervousness came rushing back into the pit of my stomach, my head shot around fearfully in every direction, trying to locate the cause of my sudden panic. Something was definitely wrong.

Then there it was, the last thing that I'd want to see. My nightmares had manifested themselves, black snakelike creatures wormed their way around the red void like eels. Luckily they were a fair distance from me, but they were all swarming in a group the exact direction I was moving towards. The sight disgusted me, the very nature of them made me feel sick to my stomach. I tried to break free of the magnetic pull of Josh's subconscious, and for a second didn't think I was going to be able to. But in the end I managed, and I floated while staying alert in a terrified fascination. I hated them, they were awful.

Thinking through the situation, it seemed hopeless. Did they know? Did they know that I would be heading for Josh? They began to disperse, like there was an explosion in the center of their swarm, they all flew out in different directions. Like giant leeches, they attached themselves to the dreamers within the void. I turned back and stared through the path of floating subconscious leading back to my own.

What are they doing? Do I brave it and break for Josh? Or do I retreat? For a short while, my intuition had abandoned me. But then thank god, my indecision made sense. I heard a voice, it boomed through the red void with an almost deafening loudness, but I knew somehow that it was directed at me, and me alone.

"Turn back. Stay where you are, I guarantee there is no safer decision. Turn back now."

"Who are you?"

"The streets of Vickerdon are dangerous, and your inability to leave the hospital is for your own good. You are painfully impatient, turn back Steven."

I turned around and swam as fast as I could towards my own floating subconscious. It looked like liquid in zero gravity, a sentient globule that slowly drifted along an endless ocean. In around half a minute of frenzied swimming I finally reached it, and I threw myself into it like I was trying to hip and shoulder my way through a sheet of drywall. My mind tumbled around violently, slamming me back into my body like a rag doll. I was covered in sweat and breathing like I'd just ran a marathon. My eyes shot open and I stared at the ceiling of my hospital room.

"Jesus…"

I sat in bed thinking, devising theories on what the hell was happening. What were the black spirits? Whatever they were, I didn't assume that they were particularly friendly. The nightmares that I'd had when I'd arrived in the hospital came to mind, were they the same spirits? Leeching themselves onto my subconscious to taunt and torture me from within the red void? I guess I'd discover it all in time, for now I suppose it was simply just a matter of waiting. The booming voice had told me that I was in the safest place. There was no reason to trust the voice, but in any case, I did.

"Hopefully I'm not stuck here for too long... May as well go see if I can score a cigarette in the courtyard."

CHAPTER 18-

"I wouldn't imagine that we'd have long Josh, are you ready to move?"

Josh nodded, ready to move. The idea of waiting any longer was much worse than running into danger, he was glad that the time had finally arrived. As he walked with Edmund towards the streets, he quizzed him.

"So are they distracted again?"

"Not quite, they simply just don't seem to be around at the moment."

"Well that's good right?"

"I suppose, but to be honest, that's what troubles me. Ok, same as last time. Do exactly as I say."

"Right."

Edmund faded out of sight as Josh broke into a sprint, running out of the factory and into the moonlit streets of Vickerdon. The night was cold, and Josh felt the ice of the wind slide straight into his bones. But he doubted that he'd be feeling the cold for very long, he'd most likely be doubled over sweating in just a matter of minutes. As he bolted across the road, Edmund's voice boomed with the first instruction.

"Move downhill, then turn left onto the main road."

Josh did so, feeling a spike of energy surge through his legs.

'Thank Christ for downhill...'

Just like last time, Josh's legs pounded away in front of him, left right left right. For a moment Josh caught sight of the moon in the night sky, it was an enormous white pancake, throwing a glowing white radiance down into his face. Obviously, Josh knew the moon couldn't grant warmth in the way that the sun did, but somehow it was seeming to. A lukewarm glow that covered Vickerdon. Unfortunately, Josh got so caught up staring at the moon that he failed to notice the pothole in the center of the road. In one ungraceful motion, he was sent hurtling face forward towards the ground. He threw his arms in front of him, feeling the asphalt tear into his palms.

"Goddamn it..."

He sat up, reeling in disorientation for a few moments. Then rose to his feet in a fit of embarrassment.

"Eyes peeled Josh, make sure to watch for obstacles on the road."

Josh sighed, and picked up his pace once again.

"Helpful advice Ed."

Josh worked back into his pace, and kept moving for the main road ahead. His hands throbbed, and droplets of blood flew off his hands making tiny little sounds as they hit the concrete. Josh payed no mind, he just continued to thunder along with his eyes fixated on the road ahead like a hawk watching its prey. Left right left right, almost there.

"Ok Josh, remember this left."

"Gotcha."

Josh bolted out into the main road and threw himself left, unprepared for the steepness of the main road. For a second, he thought he'd hit the ground for the second time that night, but he managed to retain his balance, steadying his motion downhill. When he was half way downhill, he grew anxious. Despite his lack of all things intuitive, something was clearly wrong. He yelled to Edmund, in big gasping breaths.

"Somethings wrong man, can you feel it?"

"Yes, slow your pace Josh. We need to stop for a while."

Josh did so, quickly jolting to a stop. Edmund materialized before his eyes, a deep look of concern on his old face.

"What is it? What's happening?" Asked Josh between rasping breaths.

"I don't know, it's incredibly odd."

Josh looked around, trying to spot something off, anything that seemed unusual. Before his eyes could pick anything up, Edmund spoke up.

"There! By the streetlight."

At first, Josh couldn't make anything out. But slowly, a figure slowly made its way into the light from the streetlamp. Slinking along, as if badly wounded.

"What is it?"

"That is a spirit of Zugai."

"What...? Ed, they're the enemy! We need to go right??"

"No... Trust me, this is different. It doesn't appear like any of the others, we could learn something here Josh. I can feel it."

Josh slumped down and slowly shook his head.

"Ok man, fine. But if it eats us or something it's on you."

They moved towards the spirit, still hesitant despite Edmund's feeling towards it. It turned its head and stopped, staring them down through its smoky black face. Josh stopped, the sight of it brought back strong memories of Jessie, they washed through his mind.

"Why aren't you with the rest of them?" Edmund asked.

Instead of answering right away, the spirit laughed a pained cackle. It was truly horrible, Josh thought of it to be the most unsettling sound he'd ever had the displeasure to witness. He backed away, afraid.

"Rest of my kind? I have no kind, no kin to call family. I despise the pitiful souls of Zugai, they are pathetic sheep searching for answers amongst wreckage. But I can accept the real truth we are burdened with, it is the *only* reality."

Edmund considered the spirit's reply, then continued.

"Since when does any spirit of Zugai think for themselves?"

Even though it's face was nothing but a dense mist of jet black smoke, Josh could still tell that in some way, it was smiling.

"Since I heard the calling of Coda's rightful king."

Edmund flinched, clearly unnerved by what he was hearing.

"Coda no longer has a king."

Once again, the spirit laughed, the sound cutting into Josh ears like knives.

"Well I know otherwise. The great drum grows louder. His time returns, the rightful leader—the rightful and true leader."

Josh's stomach dropped to his knees, paralyzed with fear his mind trembled. The true and bleak reality of the situation hit him hard, and that dream was the very *last* thing that he wanted to be real. He didn't speak, instead he just turned away from the spirit and buried his head in his hands.

"Where are the others, where are the other spirits of Zugai now?"

"They swarm like moronic bees within the ocean of dreams, pathetic... But not me, I defected from their ridiculous display of order. I was tried for punishment, and I made it out. I had to try, because I know better... I know, *so much better...*"

Edmund turned and faced Josh, his face blurred and fierce.

"Ok... Let's move."

And like that, he disappeared from visibility, leaving just Josh and the horrible black spirit in the white glow of the moonlight.

Josh looked back at the spirit, feeling a small surge of anger heat up the back of his head.

"You won't win this... You'll lose, and I'll be there."

The spirit looked leered at Josh, calculating what he'd said before spitting back its retort.

"You don't understand what we want, you understand nothing. Have you ever been lost? Broken apart? Nearly disintegrated by the weight of misguidance?"

Josh had no words, stunned he turned away and began to walk downhill. Little Marron ran beside, soft moonlight bouncing off his black fur.

"Quicker Josh. It's not too far now, move your feet." Boomed Edmund.

Josh picked up his pace and continued to run downhill, while the words of the Zugai spirit bounced around his thoughts.

"Oh I've been lost... All my life I've been lost." Josh said to himself.

The rest of the journey to the hospital raced by, and the further he traveled, the further that thoughts of the spirit went from his mind. Steven was close, Josh even felt excited about the prospect. Seeing an old friend. His very first friend, and probably his truest. "Right there Josh, just up ahead." Said Edmund.

The building didn't differ too much from the factory they'd come from. It was old and weathered, with a tall red, cracked brick fence surrounding it. Josh stopped outside of it and dropped his palms onto his knees. Wheezing for air, covered in a thick film of sweat.

"Goddamn we made it. Man, he better be in here."

Edmund stood beside Josh, semi-translucent.

"He is." Edmund said while slowly drifting towards the entrance.

Josh nodded, catching his breath. "Let's do it."

CHAPTER 19-

A voice had spoken to me in the void.

I thought about it again and again, racking my brain to think of an answer. I'd been helped, someone or something was in there with me, and had warned me of the danger. But who? Or what? I had no idea, it was like trying to remember the name of a song, the more you try to remember, the more it slips away. I shook my head and tried to throw the thought from my head. Hopefully, I'll find out at some point.

I jumped out of the hospital bed and made my way down towards the common room, hoping to find something bearable on the television. The worst thing about the Vickerdon hospital were the infomercials, just constant, never-ending infomercials that played on a continuous loop. To no surprise the staff was once again no help in my mission to defeat my maddening boredom.

"The others like them, you'll just have to manage." A nurse had said.

"I am literally the *only* person who sets foot in this room. And it's probably because they don't want to watch infomercials."

"Lower your voice, we like things calm here."

It was the one and only conversation I'd had regarding the quality of viewing in the Vickerdon hospital, and I prayed like a maniac that help was coming soon, because If I wasn't killed by a horde of evil black spirits, I'm sure the infomercials would get the job done soon enough. My plan was to somehow hijack the remote and defy the laws of the hospitals television—anything to keep my mind active.

I stopped outside the common room and stared down the long Grey hallway, the lamplight behind me cast a long black shadow down towards the large glass front doors. A feeling struck me, or rather, I suddenly became aware of a feeling. Like an elephant in the room I felt the force that was keeping me from leaving, it was like an invisible barrier that sat in the center of my mind. Then just as I'd finally become aware of it, I felt it slowly begin to fade, as if water was running out of my ears, taking a great weight out from the inside of my head.

I knew that I was no longer trapped within the confines of the hospital, the invisible barrier had lifted. But all I did was stare down the length of the hallway, transfixed on the glass doors. Part of me wanted to run and bash through them screaming freedom, but the other part was afraid of what I was being protected from. The last thing I wanted to do was let fear creep up on me now, there was too much to be done.

So first things first. I headed back towards my hospital room to change out of my gown, I'd prefer that whatever help was on the way didn't see me in an outfit that showed my bare ass. I'm a firm believer in first impressions, and I doubted that that'd be a good one.

Same as always, I threw on a pair of jeans and a black t-shirt, then grabbed my duffel bag and headed down towards the waiting room. I was nervous, after all there was still the possibility that this could be a trap of some kind, a plan devised by the old man to have me killed once and for all. Although the mysterious voice of the red void had sounded trustworthy, so I crossed my fingers in hope that my intuition wouldn't fail me, the last thing I wanted was another knife in the stomach.

I sat and waited, staring through the glass doors towards the moonlit streets. It was odd, somehow the moonlight looked warm like rays of sunlight. Growing more and more anxious to muster up the courage to go, my feet started to get ready for sprinting. Like ripping off a band-aid, my plan was just to run in the most comfortable direction until my nerves regained themselves. Unfortunately, my plan changed in the blink of an eye. Two figures were making their way up towards the glass doors from the outside. Usually anyone's rationality would just deem them as people in need of medical attention—but in my case it seemed that anything was possible, they could be deadly spirits with chainsaws for arms. For whatever reason, I didn't run, I stood my ground and watched suspiciously instead.

"Josh...? I don't believe it." I whispered while watching curiously. I knew it was him, beyond a doubt.

At first, I couldn't quite make him out. But gradually, he reached the entrance of the hospital, swung open the glass doors, and stepped into the dim light of the waiting room, assuring my certainty.

It was the first time in a lifetime that I'd seen Joshua Quaid, and the circumstances couldn't have been stranger. Though funnily enough, the circumstances were in a way no stranger than the times we'd shared as children. It was great to see him again, and I felt as though no time had passed.

***

"No way, you're actually here." Said Josh.

He stared at me with a tired but smiling face that sat beneath a long mop of sweaty blond hair, which fell down around his shoulders. His face was strained with fatigue, looking like he'd seen the worst that the world could offer. It was clear that he'd been through some serious stuff, and it made me curious to know where his life had taken him after Missidnyl. I got out of my seat and returned Josh a smile of my own.

"God damn Josh, how in the hell."

I hugged him and thanked him, knowing without words that he'd gone through every circle of hell to find me, and for that I couldn't be more grateful, he'd searched for me, reached out and offered his help after all this time.

"You look terrible man, like really terrible." Josh said while punching me in the arm laughing.

"Thanks for the kind words Josh, you look like a blond mop with an old man's face under it."

Josh smirked at me cheerfully and patted his hand on my shoulder.

"So do *you* have any theories on what all this is? And where have you been all this time?"

Still smirking Josh motioned for the doorway.

"Man, I don't even know where to start."

I was sure we'd have time to discuss everything that'd come to pass, though all I wanted for the time being was to get as far from the Vickerdon hospital as possible, and I was glad that Josh felt the same.

"Let's get out of here, I've been in this place for way too long."

Josh nodded and we made our way outside, it was finally time to go.

The fresh air was incredible, it cleared my head and lifted the murky, claustrophobic cloud from my mind. For a moment I stood with Josh and just drew back deeps breaths of the gentle night's breeze.

"Hey Ed." Josh yelled.

Completely spooked, I almost ran downtown when the ghost of the crown manifested before my eyes. He approached me, watched me with his old eyes and smiled a tired and weathered smile.

"I've no idea how you escaped the nightshade, but it's a relief to see you intact. No doubt your aware there's much to be done, so I strongly suggest we move."

I looked back at Josh in confusion.

"Don't worry, he's on our side." Said Josh.

I couldn't help but laugh. So very long it'd been since the bizarre times I'd spent with Josh during the early days of Missidnyl. Then in true bizarre fashion, here we were all these years later as adults, in the company of a ghost. Josh must have known exactly what is was I found funny, as he laughed along with me. Before long I turned back to face the ghost known as Ed, and began to explain the business.

"There's some kind of horde of spirits. I saw them in the red void, everywhere."

Ed nodded, and his face turned very serious.

"The spirits of Zugai, they have found purpose. We'll talk more back at the factory, let's move."

'Zugai.. Where have I heard that word?' It struck me, I was certain that at some point that word had come up.

"Alright let's go." I replied.

We began to make our way along the streets on our way back to the factory when Josh spoke up.

"So, the red void is where everyone's asleep right?"

"Yeah pretty much, why?"

"Well, if the Zugai spirits are gonna be busy in there all night, we could stop by somewhere to grab cigarettes right?"

Edmund faced Josh in disbelief, but I cut him off before he had a chance to speak.

"For sure, I'm for that idea."

Edmund shot his disbelieving glare in my direction, then lowered his face into his hands, as if he was accompanying a couple of defiant children. Josh and I smiled at each other before crossing the road on our way to the Vickerdon 24-hour gas station.

The cigarette couldn't have gone down better, and to stroll in the open air was a miracle too. We walked back to the factory while traded stories and attempted to catch up on lost times. Neither of us spoke of the erased man or the old man, but I could tell that in the back of our heads we were just holding fast onto the short time of peace we had. Everything seemed a little better, and I felt that we deserved to enjoy it while we had it. I was hesitant to return to the factory, but when we arrived I no longer cared. The threat was gone, and my wound was healing, it was simply just time to move on.

CHAPTER 20-

"It really just throbs when the sun goes down, otherwise it just feels like a really bad scab. Definitely wasn't fun at the time though."

Josh had been asking me about my stab wound over breakfast in the factory, Edmund had ghosted up some bread and butter. I was almost overwhelmed with satisfaction to have something that didn't come out of a can, I was glad to be out of the hospital—glad to be in the company of people who didn't want me dead. More than anything though, I was glad to be with a friend.

"What a waste he was man, would've stepped over his mother for a hit. Felt good to knock some of the teeth out of that assholes head."

I watched Josh for a moment, we were the same age, and it was difficult to see how badly time had treated him. His skin was almost in the same condition as Edmund's, weathered and tired, scarred by too many bad times.

"I gotta thank you again Josh, if you didn't come I might've been stuck in the hospital until the end of times. I owe you a big one."

Josh placed his bread back down on the table, and looked at me with a face full of questions.

"So, there was some kind of invisible wall trapping you there?"

"Yeah, but more like it was in my head. Like some kind of mental barrier."

"Weird, think it was Solus?"

Josh and Edmund had updated me on almost everything that I didn't know throughout the course of the morning, including the name of the wretched old man, and the horrific display that'd occurred over Josh's final breakfast with Hans. I felt for him, it was awful to hear.

"I don't think so. To be honest, it felt like it was done by someone who was helping us."

"Like a guardian angel?"

I picked up my last piece of bread and nodded my head.

"You know, I kinda think so."

Josh raised his head solemnly, and spoke quietly.

"You never know man, it could've been Jessie."

It struck me hard, and I was overcome with sympathy for him. This whole thing was a nightmare, I wished that none of us had to be a part of it. Earlier, I'd told Josh what'd happened with Jessie when I'd returned to Missidnyl, and he hadn't opened his mouth during the whole explanation. But he seemed happy about the prospect of her being taken by a beautiful white void of pure light. But I could tell that the suffering she'd gone through outweighed his peace of mind, and in no way did I blame him.

"It could be her, I wouldn't discount it."

Josh lowered his head and gathered his posture.

"Thanks for telling me what you knew. It means a lot for me to know the truth about things. I really appreciate it."

"You would've done the same for me Josh." I said.

Josh handed me a cigarette and grabbed one for himself, smiled, and looked over towards the window on the far side of the factory.

"True."

I lit my cigarette and took a deep drag, holding it in my lungs. Speaking as I slowly exhaled.

"Too bad our reunion's under such garbage circumstances."

"Yeah but you know what? We'll win. I'm gonna personally rip that old mans wrinkled head from his shoulders."

"I'm looking forward to it, just make sure you let me get some good hits in too."

"Sounds like a good deal."

We sat in silence for a while, each of us thinking our own individual thoughts. Edmund appeared before us, and by the looks of it he'd been thinking too. His face was wrought with impatience.

"Ok, I think it's about time that we formulate some kind of plan. I've come up with some ideas, but we're all going to have to do our part."

"Lay it on us Ed." Said Josh.

He paced about the room while he began to explain one of his ideas, though it didn't take long before I had to interject. His idea was to send me into the realm of Coda, then essentially fast travel to an eastern location within America. Once there, I would contact Josh and Edmund, then rendezvous with them near wherever Solus was located.

"I'm sorry Edmund, first of all. I don't have the crown anymore. Also, I have no idea how to actually end up where I want when I leave Coda, and last time I ended here, and I got stabbed. I just don't think it's possible."

"But think about it Steven, you were delivered to the exact town that we were located. Does that seem like a coincidence to you?"

When I thought about it, Edmund wasn't wrong. There was no doubt that during recent events, some kind of sentient force had been lending a hand. The problem though was my inability to rely on such a force, it scared me to imagine my fate being given up to some spirit we didn't know from a bar of soap.

"I know what you mean Edmund, but is that something we should trust right now? And the main point is we still don't have the crown, how would I even be *able* to make it into Coda without it?"

Edmund continued to pace around the alcove, thinking deeply.

"Well, the crown is essentially mine. It's possible that there's a way to replicate it through *me*, and for me to act as a conduit similar to the way the crown works."

"Have you ever tried to do anything like that?"

"No. I haven't. It would take the voice of Coda to accomplish such a feat if we were to do so, Josh may have the ability."

As Edmund spoke, he turned his attention to Josh, who was sitting with Marron smoking a cigarette. He eventually gazed up in confusion, looking back and forth between Edmund and I.

"What?"

"Have you been listening?"

He stumped out his cigarette and let Marron down from his lap.

"To be honest, I didn't really catch much of that. What'd I miss?"

Edmund buried his face in his hands and sighed in agitation, and I couldn't help but find it funny.

"I can't have you like this while such an important discussion is taking place, it won't do. Open your ears."

"Sorry Ed, I was thinking."

Edmund turned and faced the window. So naturally I began to catch Josh up on what he'd missed, nodding along as he listened. He then went on.

"Okay, but. How am I supposed to go about this? I mean, I barely even know how my painting stuff works as it is."

Edmund considered it, still straining his face in deep thought.

"Honestly I'm not sure, but I feel that it's possible. Steven?"

"Well, I guess there' s no use in *not* trying."

Josh nodded. "Yeah, let's try I guess."

It was growing late, for the remainder of the night we swapped more stories and filling the hours smoking cigarettes and eating bread. It was interesting as well as heartbreaking to hear about the way things had gone for Josh. There was so much death, it had almost seemed to have followed him like a dark swollen, black cloud—striking anyone close to him with a fatal bolt of lightning. I told him about my extensive brush with drugs, and the impact that it'd had on me following the death of my mother.

"I remember her you know?" Josh had said.

"She'd always invite me in for food even though I smelt like piss. That's one hell of a woman right there."

I laughed hard, feeling it heal me inside and out, truly the best medicine that one could ask for. Josh at one point had also asked me.

"So if you don't mind me asking, did you ever learn anything about your dad?"

I'd answered him without much hesitation.

"Nah, I guess those answers wont along with mom."

Josh punched me softly on the shoulder.

"That sucks man, but hey, you never know what you can find out."

"Yeah that's true."

"Hey by the way, I've been wondering something, do you remember that little pine forest around the back of the old housing estate?"

Instantly I knew where Josh was going with this, and the memory felt completely bad. I hadn't thought about it since I'd seen the photo of Josh in his old Missidnyl home, and for him to bring it up here and now threw me through a loop. But I listened to his half of the story, out of curiosity more than anything.

"Yeah, I remember it." I said

"I just can't help but shake the feeling that what happened there was real, I just can't get it out of my head. With the old guy."

I thought back, way back to our earliest years, about this particular event that'd taken place in the Missidnyl tall pine reserve. We'd spend many afternoons climbing the trees there, and each time we'd gather just a little more confidence to go higher than we had the previous time. By the end of it, we'd be shakily sitting atop the tallest branch, howling like wolves as the afternoon sun fell. But one afternoon, Josh had misplaced his footing, and had fallen from the highest tree branch of the tallest pine tree, an enormous fall that would in most cases be the untimely end of anyone.

I remember scaling down the pine tree while yelling Josh's name again and again, panicked and scared. I pictured him on the ground, covered in blood with bones sticking out every which way. But when I'd finally made my way to the base of the tree, there was nothing there but a bed of pine needles. I looked back up the tree and saw Josh at its peak, white as a ghost, and shaking like he'd seen one. Slowly I'd made my way back up, and sat on his side. Swearing that I'd just seen the demise of my best friend. What he had said next frightened me, and was the last thing that I'd expected.

"I fell down Steven, I was so scared. I fell down so fast, but when I got to the bottom. I felt giant hands hold me, and I saw him. He was old. Like, real old.. And he put me back on the top of the tree, right here."

I can't remember what my reply was, but was probably along the lines of claiming that it must've been our imaginations playing tricks on us. We never went back to the Tall Pine Reserve after that day, Josh would always insist that the old man would kill him if we did.

I looked back over to Josh, and hesitated on making my suggestion, but ended up doing so.

"Do you think it was *the* old man? Do you think it was Solus?"

Josh instantly shook his head, looking as scared as he was all those years ago.

"No. But I keep getting this terrible feeling at the moment, as if he looks for me, like he's pissed off that we never went back to the forest.. But the weirdest thing is, the first time I heard about this Coda thing, *he* was the first thing I thought about. The first time I'd thought about him since we were little kids."

We sat in silence for a while, and listened to the rain fall against the roof of the old Vickerdon factory before mutually deciding it was time to get some sleep.

***

I had trouble getting to sleep that night, I'd toss and turn during fits of confusing semi-lucid dreams. Every now and then I'd sit bolt upright in the gold linen bed, trying to recount what was going through my head, but it would always slip away. Like a rock was sitting in my stomach, something kept playing on my intuition, it wasn't until I finally managed to remember a portion of my tired thoughts that I knew what'd been knocking around my head. It was Edmund, my intuition was warning me about Edmund. It was a hard decision, but ultimately I decided not to trust him. Soon after, I finally managed to drift off into a deep sleep. A pitch black, heavy deep sleep.

"Tea? It's not coffee but at least it's something."

Josh stood over my bed holding two cups of steaming tea, his face was groggy and more tired than it was yesterday. He looked like he hadn't slept, but instead spent the night on a bender. But he seemed cheerful, and his mood was good.

"Thanks, that's perfect." I said.

We walked into the only spot of sunlight spilling into the alcove, then dragged two chairs to sit. They were the first rays of sunlight I'd seen since my time in Coda, and it made me think of Pito. Little Pito Marron.

"How'd you sleep?" I asked Josh.

He took a huge swig of his tea and winced, spilling the majority of his tea over his lap.

"I think I just burned my damn tongue out of my mouth."

I couldn't help but laugh.

"Still clumsy."

Josh laughed and set his empty tea cup next to the chairs before pointing towards a pile of canvases sitting in the corner of the room.

"I think I slept for maybe two hours, them boom, it was art time. So I started painting, and before I knew it the sun was up."

"Can I have a look?"

"Yeah go for it, you might be able to make sense of them."

My eyes had already caught a glimpse of what was on one of the canvasses, and I prayed that my eyes were deceiving me. But of course, they weren't in any way.

I held the painting in front of me, and studied it. It was a barren desert setting, smoke rising from the sand as like boiling water. In the middle of the picture was the crown, the cursed crown that I'd last seen within the very factory we were now sleeping in. The most unsettling part however, were the spirits of Zugai, they swarmed around the crown like a jet black hive of pissed-off bees. I didn't really know what it was depicting, but it obviously wasn't anything cheerful.

"Josh this is scary as hell, but it's incredible. You can seriously paint."

Josh didn't say a word, instead he stared out the window beyond me at the sight of the long overdue sunlight. I placed the canvas back down and picked up the second of three, it wasn't any less disturbing as the first one. It was a painting of literally hundreds of people, all beneath a huge heavy Grey cloud. There was little definition on the people, but my gut told me that it wasn't due to the size of the canvass. It looked more like they were all slaves, an army of faceless slaves with no personalities.

"So Josh."

"Yeah?" He replied.

"Do the paintings usually reflect future events? Things that are destined to happen?"

He thought to himself a while.

"Well, sometimes I guess. Other times they're just normal paintings of random stuff, like things from the past."

The last we needed was for the paintings that Josh had painted to come true.

"Check out the last one." Josh said.

I set the painting of the faceless slaves back down and

grabbed the third canvass, expecting something just as unnerving, and it was, but in a much different way. It was me, but a far older version of me. My face was much more aged, with a fine head of dark Grey hair. Strangely my eyes were blue as opposed to being green like my actual eyes. I looked back at Josh.

"Well, at least old Steven could scrub up worse." He said.

I laughed a little before setting the canvas back down alongside the others, they were special indeed. In fact, they were incredible.

"So what do you make of them? Do they fire up any of your intuitive things?" Asked Josh.

I sat beside him again, and reached for a cigarette.

"I don't know, I'll have to mull on them for a little while. Has Ed seen them yet?"

Josh shook his head.

"Nah, have honestly no idea where he is at the moment anyway."

My gut sparked another wave of distrust, quickly deciding it'd be best to explain my feelings to Josh, it was after all, probably best to refrain from keeping anything to myself at this point.

"Speaking of Ed, I kinda have a weird feeling about him."

Josh narrowed his eyes, and leaned in curiously. Before I had any chance to explain anything, Edmund himself spoke, booming across the room like a reverberating bass drum. An almost deafening tone that shook the very walls of the old factory.

"I know how you feel Steven. But it comes from something far worse than treachery on my end."

CHAPTER 21-

Josh threw his head around in a fit, alarmed by Edmund's sudden booming comment. My heart sunk, and fear gripped me, my intuition was burning like a bonfire in the pit of my stomach.

"Ed, where are you?" Asked Josh.

After a nervous pause, Edmund began to explain, though still without visibility. His voice still echoing loudly through the halls of the factory.

"It began a while ago, the crown is being tampered with. It is affecting me, as each and every second passes, I can feel myself fade."

I finally understood, I didn't have mistrust for Edmund, I had mistrust for what he was becoming.

"The crown is my life source, it is the crown which allows me to still exist. Solus is toying with it, and I can feel it."

Josh was completely crushed, his face was scrunched up and as red as a ripe tomato.

"Can we help? How can we make it stop?" I asked.

"Too late, nothing can be done. I can't.."

"Ed.. Can't what?"

"I can't become this. I won't, it cannot end like this."

Panic started to set in, and my thoughts began to race. If Edmund was corrupted by Solus, there would be no knowing what he could be capable of, it would without question make things far more dangerous than it already was. But my mind was blank, and no ideas came to me. While I sat hopelessly with a tight knot tugging in my gut, a sickeningly beautiful spectral flash of color lit up the room as Edmund manifested into visibility. He was blinking in and out while showing a broad pallet of bright colors, it reminded me of an old television, slightly off the proper tuning. He stared at us in fear and desperation.

"We will only have one chance, Steven come to me and prepare your mind. I'm afraid this won't be easy for either of us."

I slowly approached Edmund, unsure of what was next. But in my mind he was right, there was only one chance, and it was now or never.

"I'm going to throw every ounce of myself into this, and the result will ensure my demise. I'll never again be the man I used to be, but at least this way I can die as all men do."

I sat in front of Edmund and stared into his face, so old and so tired. He was staring down the corridor of death. Josh rose from his seat and began to scream, shouting anxiously. Every time he yelled, it ripped into me, Ed was a friend to Josh, and soon he'd be gone. He stood in front of Edmund, his face red and eyes wide.

"You can't just decide to die! Everybody I know dies!"

Edmund watched Josh helplessly. For a moment I thought he would just fade into nothing, without a word. But eventually he spoke, with his usual calm tone.

"Thank you for allowing me to remember old times Josh, but I've been alive for so long.. So unnaturally long. I am sorry. Before I leave I will give you the greatest gift I can grant, the most magnificent thing that I have the ability to manifest."

I didn't see what it was that Edmund gave him, it mustn't have been a physical thing. What I did notice though, was that for just a split second, Josh smiled. Edmund turned back to face me, and uttered his last and final warning for me to prepare in any way I could manage, then placed his hands on my temples.

Emotion yet again exploded inside of me, horrible knots of anxiety and fear wrapped up the inside of my stomach like venomous snakes binding themselves around one another. With every ounce of energy I had, I thought of my best memories, trying hard to cushion the turmoil inside me. I started screaming, air blew from my lungs and my muscles tensed.

"I'm not gonna make it this time."

I saw Josh, his face was twisted in horror, but quickly he pushed through it and ran to my side.

"Remember back in Missidnyl, that time we spent two days eating cold pizza and watching sci-fi movies? Well, as soon as this is over we'll gonna do it again. We'll have our lives back, and we'll do whatever we want. You can do this, trust me."

It wasn't as efficient as being blasted by good memories by a short spirit boy with a third eye coming out of his forehead. But Josh was helping, he continued to talk about good memories from our childhood, and the good times that'll be soon to come. Even his cat Marron joined our side, brushing his head against my side.

Everything slowly began to fade, and a washed out red light flashed over my vision. The world began to fizz out and shake in front of my eyes, while my second eyes--the special ones, began to take control. The only sight that came along with me was Edmund, his old face flashing away like an old fluorescent light bulb. Just before he finally disappeared for good, he spoke his last words.

"Take care of Josh."

Then in a grand explosion he blew out-wards in an incredible flash consisting of every color I could imagine. Along with another color that I'd never be able to recreate, it was something I'd never seen before, it was the most brilliant shade that I'd ever witnessed.

I hurled through the mysterious realm between the world I'd always known and Coda, briefly reminding me of the terrifying black void I'd spent some time in. Falling endlessly was starting to become a common occurrence for me, and I was enjoying it just as much as every other time, not at all. I felt myself drifting out of consciousness, so I held to it as tightly as I could. After some time, the exit grew near, like a mental door, only available within the bounds of the human psyche.

Breaking out into sunlight like a cannon ball crashing through thick drywall, I smashed onto the grass awkwardly, sprawling around uncontrollably. My eyes burned behind my eyelids, strong sunlight blaring into them. I had arrived, Edmund had actually done it. If only he hadn't had to die, if only he had somehow managed to keep his spirit intact without facing corruption by Solus. I felt responsible, If I hadn't have lost that stupid crown, Edmund would never have had to face his doom. If it told me anything though, it was that we had just *one* shot at this, and I didn't want to screw it up.

As time passed, my eyes began to ease into the blinding sunlight. Bright shades of green and blue started to morph and contort into the landscape that surrounded me, there was no question I'd made it into Coda now, and my journey was just as insane as every other time. I looked down at the grass beneath me and shuffled onto my knees, my body ached all over. With more time, my mind began to snap itself back to normal, and my senses started to return.

Curiously I couldn't help but think about my rehabilitation years ago, and the soul crushing panic I'd felt during it. At the time

I could never have imagined that such feelings were even possible to experience, it was a sensation that featured all of the most negative emotions in overdrive. They would stir themselves around, as though they were horrid ingredients handpicked by a deranged scientist.

If I was a puzzle, all of my pieces had been blown out in all directions. But slowly, one by one they placed themselves back into the picture making me whole again. After a long time, I had healed, but not without some deep scars that would always sit beneath my flesh. So at the best of times I'll always think to myself.

'No matter what happens, I can always heal. And the pieces of the puzzle, can only become scattered, never destroyed.'

Looking up towards the trees that surrounded me I scanned the area, it was strange to think that at a glance anybody would assume it could be a location not dissimilar from somewhere on Earth. But on closer inspection there was something different about it, something that quite literally felt 'otherworldly'. I picked myself up from the grass and made my way towards the only clearing I could spot between two tress in front, as I made my way closer something began to glisten—like a light source reflecting off of a piece of glass.

I quickly started to realize that it in fact *was* glass in the distance, and by the looks of it, a lot. It was a structure of some kind, and it was enormous. It stood at least the height of a two-story building, if not higher. The sunlight's reflection bounced off in every direction, lighting small specks all across the emerald green grass that surrounded it. It was like looking directly into the sun, a gleaming beacon emitting more light than the brightest lighthouse.

When I made it closer to the weird structure, I managed to get a quick glance and saw that it was a statue. A seemingly gargantuan statue depicting what could be some sort of historical figure of the realm of Coda, possibly even a figure of worship. It made me think of the statue of liberty, had she be made of pure glass as opposed to copper. It dawned on me at that Coda may have all kinds of religious sects of its own, little cults scattered across its vast lands that preyed to all kinds of different gods and goddesses. The thought was disturbing, mostly due to the fact that in a way it was essentially what Josh and I were up against, the hideous cult of Zugai, mislead by their sick and twisted leader Solus.

I shivered a cold shiver before turning my back on the giant glass monument, and began to head back through the little clearing. I'd made it only a few steps before a voice spoke to me from behind.

"How very curious it is to see you about, surely you're from a land disconnected from this one I have no doubt?"

I whipped my head back towards the source of the voice and immediately had to shield my eyes from the laser beam rays of sunlight, scrunching my face and wincing, I tried to spot whoever was talking between the gaps of my fingers.

"The sun dances like fire off the glass that stands tall, but you'll see all its beauty when the sun starts to fall."

I couldn't fixate on him, the sunlight was simply too much.

"Who are you?" I asked.

For a terrifying second, I got the notion that whoever was speaking to me was running towards me with plans to bury a knife in my stomach. Fortunately, the mysterious figure brushed straight passed me and into the clearing beyond the two tall trees. I waited for my vision to return, while worrying that I was blinded. When my sight did return, an outline of a tall, slim man wearing what looked like a Japanese straw hat stood in front of me. I stepped a few paces closer and repeated my question.

"Who are you?"

Before he answered me, he sat down on the grass, crossed his legs, and placed his head in his hands.

"I'm passionate about your culture and your need for a name, and I find it quite odd that to lack one's a shame."

As my sight returned I began to make out the features of his face. He looked young, early twenties maybe, possibly even still a teenager. Small locks of light blond hair hung out from beneath his hat, with his skin looking to be only a few shades darker.

"Okay, so what *are* you then? What kind of spirit?"

He laughed an exuberant laugh, sounding more like a mischievous sneer.

"I've seen eyes like yours before, and the man I speak of knocked on deaths door. He held his bleeding eye-sockets as he stumbled, and it was soon after that the house of Coda crumbled."

The longer I stared at whatever this spirit was, the quicker I was beginning to think he was of ill intent. I contemplated running, but considering the speed he'd demonstrated when he'd ran past me, my chances were slim. Besides, there was still the matter of the barely healed stab wound on the side of my stomach. Before I could act in any way, he continued with his strange rhyming way of speaking.

"Please remain calm, as I mean you no harm. You can name me whatever you choose, however ridiculous I'll not refuse."

I stared at him a while longer, still recovering from the blinding sunlight. Then shook my head in defeat.

"Can I go just one hour without this kinda crap happening? I'm not going to name you, so how about you come up with your own? You can call yourself anything you want."

He rocked back and forth, smiling up towards me from beneath his large straw hat. His eyes large with fascination, they were the most arresting shade of blue that I'd ever seen, like little crystals sitting beneath strong sunlight.

"Very well then." He replied without rhyming his words.

In a startling display, he pulled his straw hat over his face and began to hover off the ground—literally floating a matter of feet above the grass. In a horrific way, he compressed his entire body within his hat and spoke. His voice reverberated loudly, despite being in the middle of an open field, he spoke similar in the way Edmund did during his last times in the old factory.

"And what is *your* name brother? Does it glisten red like the name of your mother?"

He caught me completely off guard, all I could do was stand in silence. How on earth could this spirit know anything about my mother?

"Ruby red, had breathed her last breath. But she watches young Steven, even in death."

He emerged from his hat like a turtle coming from its shell, and walked towards me, with his piercing blue eyes locked firmly onto mine.

"What is it that frightens you? Is the word *death*? Is it my knowledge of your little family tree? ..I can see straight inside you, as though your eyes are small portals. There is so much that dwells inside people, so very passionate I am to understand the way in which you function..”

I backed away from the strange spirit, and almost lost my balance. He was as unsettling as he was confusing, and he was *incredibly* unsettling.

“Alright, stay where you are. What are you?” I asked.

He frowned in an almost apologetic manner before kneeling down onto one knee, he then laced his fingers behind his neck.

“Simply put, I just like to observe. I walk through these lands, just me and an endless wealth of insatiable curiosity.”

“But how did you know those things about me?”

He looked back at me as he answered, his thin and pale lips seeming not to move as he spoke.

“Eyes tell it all, they are the windows to the soul. And yours tell much.”

“Okay, fair enough.”

I started to make my way past him and towards a dense mess of trees that sat at the far side of the clearing, while being well aware that the strange spirit would follow me, and of course, he did. As he trudged beside me, he chanted small incoherent chants to himself. Every now and then, he’d look over at me silently, then continue to mutter to himself again.

When I made it to the clearing between the trees, I stared down a valley that stretched on for what looked like an entire American state. As I surveyed the immense landscape, my eyes fixated on the very last thing I’d expect to see. It was a train station, an ancient looking, most likely rusted over train station that sat far away in the distance. I could even see a plumes of steam rising from its location.

“Yup. That’s the Alven Valley train station down that way, and in case you wondered, Alven Valley’s pretty much all the same. Just an endless stretch of grass and trees, it was once far more interesting. But not so much anymore.”

My eyes narrowed.

“Why’d you stop with all the rhyming?”

Almost in a frenzy, he jumped over and landed directly next to me, looking straight into my face, narrowing his eyes as if to mimic mine. He smiled a cheerful smile before once again jumping back over to where he was.

"Curiosity. I love it Steven! Truly, I adore the very nature of it. At first I rhymed, but now I'm not. And by Coda, you're now wondering why that is so."

Instead of replying, I began to make my way down towards the train station that sat far off in the distance within this so called 'Alven Valley.' There was no doubt that I'd most likely need the help of this odd spirit that was in my company, but there was something about him that sent my senses into alarm, for whatever reason, my intuition told me that the less he knew about me the better. Though despite my feelings about the situation, I queried him while we walked down the decline to Alven Valley.

"So why's it called the Alven Valley anyway?" I asked.

"It was named after the failed prophet Alven Oraag. He was chosen for a grand purpose. But instead, boom! Failure.. Hopeless failure."

"Was he a spirit?"

"Nope. He was a human."

Instantly I thought of Edmund, wondering whether it was possible that this 'Alven' was chosen for a similar purpose, but I kept my mouth shut as tightly as possible, and more importantly my eyes out of his sight.

CHAPTER 22-

Marron the Cat was hungry, and for the last few days Josh was having to use what was left of his dry food as sparingly as possible. But Marron wasn't alone, Josh himself was now facing the problem of hunger. Without Edmund around, there was no one with the ability to ghost up bread and butter. Worse yet, no one to create painting supplies anymore.

"Don't worry buddy, I'll think of something."

Steven was in Coda, and Edmund was dead. In true Josh fashion, he was the one left on his lonesome with nothing but his dark, festering thoughts. But at least there was Marron, the little companion who'd come back to him.

"Maybe I should make a break for the milk bar again, I survived last time, maybe I'll survive this time."

As each hour ticked by, Josh slowly felt more and more hopeless. But the main issue was his anger, it grew like a garden weed on steroids. He felt completely useless, like he was letting the team down.

He lit a cigarette and paced about the factory, trying to think up a plan. Could he now offer any kind of help? Was it even possible to lend a hand? Josh had no idea, nothing came to mind no matter how hard he thought about it. He studied the graffiti that littered the walls of the run-down factory, reading them out loud, small puffs of cigarette smoke escaping his mouth with every word he uttered. Then he read something that sparked an idea. A light bulb had appeared above his frustrated head.

'CODA IS KING.'

Josh repeated the words to himself again and again, feeling like each time they ran through his head, his idea would surface just that little bit more.

He somehow had the grasp of Codas ancient voice, and in his mystical, meditative state he could weave his wrists about like a skilled surgeon. So, why the need for a canvass? The graffiti that littered the walls of the factory needed no canvass, so why should his paintings? He looked over towards the remainder of painting supplies that lay in the corner of the alcove. There was more than enough to last him at least a few days of continuous painting, and Josh would have no problem with that.

He didn't know exactly what it was he was going to paint, but he guessed that some part of him did. Josh approached his arts supply table and immediately locked his gaze on a tube of red oil paint, he grabbed it and spoke to himself.

"Yes. Something about this colour.."

He grabbed the largest paintbrush of the set and sat cross-legged in the center of the alcove before pushing all the furniture out of the way. He then continued to speak to himself, without even realizing what it was he meant.

"This alcove is the heart, heart and vessel."

Then it began. Josh painted like never before, like a crazed scientist he ducked and weaved around the floor, creating all kinds of strange symbols that all seemed to balance out into one large and intricate picture. It would be some time before it was completed, but that was the beauty of it for Josh. The longer the better, he relished every single moment that the brush sat firmly within his hand.

All of his festering anger and thoughts of rage diminished almost immediately, he'd slipped back into that place that existed between two places. Josh smiled as he worked, his eyes gleamed bright with love and adoration for the sake of his art. He was untouchable, completely hidden from every weight that the world could throw on top of his back.

Little Marron sat in the corner and munched on the last of the day's dry food, before strolling back over to one of the gold linen chairs for a doze. Luckily, even though Edmund was no more, his furniture and the protection that he'd placed on the factory still seemed intact. It was unknown to Josh for exactly how long, but right now it didn't matter.

CHAPTER 23-

Complete. The task of the crowns restoration was finally complete. Solus stepped into the circle of Zugai and raised his arms with his eyes closed.

"Faithful disciples of Zugai. I thank you all for your efforts. The time has finally come for me to join you within the realm of Coda."

Solus reached down and picked up the crown, and with no painful sting of insanity he placed it on his head. He opened his eyes and began to chant, then within a matter of seconds the world around him began to shake and fizzle.

"Yes. Yes! My destiny begins now! The new age has arrived! The age of Solus. The endless and pure age of Solus!"

With complete ease, Solus once again closed his eyes and left the realm he'd always resided in. When he opened his eyes he stood on the sands of the island of Zugai, and looked out over the crimson red dream sea.

He raised his hand and thought of a stone sitting on the sand.

"Let it be done."

And just like that, a large stone manifested itself on the island of Zugai. Next, Solus thought of another stone, but this one, shaped and crafted as himself.

"I *am* the one true god!"

A monument of Solus blinked into existence, standing exactly in his manner. Eyes closed. Arm raised.

The spirits of Zugai stood around Solus forming a perfect circle, their heads were bowed down with their fingers laced in front.

"There is very much to be done. So, as your just ruler I command that you take these lands. Leave this island and search every stretch. I'd like to know my new world. I want it all, every inch."

The spirits of Zugai flew in every which way like fluttering bats, weaving in all directions. And Solus went about constructing the new house of Coda, the *true* house of Coda. A building that would stand as tall as his brilliance, all the way up to the dark and thundering sky. But there was *one* matter that needed to be addressed, a matter of which Solus didn't like the smell of.

"Amicus."

The erased man appeared beside Solus, his blurred face revealing nothing but an expressionless glare.

"Something stinks in Vickerdon. I feel the voice of Coda and I do not like it. Go there, and eradicate the source."

Amicus bowed his head and blinked out from the realm of Coda, an ability of which Solus could now perform himself. He stood proudly for a moment.

"When that blurred out rat returns. I'll finally erase the rest of his pathetic soul."

He smiled and looked back over the sands of Zugai raising his arms.

"So let it be done."

CHAPTER 24-

The sun was falling, a mess of swollen orange clouds floated over the sky of the Alven Valley. Despite every circumstance, I couldn't dispute that it truly was a beautiful sight. Perfect strains of deep violet and crimson red streaked through the enormous clouds as if they were living organisms floating peacefully like giant creatures with no purpose other than to demonstrate their flawless beauty. The clouds in Coda were different, along with everything else. There was no argument that the lands of Coda were quite literally a perfect embodiment of an immaculate piece of artwork.

The Alven train station stood in front of me, it was a long Grey brick platform with an orange and yellow train that sat docked in the terminal. At the back of the station platform was a weathered old yellow picket fence that ran its entire course. I got the notion that I'd be aboard this train for some time, and my imagination went wild thinking about the kinds of things I might see from outside the train windows during the long journey ahead.

"The Alven train will depart quite soon, I suggest we climb aboard."

The odd spirit of curiosity was still in my company, and it was getting harder and harder to avert my eyes whenever he spoke to me. I didn't trust him, in a strange way he reminded me of one of the spirits of Zugai, all snakelike in their movements.

"Well let's get on then." I said.

"Ah! Yes. Let's, you and I, Steven Marron and old nameless spirit. After you."

I scanned the length of the train and noticed a problem, there was no door.

"Where's the door?" I asked.

The spirit jumped next to the train and slumped his posture while placing his hand on his chin, as if he was mocking the very act of thinking itself.

"Well... It seems I can see something that your *ever so special* eyes cannot. What does that tell you?"

When he looked back at me, I stared past him and wondered whether this was some sort of trick, a trap that he'd led me to.

"What're you talking about? I don't see a door, so if you do, just open it for me and we'll leave."

The spirit laughed and once again jumped directly next to me, he was so close that I could feel his breath against the side of my neck. He spoke softly.

"This train, needs an offering. You need to give it something, something dear to you. Something sentimental.."

"Like what?" I asked.

"I don't know Steven.. And you don't know.. So think..."

I pushed the spirit aside and approached the train, still scanning the length of it, trying to spot any sign of a door to enter through. Then strangely, my eyes began to water, like I'd just had a plume of smoke from a campfire blown into them. Something in the front of my head felt like it twigged, and somehow, in that bizarre moment, I knew that the spirit was lying. I turned back to face him, unafraid of meeting his eyes.

"Your lying."

The spirits eyes lit up, and somehow his piercing blue eyes grew even more intimidating than before. His thin lips curled into the most discomforting smile that I'd ever seen.

"Ha! Yes.. Clever, clever little Mr. Marron. You're really something aren't you? By Coda I think I've grown obsessed..."

He edged closer to me, but this time I didn't back an inch. He stared straight into my eyes and narrowed his. Again he spoke softly, each word chilling me to the bone.

"You certainly are just jam-packed with surprises.. You've done me a very fortunate service, what I thought in fact isn't, how so very long it has been since a time like this has been. And I'm quite sure that your family tree isn't quite what I suspected..."

I turned my back on him and saw a door that sat at the front of the train carriage, I'd broken whatever illusion it was he'd put on me.

"Alright. Let's go then." I said.

"One thing first please." He replied.

I turned back to see his smile once again spread across his face, though not so discomforting this time.

"I have decided on a name."

"Yeah?"

"Yup. From now on you shall call me Oak."

"Okay, no problem." I said.

"Within the secret and mystical groves of the oak trees, the druids of long ago would perform their secret rituals. I still remember their voices, chanting their rehearsed chants. The first word ever to pierce the holes on the sides of my ancient head was Oak.. I remember it all like it was yesterday.."

I nodded my head slowly trying to process what it was he was saying, it made almost no sense. But there was a small part of me, a tiny part somewhere in my brain that was intrigued by his tale. It didn't feel anything like my usual intuition, but I believed it may be knit from the same cloth. I did my best not to forget his words, because my usual intuition *did* me that it'd be best to remember. For whatever reason.

"Okay Oak. Let's go."

"Gladly."

We boarded the train and sat idly for around five minutes. Then, we were off, thundering along through the realm of Coda inside one of Earths most common means of transport. Although it *was* the first train I'd ever seen to have a deep purple interior, aside from the seats which were orange like the outside of the train. Soon, we swiftly glided away from Alven valley. And the last thing that caught my eye was the giant glass monument that sat on the summit where I'd entered, far off in the distance.

"So what is that glass monument anyway? Is it a statue of Alven?"

Oak slowly shook his head.

"No. It isn't." He replied.

After a short silence I pressed him further.

"Well what is it then?"

"A man who made me very sad a long long time ago, and that's all I'm going to say about it Mr. Marron."

Aside from his comment, he still smiled as he spoke. He then pulled his straw hat over his eyes and slumped lower into his chair, and I wondered to myself as to whether spirits have the need for sleep, I doubted it. Oak was nothing short of being the strangest being I'd ever happened to come across, and I almost got the feeling that a lot of the time, he'd like to consider himself as human as anyone. Maybe that was his quest? Maybe his ultimate goal in his existence was to attain some kind of a mortal existence?

Still though, in no way did I trust him, there was without question, something very off about him. I got the notion, that if I had his ability to see the depths of someone through their eyes, I'd see a being of infinite complexities.

After about an hour, (well away from the Alven Valley) the landscape changed dramatically. I saw a thick mess of deep emerald green forestation with all kinds of alien flowers blooming all around. There were hundreds of tiny little spirits dancing and weaving amongst the branches, like small translucent ghosts that were only aware of the very forest they were dwelling in.

It was breathtaking, and had I brought a camera with me, any photographer would marvel at the pictures that I'd bring back. But that was another thing though.. *Getting back..* With no crown and no Edmund, how was I even supposed to be *able* to make the journey back to my own realm. Then again, I'd just have to cross that bridge when I came to it, no point in worrying about something I couldn't help at the moment.

Oak stirred and raised his straw hat, then stretched his long spindly arms like he was waking from a long night's sleep.

"Good sleep?" I asked.

Oak smiled and vigorously nodded his head.

"Convincing? Or did you see straight through it like the great glass statue of Alven Valley. But then, you *were* quite blinded by the sun. You have your weaknesses Mr. Marron, I'll admit they're a mystery, but they are there, little holes sitting on the cloth of an old sweater."

I raised an eyebrow and shook my head.

"I *was* sleeping." He continued.

"But not like you sleep."

"And how do you sleep?" I asked.

"Do you fear them Steven?"

His question was irrelevant, but I still knew was he was referring to anyhow.

"Black and snaky.. As if someone had given life to the plumes of smoke from a chimney. And it's odd too, because that *is* somewhat the case."

I looked into Oaks eyes, trying to pull the same ability he'd pulled on me, but all I saw was his piercing glare shooting back at me. Having to look away, he'd won, I had watch something else, there was something truly awful about his eyes. But not awful in a malevolent way, it was almost the opposite. They were full of sadness, but more than just simple sadness. Then again maybe it wasn't sadness, maybe it was something else. What his eyes *did* tell me though, was that Oak had surely seen things that nobody should ever see.

"What do you see in me Steven? Nothing? No.. You felt something, something that your mushy brain cannot possibly think about rationally. There are other things aside from the brain that think.. I see that part of you, and *it* thinks. *Its thoughts rattle on and on and on...*"

I decided the best course of action was to throw the topic out the window, mostly because I couldn't be more uncomfortable if I tried.

"So Oak."

"Yes?" He replied.

"What are they?"

Oak shook his head and began to speak, but I was growing frustrated, and my patience with him was fading fast.

"What exactly do yo—"

"Oak. The spirits of Zugai. What are they?" I interrupted.

For the first time, I felt the tiniest hint of hostility in him. But as he began to explain, it left as quick as it'd come.

"Simply put. They are just people." He said.

"What do you mean *people?* You mean like spirit people?"

"No."

Once again, his hostility returned, and I decided it was probably best to drop the subject. God knows what he could be capable of, and I didn't really want to challenge that. So instead I slumped back into my seat and looked back out the window.

"I guess I'll find out soon enough."

"Yep. Real soon actually." He replied.

I felt his smile hitting me on the side of the face like a slap, making me uneasy. Mostly because he was right, I *was* afraid of them. More afraid of them than anything else I'd encountered during the insane journey that'd begun upon my return to Missidnyl.

CHAPTER 25-

Josh couldn't help but marvel at his own work, he didn't know what it was he'd created, but he smiled with pride nonetheless. He'd felt his soul, pulled it out from his chest and had let it swarm the alcove of the factory. He followed it around in a blissful meditative state and painted the path that it'd shown him. His metaphor sounded ludicrous, but that was how it'd felt. It was the best feeling, Josh's favorite feeling.

Perfectly intricate symbols surrounded the entire room, and in the strangest way, it was like they each had their own small eyes to see. They looked at Josh like they were his children, and the sensation was good, *really good.* There was no malevolence, in fact it was the opposite. Warming. Loving and pure, a white glow that filled the decadent and crumbled factory.

'I don't know how, but something tells me this is gonna come in handy.' Josh thought to himself as he picked up Marron before giving him a scratch on his head. Edmund was gone, and it'd hit Josh like a sack of bricks. He was so utterly sick of death, so incredibly tired of seeing anyone close to him wither away from his sad and lonely life. So Josh had decided during his frenzy of painting, that no matter what, he'd fight his opposing forces all the way down to his last breath.

"I hate evil. I hate it so damn much." Josh muttered to himself.

* * *

Directly outside of the Vickerdon factory, the embodiment of all Josh's fear stood tall with a blurred and expressionless face. Amicus, (the erased man) slowly narrowed the blood red eyes beneath his clouded face. He could feel the trace of ancient blood, not visible blood, not really even blood. It was someone he'd known so very long ago, a poor soul that should never have become as unnatural as he was. Why here? Thought Amicus. Why had the life of my student been annihilated here?

'That poor soul.. At least now he is no more, much to his favor he sleeps as he should have long ago.'

Amicus raised his arm and looked at the frail roof of the old factory.

"RIP THE SHELTER!" He proclaimed with his old and strained voice, a voice that sat low, like the deepest baritone.

CHAPTER 26-

Things were rapidly becoming more and more discomforting with Oak, for the last forty minutes or so he'd done nothing but continue to stare directly at the side of my face while I looked beyond the glass of the train window. Despite Oaks staring, I was fascinated by the wondrous scenery that flew past during our journey east. At one point there was a huge lake surrounded by glowing deer with huge and intricate antlers that resembled faces. Then was a small stretch of desert where I saw gargantuan tortoise-like creatures roaming around with not four, but more like ten feet. But most fascinating of all, was a small fairytale looking forest, where tall elongated figures seemed to be speaking to one another through intricate little dances with their long and spindly fingers.

But enough was enough, and I turned towards Oak, my face red.

"Okay what?"

"I have been interested about something." He said.

"Yeah what's that?"

"There are *all* kinds of questions that you could be asking me, but you fail to ask. I understand your mistrust towards me, but. Surely you must assume that I could be of help? Am I correct?"

He reached around me and drew me in towards him, he drew circles with his long pale white forefinger in front of us.

"You and Oak! The team of all teams! Triumphing over the deadly forces of Coda! What do you think? How about you fire a couple of questions down my way huh?"

I pushed him off me and looked into his huge smile.

"I'm assuming questions that have nothing to do with Zugai or the glass monument? Can I fire *those* questions down Oaks way?" I said with a slight hint of sarcasm.

"Well. That is disappointing."

Oak obviously had history with both things, and he was right in assuming that I was curious as to what had happened. So I quickly devised a plan, I'd ask him all sorts of questions to lift his spirits in order to soften the topics that I *really* wanted to know about. My intuition had been buzzing like a saw blade during my whole journey through Coda, it was leading me—from my chest up to my mouth it continued to direct me.

"So.. Why *is* Coda full of these weird spirits?" I asked.

"Weird..? I'll tell you what's weird, the weirdest thing in this old realm is you. *You* are weird."

"Okay but that didn't answer my question."

Oak nodded happily and moved in closer, as he spoke he wasn't whispering, his tone sat in that odd vocal range just in-between.

"The spirits roam these lands like animals in a habitat, they go about their business in the same way that anything would. It has commonly been said that they grew from art. An eternal and natural art that has always looked down on this realm like a giant paint brush with every color at its disposal. Some believe that the paintbrush has a mind of its very own, and some believe that things are the way they are for no reason at all. I myself don't know, therefore I have no opinion on the subject."

I kept on questioning.

"What is your favorite color?"

Seeming aware my intentions, he fired answers matching the speed in which I was asking them.

"Grey. Definitely, Grey." He answered.

"And why Grey?"

"A canvass is white, a blank building block for any artist to throw art on, and that's fine. But Grey just seems more interesting."

"Do you create art?" I asked

"Yes."

"On Grey canvasses?"

"No. But I watch people who do, with their stolen spray cans in the late hours of the night."

"You're talking about graffiti?"

Instead of answering right away, Oak looked beyond me and through the window of the train. He tilted his head to his side dreamily.

"That feeling of a thousand worlds each with their own little stories. Every location, even down to the inch has at some point been stained with a story of its very own. Of all these locations, the ones found in the most run down places are the ones that make my heart move."

"Well you would've loved where *I* came from." I said.

"Oh I'm certain of that. It brings happiness to my mind, but not enough happiness to speak about the particular topics *you'd* like to know about."

Oak had beaten me at my own game, I knew now that no matter what questions I came up with, he'd easily rebut them without even having to try.

The strange lands of Coda continued to fly past the window, and I began to think about Josh. I hoped he was okay, I hoped that what'd happened in the old factory hadn't sent him into a furious rage. I wondered what he'd be doing right now, probably smoking cigarette after cigarette while stewing in an inconsolable anger. There was no room to fail now, and the burden seemed to grow heavier with each and every second that passed.

'Just hang in there Josh..' I thought.

Oak shot upright and excitedly pointed a finger outside, his sudden movement made me jump and for a moment all I did was stare at him with frustration.

"On top of that summit Steven, look now." Oak said cheerfully.

I looked over a huge stretch of dead grass that eventually ended at a high summit, and on its peak stood a massive wolf. It stood on all fours as it watched the train glide by. The wolfs fur was the purest white I'd ever seen, I almost couldn't bear to look at it, it radiated a glow that was like the sun. It was undoubtedly the most majestic creature I'd ever seen, and it blew every bit of air from my lungs.

"Whoa.." Is all I could think to say as my breath slowly returned.

"Yup. That's the last one right there, and most likely the first, they once hung around these lands in large numbers. They were the white wolves, and some say they were the very first spirits to be in Coda itself. That wolf up there probably exceeds my own age by ages upon ages. Until now, I may not have even believed in its existence.. But by Coda there stands the very last white wolf. Truly unbelievable."

"The white wolf huh?"

"Yep, and in case your curious, it watches you Steven. I warn

147

you as a friend though, should you ever find yourself in its company, its very voice, even at its most gentle would tear your soul into a million pieces."

I shuddered at the prospect of being in its company, the sight of it intimidated me. The worst part about it was its complete and utter purity, it weakened my heart to even imagine comparing myself to it.

Before I had a chance to think about it any longer, Oak pointed his finger and exclaimed cheerfully.

"Our destination approaches Mr. Marron, prepare to dismount the train of Coda. Next stop."

I at Oak baffled.

"You don't even know my intentions, I know you can know tell things through my eyes. But, I'm pretty sure that there are parts of me you can't see."

Oak's eyes widened, before reaching out and hugging me almost violently.

"Right you are, your intuition is knowledge, but you have made an error."

"What error?"

"Before you head off to do whatever it is you're on route to do, you must first visit the next stop. I insist."

"Oak I really don't have any time to be—."

"You have no choice Steven."

Oaks hostility returned, but this time his smile remained. For the first time, he began to really frighten me. If there was any positive though, it was that no knots cropped up in my stomach, my intuition seemed to agree with his plan to get off at the next stop.

"Okay." I said with a stone cold face.

Then though, my stomach *did* fill with tight knots of heavy anxiety, I could see far in the distance that the spirits of Zugai were swarming and flying overhead. They flew around like a hideous barrage of black smoke, moving like a flock of birds traveling together in a group while they migrated. I wondered fearfully if they were coming for me, did they know I was here?

Panicking, I turned to Oak, and it was my turn to point a finger into the distance.

"Oak! They're coming, and you're really gonna have to tell

me what they are now, what the do we do??"

Instead of answering me, he just stared, his big dumb smile stretched across his pale, angular face.

"Oak!" I repeated.

After a few excruciatingly panicking moments of silence, Oak once again performed his circus act of retreating into his large straw hat like a tortoise. Then from within it, he spoke in a muffled and cheerful tone of voice.

"Wear the hat Steve, go on."

"What!? This is ridiculous, what is this??"

"Tick, tick, tick."

I looked around the empty seats of the train while my thoughts raced, then in a moment of desperate instinct decided to do as Oak had instructed.

The moment the hat went on my head, I could feel Oaks presence inside it, it felt like he'd retreated into a deep and infinite cave where he could watch me from the darkness. It was unsettling, I could feel him trying to pry into my thoughts and intentions, but part of me warded him away. I could still feel him managing to uncover things, and the sensation was so incredibly invasive I almost couldn't bear it.

"Oak! Stop. What's the plan now?" I yelled.

"Very well." He replied from within my own thoughts, like an alien echo.

"Okay that great, but what's the plan?"

"They won't see you now, very simple really. But don't forget to leave the train when it stops. Because if you don't.. Well then. Boom! Off comes your fancy new hat!"

"Fine! Okay." I replied angrily.

After a matter of minutes, the train slowly halted to a smooth stop, and the doors burst open. I quickly walked over to the exit and almost lost my balance in the process. The hat was a burden, it carried a weight, not a physical weight, but a mental weight pushing heavily against the borders of my mind.

The spirits of Zugai had closed a great deal of distance and they approached with incredible speed. They looked less like typical birds now, but more like Eagles, soaring with a dangerous velocity.

"You're sure they won't see me?" I asked Oak.

"Yeah, yeah, don't worry your little head."

"Okay good.."

After nervously watching the spirits of Zugai, I looked around and noticed that we'd arrived in a garden, unlike any I'd seen before. It was lit up by an immaculate array of colors. Colors that shone like bright lights all mixing into one incredible shade of deep violet. Then a little deeper into the garden was a stone circle, featuring one much larger stone in its center.

"Oak what *is* this place…?"

"It is the glorious shrine of Ante. Approach the stone."

In a daze, I walked towards the stone circle, completely transfixed on the larger stone in the middle.

"That's it Steven."

Besides the fact that it was clearly just made of rock, it still gleamed like a gemstone. It had a presence about it, like the rock itself had a consciousness.

"Oak, what is it?"

"The stone of Ante helps people. It shows you things, things you might have happened to forget. It uncovers small clues that sit in the faraway pockets deep down within the brain, it is an aid to those who seek victory for whatever battle it is they may be fighting."

Almost drooling, my mouth hung open like a broken dummy, my eyes were like two sheets of faded glass. It was hypnotic, and I was well within its spell. I stepped closer and reached out towards it, feeling a sense of nervousness, but still with excitement.

"That's good. Touch the stone of Ante." Oak said from within the straw hat.

My fingertips brushed against the surface of the stone, I could instantly feel long lost emotions from my youth. Small snippets of memories began to spark up in my mind's eye, they buzzed gently through my head like the warm nod from an opiate.

"Yes, that is good. You need more though, place your palms against the stone." Oak said calmly.

Before I did as he asked, a thought shot into my mind like a bullet, and it pierced through like an arrow of lucidity, breaking a portion of my hypnosis.

"I'm gonna back away."

Just as I thought it, I felt myself slip back towards the spell of the stone. But just before I attempted to rest my palms against the stone, another thought shot into my head.

"I'm not gonna touch this thing."

Oak piped up once again, clearly annoyed by my hesitation.

"Steven what are you doing? You are *so very* close, we almost know what we need to know. Touch the stone.. You have to."

Another thought shot through my mind.

"Nah, I'm not gonna."

"Steven, times running short. Touch it now."

"No."

"Steven for the sake of Coda touch the stone."

"I'm won't!"

"Do it!"

A war exploded in my head, I could feel Oak trying as hard as he could to make me touch the stone. If my mind was a circuit board, it felt like he was smashing at it with a screwdriver. I clutched at my temples and shut my eyelids tightly, like I was battling the most intense migraine of all time.

"How dare you! I offer you protection, and you decline your end of the bargain! Pathetic!" Oak screamed.

I dropped to the ground in mental agony, flopping around the deep green grass beside the stone of Ante. For a moment Oak seized control of my arm and reached towards it through me, then the next moment I'd recoil and scream against his control.

"Okay! That is it!" Oak shrieked.

The straw hat bounced from my head and rolled away from the stone circle, and Oak emerged from it in a quick and disturbing motion. His face was bright red with anger, and his eyes watched me like perfectly sharp blue knives.

"Well! I suppose that part *one* was an awfully disappointing failure. But part two, I assure you, will *not* be." Oak said while breathing heavily.

He turned towards the spirits of Zugai, which were now no more than one hundred feet away, and pointed directly at me as he screamed.

"Hey! I have here an exquisite prize for you! Have at him you flying rodents!"

The spirits of Zugai grew closer, and panic lit up in my chest like a fire. Oaks intentions were obviously to have me killed after attaining something from me, and it was obvious now that it had everything to do with this stone of Ante. As he'd explained, the stone *revealed* things, things that one may have buried in the deepest corners of the mind.

Oak looked over at me one last time with another of his wide grins, this time full of malice. He turned away and darted like a rabbit back towards the train tracks with speed to match.

"Well.. At least I didn't touch the stone.." I said to myself as my panic grimly morphed into a morbid sense of defeat.

But just before I shielded my face and awaited being mauled like a lion would a gazelle, another thought shot into my head— just like before.

"Don't worry brother."

I slowly looked up towards the horde of black spirits, and it looked like they'd all slammed into some kind of invisible barrier. They dispersed in all directions and began to smash into each other in a bizarre frenzy of mad confusion.

"There ain't too many of 'em, shouldn't be much trouble."

They continued to crash amongst one another like blinded birds for about thirty seconds before retreating as though they were wounded—like a bird limping while still being airborne.

I stood beside the stone of Ante, dumbfounded. Something had managed to ward them away, something had come to my aid and saved my life. Then I heard the voice of my Saviour, this time outside of my own thoughts.

"Hey Steven! Ya came back!"

I turned around to see not just a friend, but a member of my family. I smiled and ran to him.

"Man you saved me!"

"Well I *am* the best spirit around here remember?"

CHAPTER 27-

Josh hit the floor like a military solider hearing the sound of gunfire, debris fell like concrete rain onto the floor as the old Vickerdon factory roof was ripped from its very walls. He waited nervously as the remains of wreckage showered violently around him, while thankfully, nothing struck him. He picked himself up from the ground and stared at the cloudy Grey sky that had revealed itself above his head.

"What was that...?"

He brushed the dust from his clothes and looked around the room confused, even without a superior sense of intuition like Steven, Josh knew with a dreadful certainty that something was about to go down. Something bad.

He studied the artwork that sat beneath his feet, and despite the lack of sunlight, it somehow gleamed like light hitting a metal surface. Before Josh had more of a chance to collect his thoughts and make sense of anything, a horrid voice boomed from the entrance of the factory, an awfully deep tone that threw him back to his earliest fears—the fears he'd felt during the bad times.

"What gives you the right?.." Asked the ancient voice of the erased man.

Josh's stomach dropped, and his face turned bright red with a paralyzing fear.

"I sense the death of an old soul. Explain." He said, now sounding closer than before.

Josh's mouth was frozen solid like the rest of his body, all he could achieve was a small whimper. After a few moments, the erased man stepped into view and stared at Josh through his old and blurred face. He was at least six and a half feet tall, covered in rusted chains from his neck to his feet. Only his head and arms were exposed, and they featured the same cloudy black quality similar to the spirits of Zugai. His entire body radiated dark, murky smoke like a campfire being smoldered. His eyes were like two strong lasers that shot out from his face.

"You.."

Just before Josh felt himself about to literally faint from fear, he caught a glimpse of Marron perched up on one of the chairs sitting in the corner of the alcove, and he thought of Steven, and his uncle, and everyone he'd been close to over the course of his sad and obscure life. Then through these thoughts, Josh managed to regain his voice.

"I hate you." Josh said quietly.

Even without eyebrows, the erased man somehow still furrowed his brow, and like a dog hearing a strange noise, he tipped his head subtly to the side.

"Hatred. You use that word as though you understand it." Said the erased man.

Josh felt a surge of angers.

"*Oh* I understand it. And I hate you, you ruined everything, you completely destroyed my life. And if there was a word stronger than hate, even that wouldn't be enough." Said Josh with his fists clenched tightly by his sides.

"At my age, years tick by like days. The wheel of time spins like a pinwheel of festering death.. And you speak to me of hatred, and you even dare to direct it at me. You are so very young, you are s—"

"Shut up,. I'm so goddamn sick of all this evil and all this death. I hate you, and I don't care about *anything* you have to say. You killed my sister.. You ruined everything."

Amicus strained his face in frustration and raised an arm towards Josh.

"YOU UNDERSTAND NOTHING!"

Suddenly Josh felt the ground beneath his feet shake, and the walls of the factory began to split and fissure. Josh held firmly onto his anger, and didn't move a single inch.

"I'm not running this time." He thought to himself.

"TO THE NIGHTSHADE!" Screamed Amicus.

The floor beneath Josh warped and split, revealing a black void that stretched on endlessly, Josh screamed as he prepared to plummet down into its depths. Oddly though, his footing remained. The artwork that Josh had created was lit up and glowing like a white neon light, he stood on its surface while looking through it and towards the darkness of the nightshade.

"What is this?" Amicus demanded.

Lost for words, Josh just stared at the erased man with a

stunned expression.

"Fine! You like painting? Then how's this??"

Again, Amicus raised his arm and directed it at Josh. A horrible pain shot into Josh's wrist, and he grabbed at it as he screamed in agony.

"How's your wrist now?" And how about the other?.."

Searing pain rose into Josh's other wrist, he screamed, but his rage still shone through, his hatred staying completely intact.

"That it? A couple of broken bones..?" Josh panted weakly.

The eyes behind Amicus' blurred face grew into a burning rage, he stepped closer, just a few feet short of the shining glyph that Josh had created.

"FINE!" Amicus boomed.

Josh screamed desperately as he felt the very skin on his wrists split like a bursting balloon, and blood poured out and onto the floor beneath. The erased man was literally ripping Josh's hands from his arms.

"If the breaking of bones doesn't impress.. Then I'll remove your limbs.. One by one."

The pain was too great, and Josh felt himself passing out. His vision wavered, and began to fade as he felt himself slip out of consciousness.

"This room is a mockery! You have no right to create this!" Said Amicus.

During what Josh thought was his final moment, he by miracle felt relief. The agonizing pain at the ends of his wrists subsided, and was replaced by something that actually felt pleasant. A pure white glow grew from his bloodied stumps and formed into two hands of bright shining light. A single word crossed through Josh's thoughts as his lucidity returned.

"Jessie.."

Josh raised his head and stared back at Amicus.

"Is that it?"

Amicus screamed with fury and again raised his arm, this time tearing Josh's entire left arm off of his torso. But in no time, glowing light once again replaced where his limb had been torn off.

"This is impossible!" Said Amicus as he unleashed every bit of power he could muster. Concrete and debris crashed around the factory like a deadly whirlwind. Josh felt himself being pummeled, and could feel his body being smashed by it as though he was swimming in a pool of knives. But still, there was no pain, only a buzzing pleasantness that radiated from within his body. When the whirlwind of destruction finally subsided, all that was left was Josh's torso and one single leg. All the rest was pure light, shining bright like the sun.

Amicus approached him, and stepped within Josh's glyph of light.

"This cannot be. You *will* be destroyed. I am death personified! I AM DEATH!"

Amicus lunged at Josh and forced his palm into his chest, impaling him with his entire arm. He raised Josh high into the air and screamed an ancient chant of Coda, a chant that had existed since the reign of its former king.

"LUPUS AD MORTEM ALBUM! DEATH TO THE WHITE WOLF!"

The words tore at Josh, though not physically. They pierced into his soul like a razor blade, and he screamed. Amicus laughed and again chanted the ancient words over and over, annihilating Josh with every word.

"True power. I am true and pure power! You will die at my hands, and you will suffer with every passing second.. And I will count them with my words.

The glyph beneath Josh was beginning to crumble, and small parts of his most prized piece of artwork began to fall into the black depths of the nightshade. Josh stared at Amicus with rage and thought again of everything that the horrid beast had taken from him. He reached towards his face and tried to choke him with his hands of light.

"NO!" Josh screamed.

The erased man was too strong, and there was no hope that Josh could manage to actually harm him physically. But whatever Josh now was, completely opposed the crippling darkness that was the erased man. The light of his hands burned into Amicus, and for a moment he staggered back in pain. Josh gripped harder and screamed into his face, leering down directly into his crimson red eyes. They struggled against each other, the darkness of Amicus, and the light of Josh. Finally, Amicus lost his grip and dropped

Josh to the floor.

And stared back at him panting.

"You cannot win this. This circus you've created here is useless!"

Josh picked himself from the floor and stumbled towards Amicus.

"I dunno... Seems pretty effective to me."

Amicus rose tall on his feet and raised his arm, preparing. But Josh suddenly ran and jumped onto him in a bear hug grip, screaming and cursing him.

The pain that Josh had felt before, the pain that'd felt like a knife cutting into his soul returned almost tenfold as Amicus tried to pry him away. Though as Josh screamed, he knew that the pain was mutual, that the erased man was suffering the same feeling that he was.

Finally, Amicus managed to grip Josh by his neck, lifting him up and again began to chant the ancient voice of Coda. The words tore at Josh, crippling him with every syllable. He writhed and kicked his limbs of light like a glowing rag doll, trying to escape the death-lock that Amicus had on him.

For a moment Amicus stopped his chant and looked into Josh's eyes.

"This is it.. This is where you fall."

The erased man had made an error, because the moment he ceased his chant, Josh found his last burst of energy. He forced his hand onto the erased man's face and gripped his wrist with the other. Amicus was caught off guard, and his hands lost its grip on Josh's neck.

"GET OFF ME!"

Instead, Josh placed his other hand on the side of the erased man's head, and squeezed as tightly as he could manage. Then in a moment of instinct Josh thought of everyone he'd lost, the people he'd loved.

"I'm gonna need help with this." Josh said fatigued.

The white glyph shone bright and Josh felt a surge of strength run down the course of his arms, and as the light shone brighter, his grip tightened more and more.

Josh could feel all those lost to him, their spirit ran through his body like an immensely powerful current of electricity. Amicus screamed a blood curdling scream while unsuccessfully attempting to rip Josh's hands from his face.

Josh knew with certainty now that he could destroy him, in one swift and final motion he could literally erase Amicus, obliterating him to nothing but a pile of old, rusted chains. But he couldn't help but to think of Edmund, and his hopeless ambition that'd stretched on for all those years. Josh would fulfill his wish, and for the first time he saw the situation without rage.

In the span of a millisecond Josh removed his hands from Amicus and instead gripped onto the chains that covered him, and with every ounce of his strength he ripped it out-wards from the neck down. The chains snapped and flew out in all directions, making loud pinging sound as they ricocheted around the alcove of the factory.

Amicus stared at Josh in shock and amazement.

"Those chains were impenetrable. There is simply no way.." Amicus said quietly.

"There was once a spirit, so very long ago, who I'd have thought to be the only one capable of such a feat. But he was destroyed, utterly annihilated by wolves.. He, in his naivety thought he had an ability to tame them—the ability to *use* them for the purpose of purifying the lands of Coda. He was sorely mistaken, and they destroyed him, tore his soul into pieces."

Josh stared back at Amicus, unchained and free. He didn't really have any clue as to what he was talking about, but it didn't matter. All that mattered was that the threat had finally been defeated.

"It is astonishing.." Said Amicus

Josh looked back down at the glyph radiating beneath him, its light was slowly dampening to a dim glow. A whole mess of thoughts ran through Josh's head, all kinds of memories and experiences that he'd lived through. It was unfortunate that so many of those times were bad, but not all of them. Some of them were beautiful, and it was these memories that Josh focused on.

"Your name is Josh?" Asked Amicus.

Josh nodded slowly.

"You shine like the wolves used to, I truly cannot fathom how.. But somehow, you do. This spirit that I speak of, the spirit of long, long ago shone just the same. Coda suffered an immense loss when he perished, so much so that I even took it upon myself to immortalize his image. When the sunlight of Coda hits the glass, it shines like the sun itself.. The way *he* used to shine."

Josh was having trouble retaining what the erased man was saying, as the light beneath his feet dimmed, so did his consciousness. He began to sway back and forth, as his balance started to fail. There was one last thing to do though, he looked at Amicus and spoke weakly.

"Come a little closer.."

Amicus approached Josh, while Josh quietly laughed at the prospect. His greatest fear and the sum of his nightmares had been intimidated, literally afraid of what Josh was.

Josh placed his hand on the erased man's face and closed his eyes, and in a burst of bright light, the last power that resided within the glyph ran through Josh like an electrical current and straight into Amicus. Again, they both screamed a scream of complete agony. But for Josh, it was the last pain he'd have to feel. All that was left of him was his torso, one leg and his head. The light was fading, and Josh decided to give it to someone who could use it. Someone who despised Solus as much as he did himself, Solus was, after all the true cause of all the madness that'd plagued Josh's life.

After the light had been given to the newly freed erased man, Josh fell onto the floor in a heap, panting and wheezing his last breaths. He thought briefly of Edmund, and the final gift that he'd bestowed upon him. It was an image, a beautiful image of his family, their arms open, ready to see Josh when the time came. Josh smiled as he thought of seeing them again.

"Jessie.."

Amicus looked down at Josh after recollecting his posture, and he spoke to him with pure sincerity.

"I am sorry Josh, for everything that has happened. I will gladly carry the heaviest of guilt for the rest of my days."

Josh managed to squeeze out a raspy and croaking response.

"Just kill Solus."

Amicus nodded.

Marron ran over to Josh from the debris and nestled himself next to his owner, and Josh was reminded of the night they'd met at the Vickerdon train station and the way that Marron had come back. He then thought about his early days in Missidnyl, times with Jessie, times with Hans, and long summer afternoons he'd spent playing with Steven. Joshua Quaid's eyes slowly closed, and he rested with a peaceful mind, and a big smile on his face.

Amicus knelt down beside Josh's body and performed a ritual he hadn't performed since the old, wretched king of Coda had taken his purity—he prayed. With his fingers laced in front and his eyes closed, he rejected the darkness of Coda and proclaimed his hatred for all that was impure within the lands of his ancient realm. He opened his eyes and looked at Josh once again.

"I owe you everything. Down to my last breath, I will kill everything that opposed you..."

Amicus rose to his feet, and prepared to return to Coda.

CHAPTER 28-

I could tell after a little while that Pito had changed, it was odd to make such an observation after knowing him for only a short while, but I could tell that he had grown. He was still the same bubbly spirit of a child with boundless wonder gleaming in his eyes, but he now spoke with more conviction, he'd become more serious about his beliefs and ambitions. Pito had traveled an enormous distance since leaving his forest, and what he'd seen along the way had opened his eyes to the true and decaying state of his realm.

Little Pito Marron, had saved my life. In his mind it was simply just what family members would do for one another, a relative being there for someone in a desperate time of need. I in all accounts, now had a brother, a courageous brother that I literally owed my life to. Together we walked along the old, rusted train tracks, while we caught each other up on what'd happened to us on separate accounts.

One of the first things that Pito spoke of was the stone of Ante, he didn't know anything about it historically, but what his third eye had revealed was in no way good. He'd told me that it was dangerous, a dark tool that's use would surely have caused my demise, even though he didn't know exactly how.

During our walk we'd seen at least another half dozen spirits of Zugai flying in the distance, fortunately they hadn't headed in our direction this time. Pito had used his third eye to attempt to uncover their motives, but they were too far away, and he couldn't get a clean lock on them. I had my intuition though, and I felt like they were scouting, and surveying the old lands of Coda like a smoky black, flying search party. Each step we took caused my fear to grow little by little, we were heading directly into the belly of the beast, and I knew that at some point soon I'd be having my first and last confrontation with Solus. All I wanted was for Pito to be safe, but sadly, I needed him. But then again, for all I know, maybe he really *was* the strongest spirit in all the universe.

For the last hour or so, the grass beneath had slowly gone from a lush green to a deep orange, and the train tracks had veered off in a different direction. I tried not to, but I couldn't stop myself from pondering about why things the way they were within Coda. I turned to Pito.

"Why *is* Coda like this?" I asked him.

"I dunno, why is where *you* come from the way it is?" He replied with a big grin on his face.

"Well I can't argue with that." I said smiling back.

Far, far away in the distance, the clouds swarmed like a dark spiral—a black tornado in slow motion, in my heart I knew that Solus was in its center. I swallowed hard and continued to plant each foot in front at a time, keeping the pace quick and steady. Pito must have seen the fear on my face.

"You scared?" He asked calmly.

"I'm not going to lie to you Pito. But yes, I'm pretty damn scared. What about you?"

Instead of answering straight away, Pito instead gave me another big smile and stopped walking for a moment.

"Whether or not we come outta this. I wouldn't trade these times for anything.. I feel like I'm a real human. I *am* scared.. But, it's worth it. We're trying right? So no matter what we'll always have made that mark."

"You're absolutely right, and you know what else? You have more humanity than most people I've known."

Pito motioned towards me, about to hug me, but suddenly he stopped. His forehead split open to reveal his third eye, and it darted around crazily in the direction of the black spiral way off in the distance.

"What is it?" I asked warily.

He looked at me with a stone cold expression and spoke slowly.

"He is *so* bad Steven. I can hear some faint things.. And there is no good in him at all.. He's horrible. It's like he's hollow.."

I slowly nodded and put my hand on his shoulder.

"Close your eye Pito, you don't need to listen to it. Let's keep walking."

Pito's eye closed and we continued forward. For a while we walked in silence, but soon enough we lifted our spirits back up with more stories. I told him about funny things that'd happened during my life and recited literally every joke I could think of. We laughed and smiled on our journey forward, but I knew we were both thinking about the same thing in the back of our minds. Solus, the terrible man that lacked any sense of good. Mad, ancient Solus.

The dampness of the orange grass started to become increasingly difficult to walk in as we continued trudging through it, and the very smell of it started to make me feel sick to stomach. After about five minutes I was almost losing my shoes in the muddy grass with each and every tedious step.

"Goddamn it." I said in frustration while looking at the long stretch of orange grass in front of us.

"Should we try and find a way around it?" I asked Pito.

We stopped for a moment and looked into the dense bush that sat on our right, and by the looks of it, we'd have enough trouble just trying to take one step into it. On the other side of the path was the same thing, just a tangled mess of impassible bushland.

"Screw it, it'll most likely get less muddy soon, let's just keep going," said Pito.

We kept trudging through the mud, and soon enough each step was almost submerging me half way up to my knees. But we kept moving, and hoping that soon enough the mud would harden up again. I started to imagine myself drowning in it, and the more I thought about it, the more unsettled the orange grass started to make me feel. Butterflies rose in my stomach and I stopped, noticing that Pito had stopped swell, once again his third eye was darting around while he looked at the ground nervously.

Pito.. What's up with this mud?"

"Hmm..."

"What?"

"I don't think it's just us here.." He said quietly.

I stared at the ground, my heart racing. Then, afraid of what Pito's answer would be I brought myself to ask him.

"What do you hear...?"

Pito looked at me with wide, fearful eyes.

"Pito..?"

"Steven.. We need to somehow get into the bush ok? Really, really slow.."

"Ok.." I replied after swallowing hard.

As Pito had instructed, we very slowly trudged towards the thick bush land to our right. I tried as hard as humanly possible to rule out the idea of some giant beast spirit biting off my feet.

"Almost there.. Keep going.." Pito said with his voice shaking.

Finally, we made it to the bush. It looked like the only option we had was to climb it and then just hope we can make it through and away from the mud.

I reached out and grabbed a thick vine, then turned to Pito and took his hand.

"Ok, I'm going to start pulling us out." I said while Pito nodded fearfully

Luckily, a large root was sitting at the base of the bush, after managing to plant a foot on it I turned back to Pito.

"Pito, climb onto my back ok?"

I gripped the vine with both hands as he started to grip my shoulders, then managed to wrap his arms around my neck in a bear hug.

"Alright, here we go." I said.

With all my strength, I started to pull us up and out of the deep mud. The healing stab wound on my stomach flashed in pain and I winced as I strained with the weight from Pito and myself. Then, catching me completely off guard, Pito screamed.

"Steven! Hurry!"

I kept trying as hard as I could to pull us out, but the pain in my side was becoming too much.

"Pito, give me some good thoughts!" I yelled.

Pito blasted a barrage of warm thoughts into my head, and it just managed to give me the strength I needed to pull us from the mud, it was like a thick pool of glue. I stood on the root of the bush's edge, gasping for air.

"It's ok.. We should be safe now.." Pito said anxiously while slowly climbing off my back.

"What the hell was it??" I asked Pito panting.

Before Pito had a chance to answer, the surface of the thick mud started to bulge just a few feet in front of us. We both stared, eyes wide and hearts racing. The surface of the mud split open to reveal a hand reaching out from its depths. Unlike most hands I've seen, this one had only two fingers, they were a sickeningly pale white color and looked to have at least three times the number of joints that a normal hand would have. The hand continued to surface from the mud, revealing an arm bearing the same pale color. The arm was completely covered in little spurs, they jutted out from the skin like misplaced fingernails.

"Pito.. What is it..?"

"I.. Don't really know.. I know this sounds weird, but *do not* open your mouth." He replied.

"Okay…" I replied confused.

Whatever it was, it was disgusting, but I couldn't bear to look away from it. The strange creature continued to climb out from the mud, showing more and more of its awful skin. It was so pale that it was almost translucent, like a clear balloon filled with dirty water.

Eventually its head rose sluggishly out from the mud, and my stomach churned violently. Its face looked like a bird mixed with a spider, like it was created in a horrible science experiment. For a short while it stared at us through its eight eyes, blinking each one at individual, random times. Then it began to move its beak, producing high-pitched sounds that reminded me of an Australian Kookaburra. I spoke quietly to Pito, while making sure to look away from the creature.

"Can you understand it..?"

Pito slowly nodded his head, somehow his understanding of this creatures language made me more anxious. But despite my anxiety, I still asked Pito.

"What's it saying to us..?"

"Wait." He said telepathically.

Pito's third eye appeared, and at the very moment, the creature cocked its head to the side. Pito was communicating to it, speaking directly to the creature through his telepathy.

I watched Pito and the creature stare each other down for what felt like an hour. Pito's facial expression started off as fearful, but slowly he began to look more as though he was upset. Then, Pito slowly nodded and his third eye closed, he then turned to me. He had us turn to face the other way, so our mouths were out of the creature's view.

"This stretch of mud used to be a lake. But everything here is dying, this place is poisoned. And it's all because of Solus, he's sucking every bit of life he can find."

I looked back at the creature with pity, while simultaneously feeling even *more* hatred for Solus. I turned away and asked Pito.

"What do we do..?"

"Well, we can't go through the bush, but she says that she'll help us if we can restore the lake to the way it was."

I thought it over and nodded my head.

"I'm assuming that killing Solus will restore the lake?"

Pito nodded. "Yeah I think so.."

Again, I looked back at the creature, it stared at me with its eight eyes. I was overcome with a sense of being trapped, either side of the mud was dense and impassible bushland, and we'd been trudging through the mud for at least three long hours. At this point we didn't really have a choice, but fortunately, as afraid as I was of the strange creature, I took solace in the fact that it despised Solus as much as we did. I turned back to Pito and thought out loud while his third eye darted around.

"Ok, so how can she help us?"

"There are two more of her kind, and they're making their way to the surface now. They're gonna take us through their lake."

I pondered the plan for a moment.

"How exactly are they going to take us through it..?"

"We're gonna ride on them.."

I took another glance back at the creature and shivered. On one hand I hated the idea of offending them, but as rude as it was they were possibly the most grotesque things I'd ever seen. I'd always *hated* spiders, and the thought of riding on something that resembled one, let alone with a beak, put me into a cold sweat. But at the end of the day, it was a creature just the same as I was myself.

"Ok.."

We stood on the tree root as we nervously waited for the other two creatures to reach the surface, I placed my hand on Pito's shoulder as the mud began to bulge again. They clawed out from the mud in the same fashion as the first, but unlike the first one these two continued to pry themselves out from the mud, revealing the rest of their bodies.

As I'd feared, they had eight long spindly legs just like a spider. Their torso's stretched on to about three times the length of my own, and just like their arms, little spurs covered their stomachs completely. Instead of having abdomens like a spider would, they had great long tails that split off into two halfway along, with big red pincers on the tips.

"Hold on a second." Pito thought to me.

For another while, Pito communicated to the creatures until finally reaching a conclusion. He turned to me and motioned towards them. It was time.

"Well, never saw myself doing something like this." I thought as I gave Pito a smile. He smiled back, but his smile was as shaky as my own.

Together we began to trudge through the mud with our arms linked together, and towards the creatures waiting for us in the middle of the poisoned lake.

"So why can't we open our mouths anyway?"

"It's their cultural etiquette. Plus, they'd peck out your tongue like a bird eating a worm."

CHAPTER 29-

Amicus walked through the broken ruins of the old house of Coda, it was a structure that once stood as high as a mountain. In years long, long gone, he would spend most of his time in the house of Coda, he would serve as the king's right hand man. Amicus had always been under the command of someone else, and it was the same thing every time. Power, it was *always* about power.

Amicus was hated for his purity, for the majority of his time serving for the king, there was never a moment of trust, never a moment of good sincerity. When he was banished, Amicus had walked the hall of the house of Coda for the last time, and the king smiled a snakelike smile, smirking at the prospect of defiling a spirit of such purity.

His memories of the king were hazy, unfortunately so were most of his memories before his final punishment. Anger rose in his heart like a red hot dagger. Not a rage that was driven by madness though, his anger was driven completely by pure and lucid hatred.

"All those children.." Amicus thought to himself.

"All those children, lost.. Erased by my very own hands.."

Amicus was free, his chains had been destroyed by the spirit of the white wolf. And the deed was done by the most peculiar of people, Joshua Quaid. Amicus owed him literally everything, he was his Saviour.

The king had always been impure, he was utterly warped by his greed and envy. He'd always wanted everything for himself for the sake of power, every last drop of power that Coda could manage to offer him he would hunt fiercely with violence and malice. Then there was Solus, a man almost exactly the same. But the difference was that Solus was *completely* devoid of any good, he was everything horrid and grotesque all wrapped up into an old, wrinkled man.

Even without having heard his Josh's final wish, Amicus would have vowed the harshest vengeance upon Solus no matter what. A good hearted soul would never look towards violence for the sake of solving a problem, and once upon a time Amicus lived by that rule with a pleasant sense of warmth. But Solus was a man who was incapable of redemption, he was a black void that only cared about propelling his own power and gaining control of as much as possible. As if he was a disease, Amicus swore to cure it.. Down to his very last breath.

Amicus walked down the broken steps and towards the Ante forest, a cursed ground once watched over by a twisted spirit Hell bent on uncovering the dirtiest secrets buried in the minds of spirits. A long time ago, the king himself had used her for the purpose of learning everything he could. But when he grew jealous of her magic he had her construct a shrine to carry out the deeds before proceeding to destroy her. She'd been tricked, and played like a pawn in the king's sick game of chess, and she was by no means the first powerful spirit to fall prey to the king. He was always the most cunning and underhanded spirit there was, and when his tricks were of no use he would simply just threaten those with the raw power that he possessed. Such was the case with Amicus, possibly the first spirit to be born pure within the realm of Coda.

He would often wonder if there were others out there, spirits with good nature in their hearts. Maybe the day would come when Coda could be run by a force of light, maybe that new era would shine life over the ancient lands, as opposed to the darkness that had always swarmed the realm like a plague.

Once again, Amicus preyed. He thought of everyone he'd lost, everyone that'd fallen prey to the clutches of darkness.. Himself included.

After a while he moved on-wards through the Ante forest and towards the stone of Ante that sat at the exit, he walked with his hands clenched tightly by his sides. Solus was out there, and chances were he'd be completely unaware of what had transpired within the Vickerdon factory. It was time for Amicus to take a leaf out of the old king's book and use some trickery of his own. Before leaving the factory he'd collected what he could of the chains that had restrained him for so long, and wrapped them back over his body. The difference this time though was that they were simply just chains, chains that he'd rip off when the right time came.

"My chances are small, but I will it give everything I've got.. I will fight the hardest fight I can manage. And by Coda, it will be the last.. One way or another."

It was sundown, and the last rays of light illuminated the forest of Ante a deep orange as he moved through its dense vines and shrubbery. Had he not thrown so much power into his confrontation with Josh he could easily just manifest himself to the island of Zugai. But Amicus wasn't disappointed, in fact he enjoyed every step he took forward. For the first time in so long he felt free, and was the happiest he'd been in hundreds of years.

"Life and purity to the white wolf.." He said to himself.

CHAPTER 30-

Long ago in the year 1282, Doran lived his underprivileged life as a struggling cottager, he'd often reminisce and reflect on his days as a young man and of the good times that he'd had with his late family. Later in his life though, now on his lonesome, he grew increasingly jaded by his lack of wealth and the lowly position that he'd ended up in. He was jealous of those with wealth, and spent almost every minute of his days cursing those who were better off—those who had *more* than he did.

His days grew gradually grew worse, and slowly his jealousy turned into hatred, until eventually every night after work he would pray for death to come to the people above him. But his god didn't listen, and it wasn't very long before his useless prayers evolved into something much worse. Doran dismissed the idea of a fair god and decided to take matters into his own hands. He would sharpen his knife at nightfall while fantasizing about sliding its sharpened silver blade straight into the belly of the kings only daughter. Doran wanted everyone to see the king lose that which was the most precious to him—he wanted the king to feel true pain.. He wanted chaos.

A day came when Doran was ready, and for the last time he worked his labors as a cottager with a cheerful smile on his face. He took his knife from beneath the pillow on his bed and was about to head out when a voice spoke within his own room.

"Foolish."

Doran span his head around while stabbing his knife in all directions, surprised by the sudden voice.

"Who's there??" Doran demanded.

"You are deluded.. Do you truly expect to accomplish this? You will never make it within the company of the king's daughter."

Shocked, Doran began to panic. He feared that he had finally lost his mind, and had slipped into insanity. But after a short while, the mysterious voice proved to be coming from someone real, a man who wore a long robe that blended perfectly with the colors of the wall, camouflaging with it like a chameleon. The man stepped towards Doran and continued to speak.

"So full of hatred.. It drips from you like black ink."

Doran lunged at the man, with his knife out front. But instead of burying it within the man's stomach, he instead smashed straight into the wall. The man was gone, somehow he had evaded him. Doran looked up in confusion.

The man appeared above him, his face revealed from his long robes. He was a wrinkled old man, with a wicked smile that seemed to stretch across his entire face. Before Doran had time to act, the old man had already swung a blunt object at his head knocking him unconscious.

Unfortunately, what happened next was the beginning of all that Doran could remember until now. His dark life of jealousy and hatred was lost, even his very name was forgotten along with it. His new first memory was an awful sensation of being ripped away from something, something that he instinctively knew was important to him. Then there was the sight of an endless sea of crimson red, he floated around for what seemed like forever before finally surfacing as a newborn spirit. A jet-black, maddened spirit full of hatred.

It wasn't long before he found others like himself, others that shared his strong feelings of pure malice and hatred. Then along with his newfound kin, he answered to a voice that spoke directly to them, a great man that promised them all glory and power if they followed his wise and godly instruction.

From time to time, some of the spirits defected from their ruler, and when it could be helped, they'd be found and destroyed. But the man who once lived as a cottager by the name Doran, was never without complete loyalty. He wanted everything, and he knew that the great man could one day deliver.

On the island of Zugai, he and his kin would chant amongst each other.

"Lord Solus name our purpose."

CHAPTER 31-

During my teenage years, I did a lot of things most teenagers would do. When I managed to get my drivers license, the first thing I did was step on my cars accelerator to push it as fast as it could go. At the time I loved the rush, it made me feel alive, partly because it was my first time alone in a car, but mostly because of the sense of danger that it brought along with it.

But like everybody else, I grew older, and my urge to push boundaries slipped further and further away from me. My sense of mortality grew clearer as each year ticked by, and suddenly I didn't feel as invincible as I once did. My thirst for slamming on my cars accelerator slowly dissolved, and was replaced with looking for a rush in different ways. It was strange to look back in hindsight, as my transition didn't now seem like it was gradual, looking back it seemed like I'd simply just changed overnight. Like one moment I was one person, and a different person the very next.

These days I had no interest in moving at dangerous speeds, and here I was moving faster than any car I'd ever driven. But instead of sitting behind a wheel, I was mounted on the back of an eight legged, spider-bird hybrid creature with an enormous tail with horrid stingers on the tips.

Watching them slowly claw themselves from the depths of the mud made me curious as to how fast they could move, but as soon as they'd planted their legs on the surface of the mud, they had moved at incredible speeds.

"You alright Pito?" I thought out loud.

"I guess yeah." He thought back to me.

I looked over my shoulder and saw Pito flying along at the same speed, and just like me, his arms were wrapped around the creatures neck in a stronghold. He looked back over at me with a nervous smile, I struggled to return one of my own. Just beside Pito's head, was the head of the creature he was riding, and two of its eyes were firmly locked onto me, watching me constantly. It was scary to imagine myself opening my mouth, I pictured the creatures halting to a sudden stop sending us flying across the mud before feasting on us like we were a tiny snack. I threw the thought away and kept watching ahead.

The dense bushland raced past, and for the last half hour or so, the scenery hadn't changed in the slightest bit. Aside from the looming distant black clouds slowly getting closer and closer. I guess at the very least, the bizarre creature ride was a good distraction from Solus, because as horrifying as the creatures were, Solus was worse. He was undoubtedly the worst thing anywhere.

The closer we got, the more afraid I felt, in a rational sense there couldn't possibly be a more obvious statement. But it was deeper than that, there was something bigger at work that went beyond rationality, it was something so utterly unnatural, and it shot my nerves. Solus truly was, a man completely devoid of any good, even without my intuition or what Pito had said. It was *that,* which was most obvious.

"Steven."

I looked over at Pito, wincing against the strength of the wind.

"I think we're almost there." He thought to me.

"Thank god for that." I thought back.

I was sure that Pito had been listening to everything that the creatures would've been saying to one another, but what made me wonder was how the creatures actually *did* communicate. I guessed they must be telepathic in the same way that Pito was, but only between their own kind, of course excluding Pito—who I assumed could read the thoughts of *any* living thing.

Slowly, the creatures slowed their pace, until they eventually settled into a slow walk. I exchanged a glance with Pito before preparing to dismount the creature.

"Does their species have a name?" I asked Pito.

He looked down at the creature beneath him and spoke with his eye.

"The Kawa."

The name seemed familiar, but I couldn't quite remember how. I was sure though, that somewhere along the line I'd heard that name.

Ahead of us, the mud-river had come to an end, and a path of gravel sat in front. The bush seemed even more dense on either side of the path, and was as dead as any plantation could be. The sky above us was as dark and grey as the inside of the old

Vickerdon factory, I'd never before seen clouds as swollen and heavy as they were. I was nervous, the closer we got to Solus, the more sinister everything seemed to be. But I still felt relief, and I took comfort in Pito's notion that we were at least trying, with every ounce of our soul, we were doing what we thought to be noble.

We dismounted from the Kawa, and met with each other to face the great creatures—our mouths shut as tight as possible.

"Give them my thanks." I thought to Pito. He nodded and looked at them with a stone cold expression on his little face.

After a while, he looked back at me and motioned towards the path. As we walked away, the Kawa slowly made their decent back into the murky depths of their poisoned home, I looked back one last time to see the tips of their tails disappear like giant earthworms receding into the earth. We then spoke with our mouths, instead of our thoughts.

"They accepted our thanks, but we have an end of a bargain." Pito said.

"What do they want?"

"Well, if we somehow manage to take down Solus, they want him. They want us to drag him by the hair on his head all the way to their poisoned lake, so they can eat the man who destroyed their home."

"Nothing would make me happier."

"You 'n me both."

We moved along the trail of gravel ahead, I looked around at all the death that surrounded me. The old man had murdered and defiled what used to be the perfect image of a fairytale, leaving it as bleak and depressing as anything.

Just as Pito had, I felt that over the last while, parts of me had evolved. In fact, I felt like we all had. Years ago, death was my foremost fear, if I had a list of phobias, it would've easily been at the top of the list. But now my fears had changed, and what motivated me to do what I'm now in the midst of doing was driven by something different. I wanted to find order amongst chaos, I wanted to annihilate the sick and wretched man responsible for all the death that surrounded the realm of Coda. For the sake of everyone I love and hold dear, all I wanted was peace. My new biggest fear wasn't death, it was dying before restoring what I had a window of opportunity to restore.

My thoughts turned to Josh, I couldn't stop pondering on what exactly he was up to back on Earth. I prayed endlessly that he was happy during the long walk along the dead gravel path, I hoped with all my being that there was sense in his head. He was my first friend, and just like Pito he was family. Joshua Quaid and Steven Marron from Missidnyl, on their final adventure before retiring into a simple life. Or at least, that's what I hoped.

"Stop.." Pito said suddenly.

My feet stopped immediately, turning to Pito concerned, watching his third eye listening to something that I lacked the ability to hear.

"Somethin's weird.." He continued.

"How do you mean..?" I asked nervously.

"I'm not sure yet.. But, somethings clashing. Like, two things smashing into each other.. I dunno, it just feels weird."

Being as confused as Pito was, I didn't push for more information. Because just the same as everything else, one way or another, we'd find out soon enough.

Another hour or so passed, and the surroundings only got more and more bleak. The smell of death grew stronger by the second, and everything slowly went from a dead brown to a dead black. What was once probably a beautiful and flourishing stretch of bushland, now looked like a mountain of burnt charcoal. It was truly terrible, and it made my stomach churn with sickness.

"There." I said stopping in my tracks.

"What?"

I lifted Pito up to my height and pointed into the distance, and we stared at a black structure we could just manage to see the tip of. We both knew that Solus resided there, and it was exactly where we were headed.

"We're close."

"Yeah.." Pito replied with his mouth hung open in awe and wonder.

"Alright let's do this."

During our silence I decided that I'd die for him if such a time came, I couldn't let anything happen to him, because despite his age I still saw him as a young boy. There was so much good in him, he had more good than so many people I'd come across during my lifetime.

"It's good to not be alone." Pito said quietly.

I propped him down and put my arm around his neck.

"Brothers for Life." I said.

Pito smiled, and we walked further down the poisoned gravel path, and deeper into the belly of the beast.

"So Steven, what was your moms name?"

"Ruby."

"Is she back in your realm?"

"Nah, unfortunately she's not around anymore."

"Oh..."

"Nah, don't worry about it, I really don't mind."

I went on to tell Pito everything, I told him about my childhood, and the strange experiences that she'd guided me through. My first brushes with the dream sea, and the overpowered intuition that would always sit like a sharp rock in my chest. I then spoke about her unfortunate bitter end, brought on by the dangerous drug abuse that she'd developed over the years. I explained to him my own experiences with drugs, and about the way that it would ward off my strange abilities as a dangerous medication.

We spoke about Josh too, and I told him everything that I could remember. Starting with our early friendship all the way up to his poor sister's demise brought on by Solus. I told Pito that he'd most likely get the chance to meet Josh at some point, and chances were they'd get along just as good as we did.

The only thing that we didn't discuss was my father, and as it was I didn't know very much about him myself. I remember my mother telling me at one point when I was young that things were complicated, and then something else along the same lines a little later in my teenage years. Sometimes I'd swim through the murky red liquid of the dream sea in hopes of finding him, keeping my eyes open expecting to spot him circling around. I was certain that he was alive in some way, and I'd spent a lot of my life fighting the curiosity to seek him out. My mother told me it couldn't possibly end well, and I wholeheartedly trusted her.

CHAPTER 32-

Ruby Marron had just one month left, one more month of soul-crushing sobriety. Being without opiates wasn't so much the problem, it was the dreams that haunted her. They were merciless and utterly unforgiving, it'd gotten to the point where Ruby was almost phobic of the very color red, but more specifically a dark red, a deep crimson tone.

Her belly was enormous and the baby inside would enter the world as little Steven Marron in the next month or so, then things would finally get better, things would finally once again be bearable for Ruby. She had attended at least a dozen churches and spent every single day over the last eight months praying constantly, all she wanted was for Steven to be normal. A normal, healthy little baby boy unburdened by the horrible depths of the red sea.

There was at least 400mg of codeine below the bathroom sink, and every day Ruby fought the urge to take it. She would imagine its bitter taste going down her throat followed by the sweet opiate buzz it'd bring. But it wouldn't be fair, because in the previous eight months Ruby had made a deal with god that should she refuse to use during her pregnancy, the lord would deliver a boy without her strange abilities.

She clawed through the next month, and counted each and every long day. She continued to pray, and continued to attend church on every Sunday that rolled around. Then, in the confectionery isle of a supermarket, Ruby's water broke, and she was tended to by a dozen shoppers and onlookers. An ambulance arrived shortly after, and she was rushed off to the Missidnyl town hospital.

The next day, Ruby tried to remember a time when she'd felt happier, she tried to recall a moment when something had given her so much whole-full satisfaction. The baby was beautiful, and she fell in love with him instantly. He whimpered softly in her arms as she stared into his big, baby blue eyes, tears of joy streaming down her face.

"Mommy loves you Steven, I will always look out for you. I

love you so much. My little boy.. My little baby boy.."

The baby's father wasn't around, and for that Ruby was grateful. Though she couldn't help but think. *"How could such a mistake create such a miracle.."*

It wasn't that Ruby hated the father of her child, it was just that he wouldn't exactly be *father* material.

The next few years were the most fulfilling and heartwarming years that Ruby had ever had the pleasure to experience. She gave every bit of love that her heart could muster, and the little smile that lit up Stevens face melted her every time. She loved him more than life itself, more than anything. He slept soundly almost every night, and it was rare that he would ever manage to challenge Ruby's patience, the years glided by and they were by far the best of Ruby's life.

One day She and Steven were out for a drive in the old Ford, and the whole trip was full of laughter and smiles. At one point Ruby looked over at her four-year-old son and thought to herself.

"I will always protect you, my little baby boy."

Things took a turn for the worse a little after Stevens fifth birthday, he ran into her room in the middle of the night with tears streaming down his face—his skin as white as a ghost.

"Mommy I had a bad dream." He'd said fearfully.

It wasn't the first occurrence, so Ruby wasn't too concerned. But her heart sunk and she sweat a cold sweat when he began to describe a big red lake full of floating things.

As Steven slowly drifted off to sleep after calming down, Ruby Marron rejected the lord and cursed her faith. She felt betrayed and hurt, it wasn't driven so much by anger, it was driven mostly by fear.. Fear for her little boy. Her little boy that had wound up with the same obscure abilities that even to this day she could barely control. Around this time Ruby's opiate addiction hit its peak, every night she balanced on the deadly tight rope of her very own mortality. Though despite everything, her unconditional love for Steven only grew as time went on, more and more as each and every day bled into the next.

When she could, she would teach him everything she knew about the red sea. Oddly, Steven seemed to grasp it with miraculous ease, almost like a gifted savant with an innate ability from the word go. It made her happy, and eased her nerves to know that at least his struggles may not be as bad as the ones that she had faced at his age. He was a happy boy, and for that she was grateful.

Ruby would have regular lunch dates with her best friend Lucy, exchanging stories one mother to another. It was nice too, considering that her best friend's son was also best friends with her own. Little Steven and Josh were almost inseparable, there was rarely an afternoon that they weren't in each other's company. Josh seemed to understand Stevens wacky personality, and in some ways seemed to share it to some extent. They were good times for Ruby, but more importantly, they were good times for Steven.

One night, Ruby woke in a panic, and a horrible knot had formed in the middle of her chest. Something was awfully wrong, and she tried with all her mental ability to think of what it could be. She sat up in bed for around an hour, filing through everything she could think of, until her best friends name struck her like a dagger from the dark.

'Lucy..'

Ruby ran to the front door and peered through the window towards the house that sat on the opposite side of the road.

'Is it the baby..?' She thought to herself.

Lucy was in her ninth month of pregnancy with her second child, a little baby girl. And Ruby hated the idea of anything going wrong.

She paced around the kitchen of her home and thought about what to do, but ultimately decided to dull the knot in her chest by using the only method she knew how. One hour later she was sleeping soundly with a floaty buzz that ran through the length of her body. At the time, she had absolutely no idea whatsoever that she would never again see Lucy and her husband Carl.

The next afternoon, she wandered across the street to put an end to her anxiety. She was surprised when instead of Carl or Lucy, there was an old man holding a baby answering the door.

"Oh my is that Jessie?" She'd asked excitedly.

The old man nodded and introduced himself as Hans, he was a tall pudgy man with a glimmer of sadness that never seemed to leave his eyes. Ruby very often wondered to herself about what'd happened to Carl and Lucy, and it made her upset to have lost her best friend and fellow mother. Strangest of all though, every time she brought up the subject, Hans would evade the question and talk about something else.

For a time, things still seemed to be okay in the old Quaid house, but Ruby noticed that over time, things began to only get worse. Carl's older brother was staying in the house along with Hans, and it seemed that every time she spoke to him, his words were more slurred than the last. He was a drunk and an alcoholic, and he wore the stink of straight liquor like a terrible cologne.

But Ruby's own habits were only getting worse too, and every night she would move another inch closer to her own early demise. Thankfully, Steven seemed happy, and he was getting to an age where he could more or less do his own thing. It wasn't far off that he'd be driving, and as happy as Ruby was for her son's growth, it made her sadder than anything.

'I wish he could be my little boy forever..' She'd think to herself, while nodding off on whichever blend of opiates she was on, usually during an ungodly hour of the night. He was sixteen and full of motivation, always talking non-stop about happenings and events that he'd been a part of during the day. Ruby knew that he copped some flak from other students in his school, but in true Steven fashion, it rolled off him like the rain off a ducks back. Unbeknown to her though, an event was slowly edging closer, and it was something that Steven would have no ability to brush off.

Ruby swam through the depths of the red sea one night with a full sense of lucidity about her, floating along with the current she saw someone from the corner of her eye. She was for the first time in her life, amongst company within the murky crimson sea. She watched curiously from afar as she began to slowly understand what was happening.

'He's trying to find him. He's trying to find his father..' Ruby thought to herself as she watched her son swim through the dream sea. She had no clue how big the dream sea actually was, but considering how many people occupied the world, she guessed it was probably around the same size. It was odd though, when someone needed to be found, the trip never seemed to take all that long. Ruby felt a spark of intuition light up in her chest, and she feared nothing more than Steven finding him, so she swam in his direction with hopes to stop him before serious trouble arose.

CHAPTER 33-

Steven was fast, and Ruby had to put all of her energy into moving just to keep up with him. He was as she'd always suspected, far more naturally adept to his abilities than she ever was. Effortlessly, he ducked and weaved amongst the sleeping subconscious globules that bobbed gently with the dream sea's current. She tried to scream out his name, but of course there was no use in it. Eventually, Steven stopped to think about his direction, and Ruby finally had the opportunity to catch up to him. When she grabbed at his shoulder from behind, Steven whirled around—eyes wide and shocked, followed by a look of confusion mixed with concern.

Ruby slowly shook her head, and as if they shared a psychic link, Steven recoiled from her grip on his shoulder and backed away. Again Ruby shook her head at Steven, but again he was angered by it. He wanted to know who his father was, and Ruby felt powerless to stop him, panic seized her heart and a stream of tears ran from her eyes and into the red liquid of the dream sea— like ink floating in a body of water. Steven reacted recklessly, and immediately bolted up and towards the surface that loomed above. Ruby, frightened out of her mind, chased after him, moving as fast as she could possibly manage.

The father of her son couldn't be found within the dream sea, but outside of it, and Ruby feared that Steven knew it in his heart. After all, he had the same strong sense of intuition that she did. Her intuition said some incredibly strong things about moving towards the surface, it was utterly dangerous, but Steven was moving along blinded by his frustration and curiosity.

It hurt her to see Steven so burdened by frustration, but she guessed that it must be an issue that'd been brewing for a long time now. A big part of her completely understood that what he was feeling was rational and fair, but all Ruby wanted was for Steven to be safe. She had only wanted to protect him.

They gained on the surface, and Ruby's heart pounded madly with anxiety, she was petrified at the notion of something happening to Steven. Somehow, she managed to find a reserve of strength and propelled herself forward with everything she had. She missed Steven's ankle by what seemed like an inch, she and Steven burst out from the red sea and into the other place—the place she'd avoided her whole life.

The very moment that Stevens head emerged from the dream sea, everything within him was amplified to a maddening level. Every memory he had and every emotion that he'd ever felt was thrown around his mind like a violent spray of bullets. Steven screamed and immediately tried to reverse his direction towards Ruby, but something had taken hold of him, and whatever it was, it didn't want to let go. Ruby gripped his ankle and pulled him back as hard as she could, and for a second it seemed hopeless. But when Ruby caught a murky glimpse of what held him on the other side, a pump of adrenaline overcame her and she found strength in her fear.

The spirit was jet black, and looked to be entirely made of smoke. Even without she didn't see its face, she knew that it was smiling. She knew that her son was just a lucky find for whatever it was to pray on.

Ruby managed to pry Steven away from the spirit outside of the dream sea, once she had pulled him back, she hugged him tightly as they drifted along the murky depths. Ruby could never have forgiven herself had something happened to her little boy, he was her everything.

Sometime later, Steven eyes fluttered open, and for a little while he squirmed in terror and shock. But when he realized he was safe and within his mother's arms, he relaxed and embraced her back.

They nodded to one another before making their ways back and out from the dream sea. Along the way Ruby decided that it was best that Steven finally knew about his father. It wasn't a conversation that Ruby ever wanted to have, but the thought of Steven ever being in the danger he was just in had to be avoided at all costs. It was ironic however, considering that Steven had just met him. He tried to pull his son into the realm of Coda with his cursed arms of black smoke.

CHAPTER 34-

Amicus felt his feet sink into the mud beneath him, but he trudged forward without worry. Nothing would stop him, there was too much at stake now, even if he was opposed by every force that Coda could conjure up, he would still stand against it with everything he had.

He looked at the dense bushland on both his sides and raised his arm.

"Passage."

The bush rattled and shook, and a path slowly ripped through it. Amicus approached the new clearing and stood at its entrance, then turned back to face the mud of the poisoned lake.

"Shame."

He felt the presence of an old race dwelling beneath the depths of the mud, he cursed Solus for what they had become, he hated him for the death that was spreading across the lands of his home. The Kawa, a once beautiful order of spirits that guarded the lakes of Coda had been poisoned. He could feel their hatred swelling up inside them like an ever-expanding black balloon, it saddened him to think of what they had become.

He continued towards the dark clouds that sat far away on the horizon, marching patiently while he thought about Edmund, a poor and innocent man. Edmund was a man of purity, a man who chose to sacrifice his sanity in order to maintain whatever peace he could manage to preserve. He was a good man, and Amicus didn't enjoy the idea of someone living through something they didn't deserve.

While Solus had always hunted down the darkest hearts that the world had to offer, Amicus would look for the good ones, and Edmund was one of the best. His decent into madness was a tragic thing. He knew that he could never regain the untainted purity that he was born with, but at least the darkness that'd been driven into his soul like a rusted screw had been loosened, and he knew in his heart that his final days were upon him.

Moving through the clearing of the bush, he suddenly raised an arm and caught a rock that had flown out from the thick of the bush.

"Stop this, I am no enemy." He said quietly to himself.

After a pause another stone flew from the bush, but once again Amicus caught it with ease.

"Enough." He said.

This time, no stone hurled towards him, instead a voice spoke to him from within the bush. It was a heavily guttural, old language that he hadn't heard for too many years to count, it was pained and weak—each word riddled with rage and desperation. Amicus was a creature of Coda, and there were very few languages that he was unfamiliar with, and this was one he knew. The spirit of the bush spoke of Amicus, and his disdain for what was happening to his home and what was left of his kin. Amicus lacked the physical attributes necessary to achieve speech of their language, so he just kept moving forward, catching every stone that flew in his direction, all the while mourning over the death that surrounded him.

After a while, the stones began to stop flying from the thick of the bush, and the creature responsible for hurling the stones stepped out from the dead greenery—it stared at Amicus with large and watering eyes, full of sadness and resentment. As long as Kawa had swam through the lakes of Coda, the Boku had watched over the forest. They stood as tall as eight feet and were covered entirely from head to toe in fur. But due to the poison that Solus had brought upon Coda, the Boku that stood in front of Amicus lacked his thick coat of fur and slumped on his hands with fatigue. Just like everything else around, the proud race of Boku were dying, and Amicus felt a sting of pain.

He couldn't speak the creature's language, but at the very least he could show the Boku his deepest respect and sympathy. Amicus lowered himself onto one knee and bowed his head forward, he crossed his arms over his chest and stayed completely silent. It was an ancient ritual of Coda, and it was the first time that Amicus had performed it in an age. When Amicus finally raised his head, he was astounded to see that the Boku had returned his ritual. The great creature pointed towards him and spoke in a horribly strained voice.

"...Free.."

Amicus nodded while loosening part of the chains that

covered his body.

The Boku nodded, then turned his head to face the black, swarming clouds that sat far in the distance. Again he pointed and spoke with his pained and defeated voice.

"..Kill."

Again, Amicus nodded. The Boku slowly made its way back into his poisoned home, and Amicus continued along the path and towards Solus.

Solus had the crown, and there wasn't much that could stop him. It was a tool that should never have been created, and Amicus cursed the old king for the decisions that he'd made all those years ago. He thought back to Edmund's first struggles, and they played in his head abruptly as nightmarish flashbacks.

"I feel like my soul is dying, it's just too much.. I do not want to be like this anymore, nobody should have what this is, it isn't natural.. Help me… Amicus I want to go home.."

In the beginning, Edmund was happy. He and Amicus had walked through the realms of Coda constructing the landscape with the image of Earth in mind. It made Edmund happy to be a part of something so incredible, and they'd both cherished it for the time. But Edmund began to realize that the crowns power was boundless, and it slowly ripped the humanity away from him. He'd become something that he'd never in his life desired to be. The king laughed, and smiled delightfully at the situation. It was Amicus' first true insight and lesson about the king's dark heart, and some nights, he could still hear the sound of the old king's voice echoing through the ancient halls of the house of Coda.

Edmund was pure, and it was the goodness in his heart that'd stopped him from succumbing to the power of the crown. Solus on the other hand, had no good in him whatsoever, and it scared Amicus to the core. But it wasn't the power which Solus now possessed that frightened him, it was the fact that such evil can actually exist. That, Amicus thought, was the *truly* unnatural thing about all this.

CHAPTER 35-

"Okay, stay here.." I told Pito while nervously approaching a clearing in the dying bushland.

"I have a bad feeling about this way." Pito said anxiously.

The truth was, I did too. But even though the idea of the clearing put my nerves on edge, it still remained to be the only way we could go. It was either the clearing, or through what looked like another thousand miles of thick bushland. And I didn't even want to imagine what spirits might be lurking inside.

I peered into the clearing and saw a stretch of dead grass which led to the shore of the dream sea, I looked back at Pito and motioned him towards me.

"Do you hear anything..?"

Pito's third eye darted around for a while before he slowly shook his head. I nodded to him and started making my way onto the dead patch of grass through the clearing. The black swirling clouds were directly ahead, and one way or another we'd have to swim through the dream sea to get there. The cursed island of Zugai was close now, and the only obstacle that sat in our way was an old temple structure that sat in-between the dream seas shoreline and the island of Zugai itself. We were close, and pretty soon everything would be over. One way or another.

I understood now that being in Coda could be achieved in two ways. The first was in physical form, just like I was now. But the other was in spiritual form, achieved by emerging from the dream seas surface. When I was a teenager, I had done the latter, and if it wasn't for my mother, I never would have made it back safely. She'd saved my life that night, and it was strange to think that here I was, all these years later, about to swim through its depths yet again. But this time, I would be surfacing without her there to help me.

"Do you know what that old temple thing is?" I asked Pito.

"Nah, but whoever used to live there was worshiping something. There's been tons of religious stuff that spirits believe in, I guess that's just one of the churches."

"How do you know it was a church?" I asked Pito curiously.

"See the carvings at the bottom?"

I looked hard, but failed to see anything, and assumed that Pito's eyesight must be far better than my own.

"I can't see any carvings."

Pito looked at me with an eyebrow raised for a moment before pointing at the temple.

"It's right at the bottom."

I walked further into the clearing and continued to study the temple, but again, I could see nothing but its mossy and cracked surface.

"Nothing, I don't see anything."

Pito walked up beside me and spoke softly, sounding slightly discomforted.

"Maybe you're blessed.."

"What do you mean?"

"Those carvings were made with a skilled but dangerous hand, a *long* time before I was around. Ages ago, it's said that there were wolves, and they were supposed to be Coda's guardians. Whether or not it's true I don't know, but this temple was made by someone who definitely didn't think so. It's a mockery of them, and there's a lot more of these.."

I immediately thought back to the wolf that I saw from within the train, the beautiful but frightening white wolf that'd watched me from afar.

"I saw a white wolf, when I was on the train." I said to Pito.

Pito didn't budge, instead he kept staring deeply at the carvings that my eyes couldn't see. Then, disregarding my comment, he continued with his explanation.

"They say that those touched by the wolves are blind to anything that goes against them. I can see the carvings as clear as day. But you can't."

The thoughts in my head whirled about in a confused frenzy.

"I just want you to know I'd never trade these times for anything. I'm gonna miss you."

I was touched by his comment, but no less confused than before.

"Don't worry Pito, neither of us are going anywhere. We'll survive this."

Pito nodded slowly, and I could tell that he knew something I didn't. I didn't press him though, instead I put my hand on his shoulder and watched the last rays of the sun slowly recede into the night.

"We'll swim through the dream sea as soon as the sun rises, we won't see anything in there while its dark." Said Pito.

"Really? I've swam in the dream sea at night before, it was definitely dark, but I could see."

"This isn't the same sea, this one's heaps older. Nobody in there has been alive for a long time, the dream seas are lit up by life, and when there is no life, there is no light."

It was depressing, I knew all too well about the inevitable nature of death, but it was shocking to see it before me as it was now. Possibly millions of deceased souls, filling a liquid void.

"How old is it?" I asked Pito.

"I'm not sure, but it's a lot older than me, that's for sure."

I couldn't take my eyes off it, it seemed like the longer I stared at it, the deeper my eyes would fixate. It was terrifying to imagine Pito and myself swimming through it, wading our way through its murky red liquid.

"So.. When I'm usually swimming through the dream sea, I'm a spirit, and I don't need to breathe. But now that I'm here in physical form. How will I breathe in there? Will we just keep our heads out of it?"

Pito shook his head.

"Nah, you can breathe it. In fact, it's even better than air."

"How?"

"I don't really know, but it nurtures life. The Wolves used to run with other spirits that summoned the crimson rain, and then boom.. The dream sea came about."

"Do you believe that?"

Again, Pito shook his head.

"Nah."

I didn't ask Pito what his own personal beliefs were, part of me thought of it to be disrespectful. So instead I sat on the dead grass and let my thoughts wander, and I found myself thinking about Olive. I decided that if we managed to make it out of this, I would visit her again, in the quiet little town of Endon.

Pito sat beside me for a while before laying down on the dead grass.

"We should get some rest, big things tomorrow." Pito said.

"Yeah, you're not wrong about that.."

Pito smiled to himself and closed his eyes, and within minutes he was gently snoring as I looked up towards the night sky. He was right, tomorrow was a big day, and sadly, it'd most likely be the last.

After some time, the white noise buzzing around my head slowly grew more and more incoherent as I slipped into sleep. I dreamed of Solus, and the black spirits of Zugai. I dreamed of them slaughtering Pito before my eyes while I stood as still as stone, without the ability to move. All I could do was scream an earsplitting scream as they tore him to pieces, while Solus smiled the whole time. It was this dream that made me understand that most of my fear was for Pito, it frightened me to imagine him suffering, even just a little. I wish I didn't need him, I hated that he had to be a part of this. I tossed and turned as throughout my dark dreams, until the horror eventually fizzled, and was replaced by the sound of a choir. Millions of voices all singing in unison, all with a perfectly harmonious pitch, it was beautiful.

**

As I woke, the sound of the choir slowly faded, and my eyes adjusted to a big clear, blue morning sky above me.

I spotted Pito standing on the shoreline, staring out at the black clouds in the distance. Even without seeing his face, I could tell by his posture that he was riddled with fear.

"Pito!" I yelled out as I got onto my feet.

My mind was sent into all-out panic when I saw the terrified expression on his face as he turned to face me.

"What is it? Are you okay?" I asked as I met him at the shoreline.

"Someone came through last night." He replied fearfully.

"A spirit..?"

"Yeah, and I think I know who it was.. But it doesn't make any sense.."

"Who do you think it was?"

"Well, do you remember when I told you about that spirit who faced punishment in my forest?"

"Yeah?"

"I'm pretty sure it was him."

My thoughts burned the inside of my head like a fire of the mind, and I cursed Solus with unrelenting hatred once again.

"The erased man." I said in a pained voice.

Pito's face went ice cold, and he shot his sights back over across to the entrance of the clearance.

"He's toying with us.. He knows that we have no chance, so he didn't even bother killing us while we slept. We're done for Steven."

I put my hands on Pito's shoulders and met with his deep brown eyes. I could feel his body shaking with fear.

"No, we're not done for. I promise you that we'll come out of this okay? I promise.. I won't let anything happen to you."

"But you can't promise that."

"Well, I just did."

Eventually he stepped forward to hug me, I hugged him back tightly while my eyes unconsciously drifted over to the temple that stood in the long dead dream sea.

Pito loosened his grip and stepped back, he wiped his eyes with the back of his hands and nodded bravely.

"Okay. Let's end this."

I nodded back and started making my way towards the dream sea, with a welcome calmness. Pito walked behind me, and we slowly waded into the shallow depths. Soon after, we stood on the ends of our toes.

"So I can definitely breathe this?"

"Yeah, don't worry."

Like ripping off a band-aid, I quickly submerged my head and inhaled deeply. Just as Pito had said, it was fine, it filled my lungs like pure and fresh oxygen. I looked behind me and saw Pito staring at me with his thumbs up. His third eye was open on his forehead, and the sound of his voice came into my thoughts.

"Just move straight, I'll be right behind."

"Okay." I thought back.

It wasn't anything like the dream sea I was used to, this time around I felt the full weight of the red liquid that surrounded me, and there was no intuitive magnet that pulled me through its gentle currents. It'd been a long time since I'd swam at all, and within half an hour I needed to stop and rest. It was an odd sensation to be gasping for air when there was none, it filled my lungs with a density I could feel weighing down on my chest with each and every breath.

As Pito and I sat at the bottom of the long dead dream sea, I looked around at the floating globules. Unlike what I was used to, these ones were black, and they held no life. It was disturbing to imagine what might happen if I was to touch one of them, so I didn't even bother to ask Pito.

"Okay, I'm good." I thought to Pito as I nodded.

He nodded back as we continued to swim along, slowly weaving amongst the floating globules. My heart jolted with shock every now and then as I'd mistake globules in the distance for spirits of Zugai, but luckily it seemed that at least for the time being, it was just Pito and I.

At one point, Pito stopped dead in his tracks and looked up towards the surface with a concerned expression on his face.

"You okay?"

"Yeah.. A couple of them just flew overhead, I think we're getting close. Don't go anywhere near the surface though, just keep going Steven."

Even despite Pito's information, I could tell that we were getting close, as the knot in my chest was growing tighter with every swift motion forward. I kept thinking about ways I could exclude Pito from where we were headed, but it was useless. He'd saved me from the spirits once before, and chances were he'd have to do it again.

I tried to dismiss my train of thought, as I assumed it was all going to chalk up to instinct in the end anyway. My intuition had led me here so far, and it was really the only thing I had to go on. So I did exactly what Pito had told me to do.   *"Just keep moving."*

The dream sea grew darker by the second, until finally I was struggling to make out what was right in front of me. Pito had moved onto my side and I could see that he was struggling with the same problem I was.

"Jesus.. I can't see anything. Grab my hand Pito, let's just swim for it."

Pito took my left hand, and together we propelled forward and into a pitch black, liquid darkness.

"Let me know if you hear anything okay?"

"Don't worry, I will." Pito replied.

"Man I'll tell you what, I think I'm going to have to res—."

Suddenly, I was overwhelmed by emotion. I screamed in mental agony as my thoughts were flooded by memories that didn't belong to me. I fought the black liquid hopelessly as I felt the weight of an extinct subconscious smashing into my mind.

The memories were old, incredibly old. There were visions of campfires within the dark confines of a cave, as I'd lay on the ground beside its warmth. Teaching my children to hunt boars with a sharpened rock I'd made, then eating our prey after skinning its fur hide for clothing.

The memories bounced around my head like sharp, serrated bouncing balls, we had unknowingly swam directly into one of the globules, and it turned out that despite the person it belonged to being dead; held no bearing.

Similar to the previous time I'd worn the crown, Pito blasted me with good thoughts again, and thank god it worked again. My foreign memories of a life as a caveman slowly began to subside, and I floated gently beside Pito as he mentally nursed me back into sanity.

"I'm sorry Pito.."

"Why...?"

"I'm sorry that I need you in all this."

For a while, Pito didn't respond, but eventually his voice again filled my mind.

"I know, I can hear your thoughts remember. But Steven.. Even if I couldn't help, I'd still be here. Besides, we're family.. And it was always gonna happen this way."

A wave of relief washed over me, I could feel tears streaming from my face as I pulled him in for a hug. Then for a moment, everything was fine, part of me even managed to forget about the horrible place we were heading to. So for a while, we floated idly in the pitch black darkness of the old dream sea, until we both continued to swim off and towards Solus. Side by side.

CHAPTER 36-

We crawled on our hands and knees as far as we could before our backs emerged from the blackened dream sea, until we had no choice but to army crawl on our stomachs. Finally, we had gone as far as we could go, and there was nothing left to do but emerge onto the cursed island of Zugai.

"Hear anything?" I thought to Pito.

"Yeah a lot. There are tons of 'em, I can't hear Solus though.."

"Should we wait for a better opportunity..?"

Pito was silent for a while, and I could tell that we were both thinking the exact same thing. *"Better opportunity for what..?"*

We had no guns, no knives, no weapons. We had nothing.

"What does your intuition tell you?" Pito asked.

I lay on the shores of the island and meditated, trying desperately to feel something. Something that would answer Pito's question. But nothing came, all I could feel was a dense mess of anxious knots.

"Nothing. Sorry Pito." I said.

"No problem, we'll wait until they clear out a little."

"Okay."

We continued to lay down for what felt like three hours, until I felt a familiar surge of intuition scream at me, and I almost though that it really *was* a voice screaming at me.

"Now Pito. Let's go now." I though aloud.

Without hesitation, Pito answered promptly.

"Right."

In unison, we rose to our feet and stared directly at the island of Zugai. Then also in unison, Pito and I gasped at what sat in front of us. A tower of black stone stood as tall as the clouds, it started thick from the base and slowly thinned out as it pierced through the heavy Grey clouds that sat high up in the turbulent, dark sky above.

"Jesus. It's huge." I said.

"Yeah.. It's awful." Pito said nervously.

"At least there are no spirits outside, they must be inside the tower."

Pito nodded, and turned to me with a face riddled with fear.

"How many do you think there are..?" I asked Pito.

"Hundreds…"

My heart sank, and every bit of hair on my body shot up like needles. I knew there were going to be a lot of them, but there was still a small part of me that was silently hoping and praying that it would just be us and Solus. Even *that* scenario was a frightening one to think about.

"What should we do Steven?"

I thought over Pito's question, and was thankfully was accompanied by my intuition this time.

"Follow me."

We walked around the shoreline and across the bright yellow sand, at that moment it came to me that despite being submerged in a red liquid, my clothes were bone-dry. I was relatively clean aside from the dried mud that was stuck to my shoes, the mud from the poisoned lake. We quickly noticed that the tower had no door, there was no way for us to enter. But it didn't matter, because I knew that Solus would soon be joining us outside, his ego was too big to allow us to die at the hands of his army of jet-black spirits.

"He's coming isn't he?" Pito asked.

"Yeah, I think so."

We waited in silence for a while, the only sound was the gentle currents of the dream sea rolling back and forth on the shoreline of the small island of Zugai. Things were about to get intense, everything that we'd been heading towards was now directly in front of us. I felt sickening fear and relief, and all I could think about was my mother. At least if things went south, there was a possibility that I'd have the chance to see her again.

"There.." Pito exclaimed anxiously with his finger pointed at the base of the tower. The structure itself began to warp and shift, and where there was no door before, now stood a pitch black entrance to the tall tower of Solus.

"Well this is delightful.." Solus boomed from his tower.

I leaned over to Pito and whispered frantically.

"Pito, do *not* open your third eye. At least not yet."

Pito nodded, with his eyes still fixated on the towers entrance.

"You're a rat.. Scurrying around in search of somewhere to belong. Weak, made fragile by your undignified sense of sentimentality. Now to see you beside that equally pathetic little spirit, just makes your situation that much more laughable."

I didn't talk back to Solus, instead I stood my ground, eyes locked onto the base of the tower.

"It intrigues me.. Why do you have those eyes? Why was a rat given such a gift..?"

Solus gradually came into view from the black confines of his tower, he stood tall, with his shoulders hunched back.

"It's like giving a gun to a coward. They will stand on the line of fire, only there to be killed and forgotten. No strength, just useless…"

Solus moved closer to Pito and I as he spoke. Even without sunlight, the crown of Coda shone bright like the sun atop his head.

"I just can't seem to decide whose worse. You, or that other filthy one.."

Solus continued closing distance between us, with a perfectly confident stride in his step.

"..Did you know that he's dead? It'd make my day if you didn't."

His words stung me like a wasp.

"Untrue.. Not possible.. Not fair." I thought to myself.

"Yes.. So there it is, there's that look of shock I was after. Superb. Your ties make you weak, you are a tragedy."

A blinding rage started to grow inside me, red hot anger spilled into my veins like molten lava. I had never in my entire life felt such unconditional hatred for someone, it consumed me.

"I'm amused by you, but it does sadden me in a way to finally see you. I *was* honestly expecting so much more than this pathetic boy that stands here in my home, you're nothing in comparison to me.. Nothing.."

Thoughts of Josh flew around my head like angry birds, and the notion of him dead crippled me worse than any blow I'd ever taken. I would've happily died for him, but he was gone.

"Well. How about I introduce you and your little pet there to some of my family."

Solus turned towards the castle and waited in silence for a moment before Pito spoke for the first time.

"Nah, not right now."

Solus whirled back around and stared at the third eye that'd opened up on Pito's forehead.

"The rats rat speaks, and I see it also has a little party trick."

"Pito don't." I said quietly.

"No please do." Solus said happily.

Solus watched with a sick fascination, but slowly he raised a clump of sand off of the ground. He levitated it with the movement of his hands, and his crown shone brightly as he did so. Immediately I stood in front of Pito.

"Pito, please." I thought aloud.

"I'm sorry Steven, but I have to." He replied calmly.

"You actually care for this thing don't you? It's a lost little animal, it has no soul to even care for."

"Well he's keeping your little horde of black snakes inside that crappy tower isn't it...?"

Solus laughed an old sickly croak of a laugh and took a few steps closer towards Pito and I.

"I could completely obliterate the both of you without trying, but I think I'm going to drag this out. Nice and slow.."

A small gust of wind kicked up just in front of me and Pito, and a small spray of sand shot into me and grazed the skin on my arms.

"Little by little, the sand will strip the flesh from your body. But just you Steven, then I'll have some fun with that thing behind you."

Again, a spray of sand struck me, this time small drops of blood began to trickle from my arms and onto the sand. But I felt nothing at all, except a furious rage.

"You don't deserve the eyes in your skull, you never have. They're wasted on you, put to miserable use. You should have just gone ahead and died in Vickerdon. But at least *now* you can die in the most holy of fashions, by the hand of a god."

Another spray of sand kicked from the ground, this time much more violently. It ripped into the side of my face and cut my left cheek, blood ran down my face like tears. But I still felt nothing but anger.

"Steven, calm down. I know it's hard, but calm down." Pito thought to me.

I stood my ground and tried to regain my thoughts, and braced myself for another spray of sand. This time, I felt a deep sting of pain in my arms.

"That's good." Pito thought.

I continued to do as Pito had instructed, because after all he *was* right. Anger was a blinding emotion, and right now I needed to see as clearly as possible.

It was difficult to find any sense of meditation while gunshots of sand ripped into my skin, but somehow I managed to locate a shred of intuition; and I followed its instruction with my full trust.

"You didn't kill Josh personally did you?"

Solus raised an eyebrow and smirked.

"I know it, so admit it. You didn't did you?"

Solus stopped causing the sand to whirl at me as he walked closer, still with the same self-righteous expression he'd had before.

"Unfortunately no, as much as I would've enjoyed to put him down. You can thank Amicus for that one."

Solus raised his eyes again, a light-bulb going off above his old wrinkled head.

"Yes! We can make this a whole lot more entertaining."

Solus turned back to his tower and raised his arms.

"Amicus!"

The base of the tower once again shifted and warped to give way for a door, and the silhouette of a wounded figure began to make its way from the opening. The erased man slowly made his way over the sand of Zugai, his red eyes burning into me like little laser beams.

"Quickly, move those legs, you ancient dog." Solus said sarcastically.

"Hold it together Steven, don't lose your cool." Pito thought from behind.

"Don't worry, I won't."

"Once a grand spirit of Coda indeed, now reduced to a limping piece of black smoke. Tell my new friend here Amicus, did he scream? Did he suffer?"

Without answering verbally, Amicus just nodded his head.

"Delightful."

Solus turned back to face me, smiling like a deranged clown.

"He suffered Steven, right down to his last alcoholic stench of breath. But don't worry for a second, I'll make sure that you will both have that in common."

Another bullet of sand flew into me, and I felt the small pebbles rip into my chest. Warm blood trickled down my stomach and dripped onto the ground.

"Steven, I can't hold them for too much long—"

I stood silent for a moment, waiting for Pito to finish what he was saying.

"Pito?" I thought back to him.

"Wait.." He replied quickly.

I looked over to the erased man and into his blood red eyes, I noticed that he wasn't looking at *me,* but at Pito. Something told me that everything wasn't quite as Solus thought it to be.

"Steven.. This is gonna sound crazy, but I'm gonna let the spirits out of the tower. Trust me on this one okay?"

Without even a second of hesitation, I promptly answered.

"I trust you Pito."

Like a massive explosion, the tower seemed to erupt like a volcano made from brick. Hundreds of spirits flew out like a deathly gust of black wind, and they twirled with a sick grace through the air like winged snakes. Pito collapsed to the ground, completely fatigued, his mental batteries flat. Solus was blinded by his ego, and thankfully chalked it up to Pito's lack of ability. He laughed manically as his followers swarmed the dark skies above the island.

"Well, I guess that is the extent of what you'll both accomplish here today." He said smiling.

"You alright Pito..?"

"Yeah I'm fine, just tired as hell."

The very moment I turned my head to look at Solus, the wind was knocked out of my stomach, and I flew across the sand, taking the most powerful punch I'd ever received. When I finally stopped sprawling ungracefully across the sand, I looked back up at Pito and tried to get to my feet, but Solus pinned me down and struck me with yet another sand bullet. I gasped for air desperately as I worriedly eyed Pito.

"Dinner time!" Solus screamed as he pointed excitedly.

The spirits of Zugai all weaved amongst themselves and formed a black hurricane aimed directly at Pito. I tried to scream his name, but I felt like my ribs had been smashed into a million pieces; my whole body was in agony.

"Save your strength." Amicus said with his unnaturally deep tone of voice as he walked past me and towards Pito.

"Hold still." Amicus told Pito as he raised an arm.

Pito flew across the sand and skidded to a stop beneath the erased man, at the same time, the spirits of Zugai spiraled into the sand like an enormous black drill; right where Pito was a moment ago.

"Well this is cute isn't it?" Solus said joyfully as he raised both his arms. In a flash of red light, a rock manifested from nothing in front of him, and he threw his arms forward and towards Amicus. The rock was launched towards the erased man at a deathly speed, hurtling along like a comet.

Just like Solus had, the erased man raised his arms. The rock smashed into a thousand pieces, and Amicus stepped forward unharmed, burning lasers into Solus with his crimson eyes; and for the very first time, the smile on Solus' wrinkled old face faded a little.

"Amicus, kill it." Solus demanded.

The erased man stood motionless, not moving a single inch.

"Kill the boy Amicus."

This time, Amicus stepped closer towards Solus, hate burning in his ancient, smoky face.

"Last chance Amicus, it's kill or be killed."

A grin returned to Solus' face, stepping towards Amicus to meet his threat.

"Very well, death it is."

Solus shot his arms out in a flash, and the erased man braced himself. Amicus was struck by a terrific force, and was thrust backwards on his feet as the chains covering his body smashed and broke off, flying like bullets in all directions.

I watched it all happen as though I was hypnotized, my eyes glazed over and blank. But on auto-pilot, my thoughts had been wandering as I watched the battle between Solus and Amicus. My intuition had sparked again, and I was brought back to lucidity by the sound of Pito's worried voice as it pierced into my thoughts.

"Steven, please don't."

I looked over towards him, sprawled out bleeding on the sand, helpless and hurt. I shakily rose to my feet.

"Pito, now you're going to have to trust me."

I watched the horde of spirits circle the sky like hungry vultures, and I signaled them like I was their prey, donating myself to be dinner. Thankfully, some of the wind had returned to my lungs, so I yelled as loud as I could.

"I'm right here!"

The spirits changed formation and again began to spiral and weave amongst each other, though this time *I* was the target and not Pito; and for that I was thankful. I didn't worry about Solus smashing me across the sand again, he would most likely assume that I'd given up, and had accepted my inevitable fate. I thought out to Pito as the spirits began to drill down from the dark sky.

"Pito, tell Amicus not to protect me, tell him to let them come."

After a pause, Pito finally answered me in a pained voice. *"Fine.."*

I looked at the erased man, he turned his head to face mine and squinted his blood red eyes.

The spirits drilled down from the sky, and I stood my ground I quickly prepared to do something that I'd never done as I slipped into a quiet meditation. Then everything went dark, and I was engulfed by the smoky black spirits of Zugai.

"They're just people..."

CHAPTER 37-

Pito watched his only brother disappear in the swarm of spirits, and his heart dropped to his knees. He could hear the maniacal laugh spit out from Solus' old, wrinkled lips as he prayed as hard as he could for Steven to live.

"Please don't let it end like this.."

The spirits of Zugai had covered Steven like a black mountain, they writhed and moved around like an infestation of horrible parasites. Solus had for the moment stopped laughing, yet the silence was worse, A terrific wash of anxiety filled Pito more and more as the seconds painfully passed by.

He looked over towards Amicus, he was engaged in a stare-down with the old man Solus. The erased man looked expressionless, but Solus was still smiling his wide, sick smile.

"Amicus, I am torn between two feelings at the moment." Solus said as he stared into the eyes of his old companion.

"The first, is disappointment, it genuinely surprises me that you're doing this. Secondly, and I'll say that this is undoubtedly my favorite of the two feelings, is that I am elated at the prospect of relieving you of your long, ridiculous life.."

Amicus stood firmly, his posture tall and powerful. He was a force to be reckoned with, an ancient spirit that wielded more power than anything Pito had ever seen within the realm of Coda. But Pito feared that he was outmatched, the old man Solus was mad, and the crown that sat on his head was his doorway to boundless power that could obliterate almost anything that stood in his way.

Pito was beginning to catch his breath, and soon enough he'd be able to open the eye on his forehead. But the last thing he'd do would be to turn his thoughts to Solus, Pito could feel the madness slowly filling the crown, and to tap into it would probably destroy him in a second, its power would cripple Pito's mind with no effort. So instead he would use his last ounce of strength to release the spirits of Zugai from his only brother, just so he could see him for a final time.

"Humour me Amicus, how was it that you *did* remove your

chains?" Solus asked with a smile.

"Are you afraid?"

Solus' smile quickly disappeared, and he retorted with his first hint of agitation.

"You are completely absurd. You are quite literally, the least terrifying thing to me."

"I'm not talking about myself, I'm referring to the power that removed my chains. That is the power that terrifies you, as it should, you are absolutely nothing in comparison."

Solus' smile returned as he threw away the threat like a whisper of false gossip.

"It is sad to witness what you have become, a fearful little rat trying to fill my head with lies."

"I fear nothing." Amicus said.

"Ha! You see? Another one of your putrid lies."

Pito's mouth opened angrily, instantly regretting the words that flew out of it.

"You're the liar! You *are* afraid, I know it."

Solus laughed loudly and raised his arm to Pito, then with a twisted, toothy grin he walked in his direction.

"I'll show you your place."

Solus thrust his arm forward, and instinctively Pito shielded his face with his hands. He waited for a blanket of pain to cover his body, but he felt nothing. Nothing except the yellowed gritty sand beneath his feet.

"You are persistent aren't you?" Solus exclaimed happily.

Confused, Pito looked towards the old man, and suddenly his comment made sense. Solus wasn't referring to Pito, instead it was Amicus, who had saved Pito's life for the second time.

The two were engaged in what looked like a mental arm wrestle, both had their arms raised towards one another. Pito knew that almost anything would be instantly blown into oblivion should it find itself within the invisible crossfire.

Pito opened his third eye and thought out to Amicus.

"Thanks."

"Focus your energy on your friend." He replied.

Pito took the order without a moment's hesitation as he looked at the mound of spirits. They continued to squirm about hungrily, but something about the sight of it had changed.

"Steven..? Can you hear me..?"

Pito's heart sank lower, and he could feel tears begin to well in his eyes.

"I won't let it end like this. .....Please talk back..."

No answer came back, and Pito was left alone with Solus and Amicus. It got worse still as Amicus was clearly losing, his body strained itself painfully while Solus held his arm high without breaking a sweat.

"That damn smile.."

Pito had no plan, but he was ready to charge madly. He prepared to sprint forward as he'd scream as loudly as he could, the way Pito saw it, was that he might as well go down with bloody rage in his eyes.

He took a deep breath and began to lurch himself forward.

CHAPTER 38-

I've been called all sorts of names during my strange life as an outcast, and contrary to what some people told me, the names *did* hurt. When I got older though, the sting began to lessen, until I finally lost all care for whatever offensive slur it might be coming from someone's mouth. There were a handful of reasons that contributed to my gradual change, but the main one I'd cite would be simply just letting go, and forgetting about things that only served to make me feel worse. Whether I was on Earth or in Coda, I'd learned that they both shared one important but simple thing in common.

There's a strong gust of wind that flows through the air. Not a gust that one can feel, but a wave that flows with a strong current which never stops moving. When I find myself holding onto something that only brings me negativity, all I need to do is just let go, and let the wind will carry it away from me.

To me, part of evil has always been a disease that prays on the weakness of a good soul, but I've found that when it receives nothing to pray on, suddenly it's the evil that finds itself weak.

I almost died a horrific death on the island of Zugai, there were a few moments of desperate panic while I fought hopelessly against the spirits that swarmed around me, covering me like a smoky blanket. But just in the nick of time, I remembered the lesson that I'd learned years before, and suddenly the spirits of Zugai held no bearing on me whatsoever. *They* became the desperate ones, and in that advantageous moment, I prayed on *their* own weakness.

As I laid down with a perfectly clear mind, they tried to stab at me with their thoughts of violence and hopelessness. But I paid it no mind, instead I just observed them and listened.

They're so hopelessly lost, poor creatures stuck in the midst of an ocean with no chance of reaching land. I pitied them, as the fate they faced was so incredibly terrifying. Yet I discovered something, I saw in them a lust that surpassed any order that Solus could ever give them, a burning drive that flooded their minds like a plague.

They wanted revenge, revenge against whatever god had created them and condemned them to the life they now lived, and luckily for their sake, I had a pretty decent idea about who it might be.

I relaxed my body and focused my mind, and as I'd guessed the little mental cogs in my head began to turn as I laid on the sand patiently. Usually, when I'd meditate, my spirit would enter the red void in the realm of Coda. But this time around, my body already resided in Coda, so the result was something much different. I felt my spirit awaken within my body, but there was no disconnect from my physical self. Instead it was as if I had awoken for the first time, with everything becoming crystal clear.

I shot my hand out and felt the grip of a neck, the black spirit I held tried to release himself from my choking grasp. But there was no use to it, I wouldn't let go. I thought about family, unconditional love, and a sense of belonging. The spirits neck burned like a read-hot clothing iron, but I braced myself through the pain and maintained my grip.

Images of a life of suffering shot into my mind's eye, an angry man filled with jealousy and hatred, a life led by vengeance and heartache. The spirits of Zugai were once people, people who had suffered a life of neglect and pessimism. Solus had prayed on them, and pandered to their hunger for power, slowly recruiting countless fractured souls over the years to serve as his mislead band of sheep.

"Its purpose you all wanted, and you found it. But your god is your enemy, he stole you from your lives."

The spirits that surrounded me all hissed like angry insects.

"Senseless words!" Screeched the spirit whose neck I held.

"I can give you a much higher calling, I can show you a path to revenge."

"You cannot, you are nothing but a burden!" It replied.

I squeezed its neck harder and reeled its face towards my own, I stared into its crimson red eyes.

"You are deluded. From the very beginning of your existence there was a voice to order you, a wretched, sick voice that only wanted to use you. *Your leader..* Your *disgusting* leader did this to you, he threw you into a world with nothing but his command. So now, you're going to listen to *my* voice, and I will help you kill your false god."

"You're wrong! I know all—."

"Last chance! Do the right thing or I'll squeeze the life out of you and every one of your kind. Solus is poison, so stand against him with me."

I didn't like strangling him, but I could see a small glimmer of hope, so I clung to it tightly.

"He promised us a grand position in this new world, he told us we would gain peace.. I am full of guilt, you issue me this ultimatum, and my answer is death."

My grip loosened, and I released the poor soul from my grip, he'd been condemned to a life under an iron fist, completely lost and welcoming death.

"Solus won't ever stop doing this, more and more people will find themselves in your position. But if we try, maybe we can stop him. I can't promise anything, but maybe you'll find peace. But I promise you that if there is peace for you to find, this is the only way."

I awaited an answer, watching him thinking through his blood red eyes, along with all the others amongst him.

"Very well." He said finally.

"No, this is useless drivel, Solus is our only chance." A spirit spat angrily from within the crowd of Zugai.

The spirits began to bicker with one another, and for a moment it was just a heated debate. Quickly though, things grew progressively more aggressive, and soon enough I was caught in the midst of a sea of fighting spirits. They fluttered around like a mound of moths as I squirmed along on my back, desperate to escape. I felt like I was going to suffocate under them, they weighed down on me heavily, shoving my body into the sand beneath. Luckily, I eventually noticed a light flickering behind me. I focused all my energy, and continued to madly scoot along towards the exit.

First, my head emerged like a tortoise coming out of its shell. Then I pulled my arms out and pushed against the mountain of spirits, slowly squeezing myself out. The sky was black and full of fury, and I knew in my heart that the final leg of the story had arrived, and things would soon come to a close. One way or another.

I stood up after pulling the rest of my body out from beneath the spirits of Zugai, and looked over towards Solus.

"Let go of him!" I yelled.

Solus held Pito by his neck, and the erased man sat on his knees in defeat. Solus' eyes widened in surprise and looked at me with an expression of complete disbelief, and the thought of cutting into his ego pleased me to no end.

"I will say, you have brought a refreshing amount of excitement to the table. But I'm starting to get really sick of you, this circus is over."

Instead of sand again, a rock flew towards me like a comet. I watched it hurl through the air like a giant bullet, spinning like a car tire. But I avoided his blow thanks to a spirit of Zugai, it took the bullet without a second thought. It flew out from my right and collided head on with the rock, both exploding like a black firework.

"Let him go." I said again.

Solus stared at me blankly, then at the mound of spirits.

"Come to me!" He shouted.

They exploded in all directions, whirling around like a dark spiral. Like two owners calling to a puppy simultaneously, they all made their decisions as they flew through the sky. Then almost completely evenly, half of them took my side, while the others went to Solus. We both stood with our army of spirits as we locked eyes. He spoke angrily, fortunately after he threw Pito's body away from him and over to Amicus.

"It is an unforgivable abomination, to see the eyes of Coda sit in the skull of a rat."

"Now you're just an old man, what happened to the inflated ego? You scared?"

Solus hurled another rock in my direction, but again one of the spirits took the full brunt of its impact, and I didn't flinch a single bit as it shattered right in front of me. I felt terrible for the spirit, but things had to be the way now. My intuition buzzed along like a motor, my thoughts remained calm.

"So are you gonna stand around throwing rocks?"

"I can destroy you and your merry band of traitors with one swift shake of the wrist!" He shouted angrily.

"So are you gonna do it? Or is just gonna throw another little stone?"

Rage burned behind Solus' eyes, and he cursed at me furiously.

"Blah, blah, blah." I said mockingly.

Solus threw not one, but at least five rocks, they rocketed through the air with a savage aggression. But as I expected, the spirits of Zugai flew directly into them and they exploded into dust before my eyes.

"I know two important things about you right now Solus."

"You know nothing!" Solus screamed as another five rocks flew towards me.

"First thing. You're scared of that crown now aren't you? I'm assuming that at first your enormous ego blinded you to its danger. But you feel it now can't you? It's just going to end up tearing you into a million pieces.."

"That's enough!" He screamed.

Then again, another onslaught of rocks flew towards me.

"Every time you excerpt energy with that thing on your head, you can feel it burrow its claws just that little bit deeper into your head. I'll tell you some bad news Solus, that's exactly what's happening."

Solus screamed a bloodcurdling scream with a voice as hoarse as a one-hundred-year-old heavy smoker, and I could see more fear creep into his wrinkled, old face.

"Spewing nonsense, you're an idiot who knows nothing!"

"Edmund was a man of purity, he was a good soul.. And even *he* was driven insane by that thing. So now you call *me* an idiot while you actually thought you could wear that thing and suffer no consequences? You probably should have just killed me as soon as I'd gotten here."

In a panic, Solus turned towards Pito with murder in his eyes. But before he had any chance of killing him, the spirits on my side were just as happy to help Pito, they flew over, took him from the sand and carried him back to me.

"Get Amicus too." I instructed them.

As they headed over towards the erased man, Solus sent his horde of followers onto mine, blocking their path. But it didn't bother me at all, as everything was in motion. The spirits fought with all their strength, as me and the old man stared each other down.

"Now the second thing. I'm willing to bet that your greatest fear is judgment.. Judgment from the *true* god's of Coda. When you finally destroy yourself, something tells me that they're not gonna look at you too favorably..."

"There are no gods!! It is just me!! I AM THE ONE GOD OF CODA!"

"I *know* you don't really believe that..."

I watched Solus squirm in terror at the prospect of meeting something more powerful than himself, panic flooded his body as his eyes widened in horrified shock. The crown was destroying him and breaking his mind, literally snapping it like a pile of twigs. Despite Solus undoubtedly being the most hollow, evil-hearted man I'd ever known, it was still awful to watch someone lose their mind. But it was karma doing its work, he was a man being annihilated by his own doing.

"How many have died for this?" I asked Solus.

Solus didn't answer, instead he gripped the crown with his hands and tried to pull it from his head. He turned towards Amicus and dropped to his knees.

"Please. Help me Amicus." He pleaded.

The erased man raised his head and smiled at Solus, it was the first expression I'd ever seen on his face, and it gave me goosebumps just seeing it. Solus rose back to his feet and looked up at the spirits battling in the sky.

"Spirits of Zugai! Remove this thing now!"

As instructed, the spirits that still remained faithful to him flew down to his aid and flocked around his head. I could see his legs stumbling around underneath the mess of black spirits as the proud, firm stance he'd had before was now gone. The old man was terrified, gripping tightly to his last shred of sanity. It made me think of when I'd worn the crown myself, and the crushing fear and anxiety that it'd caused me to feel, the crown was like a shotgun designed to blow a bleeding hole right into the mind itself.

While Solus was busy trying to remove the crown I took the opportunity to tend to Pito, I knelt beside him and placed my hand on his forehead.

"Pito, are you okay??"

It was incredibly weak, but Pito responded with a beaten and croaking voice, not within my thoughts but from his own mouth.

"I'll be alright.."

His voice settled my nerves, relief flowed through my body.

"Thank god."

"It's not over yet, watch your back Steven." Said Pito.

I turned around to see the spirits of Zugai dispersing from Solus, they all immediately continued to battle amongst each other in the dark sky above. Solus stared straight at me, once again his posture was tall and proud, his sick smile had returned, and the crown lay on the yellow sand at his feet.

"One thing you will notice about me Steven, is my optimism."

His eyes darkened as he stepped closer towards me.

"I have been around for a very long time, and that time will cease to have and end. I *am* a god. I will *always* exist.. You disrespected me, and such an act isn't acceptable. But, if you bow to me as your god, things might end a little better."

His smile widening with every step, he kept gaining distance on me.

"Well..?"

I didn't respond, but I kept my eyes locked onto his.

"Good, I hoped you wouldn't. Even without the crown I still have more power than anything in these lands.. I have all the time in the world, even if it was to take more than ten-thousand years, I *will* eventually perfect the crown."

Amicus weakly rose to his feet from behind, and slowly, he stumbled over towards the crown as quietly as he could manage, all the while I didn't let my eyes wander away from Solus' glare.

"No matter what Solus, you can't avoid judgment. I promise, one day it will find you."

He slowly shook his head.

"I am the one who will make judgment.. Me alone."

Amicus retrieved the crown from the sand and kept moving up behind Solus, his eyes burned like the sun, with pure hatred written on his face.

"I would feel for anyone being destroyed by that crown. But you Solus, you are hollow, a shell full of nothing but ego."

In my peripheral vision, I saw Amicus make it a few feet behind Solus. Then subtly, he nodded his head.

"You made your bed, so sleep in it."

Immediately after I spoke, Amicus jumped at Solus. He held the crown high in his hands as he lunged from behind, he swung down hard, and smashed it onto Solus' head with full force, tearing the skin on his scalp. The old man screamed in pain and surprise as a stream of blood trickled down from his head. He desperately clawed at the crown, but Amicus held it with all of his strength.

"No!" Solus screamed with rage.

Amicus held on tightly as Solus clenched his fists, he swung backwards and into the erased man's right arm smashing into it with inhuman strength. But Amicus didn't let up or even make a sound, his face held the same stone cold and hate-filled expression. Again, Solus smashed into Amicus' arm, this time tearing into his black, smoky flesh.

"Get off me! Or I will rip off both your arms!" He screamed.

But of course, Amicus continued to hold the crown on Solus' head.

"Fine!"

In a series of swift and cutting motions, Solus hacked into the erased man's arm, spraying out thick, dark maroon blood. Then in a horrific display, his arm fell down onto the sand, completely severed from his body.

"You cannot grip without arms!"

Solus then began to hack into the other arm, with a smile returning to his old, weathered face.

In a second of instinct I began to make my way forward, wanting to help the erased man in any way I could, but Pito stopped me before I had the chance.

"Don't worry, he doesn't need help. Trust me Steven, just watch.."

I trusted Pito and stopped moving, and watched the bloody struggle between good and evil.

An incredibly strong feeling then overcame me, a deeply nostalgic feeling that was so strong I almost felt like I was going to faint.

"Pito.. What is this..?"

"Don't worry, just watch."

The erased man was missing an arm, but in a dazzling display his arm was replaced. Though not by another smoky, black one, but by an arm that was completely made from a bright, shining light. Then without thinking about it, I began to speak shortly to myself.

"Vitam alba lupus… vitam alba lupus…"

Solus screamed, it was fear in its most pure form, he was terrified beyond description. Amicus then spoke in his deep and heavy voice.

"Judgment awaits. Your broken spirit will always be condemned to your tower, and you will find nothing but guilt and misery with every step you make within its dark halls."

The arm of light burned into Solus like it was a fire, and his skin seared with its intense heat.

"NO!!! HELP!!"

His spirits flew from the sky and towards the struggle, but it was hopeless, as each of them were instantly destroyed by the pure light as soon as they made it within three feet.

"It's over.." I said to myself quietly.

The erased man looked at me and nodded his head subtly before saying his last and final words.

"I'll give my regards to Josh when I see him."

His flesh then began to fade away, and the shining light beneath exploded outward like a small supernova. For a few seconds, there was nothing but blinding light, but then it faded. Standing tall in the erased man's place was a wolf, and its infinite grace almost too much to witness.

Its jaws gripped the crown and ripped it from Solus' head before throwing it off to the side. Even without the crown, Solus was no longer a threat, his mind was broken and all he could do was ramble gibberish and nonsense in a semi-lucid state. The great wolf took him by his head and began to drag him off towards the dream sea.

"Wait."

It turned its head towards me and stared into my eyes.

"If you could.. Give his body to the Kawa."

The wolf turned away and continued into the dream sea on his way back towards the other side.

"Do you think he understood me?" I asked Pito as I turned around.

"Yep, but he would've done that even if ya hadn't of said

so."

"Oh, well that works."

I knelt down and helped Pito onto his feet and hugged him.

"You really are the strongest spirit in the universe."

Pito hugged back tightly.

"Told ya." He said smiling.

Before we could talk further, the spirits of Zugai rushed full force into the crown, each and every one of them disintegrated as soon as they made contact with it. Pito and I watched with stunned expressions while little by little, they dwindled in numbers. Once again they purified the crown of its unrelenting madness, but thankfully for the last time.

Eventually, all but one spirit remained on the island of Zugai, his eyes were filled with sadness, and for a moment I expected him to speak, but instead he turned away and charged into the crown just as all the others had done. I sighed in relied and turned back to Pito.

CHAPTER 39-

I spent around a year with Pito in his forest after we'd made our way back through Coda from the island of Zugai, they were the most loving and unforgettable times I'd ever live.

The time came though, when we both knew it was time for me to return to where I'd come from. Part of me never wanted to leave Pito alone in his forest home, but in our hearts we knew that the time had come, and it was a tear-filled goodbye that broke my heart.

On a sunny morning, I sat with Pito on the bank of the dream sea, and I wore the crown of Coda for the very last time. Pito filled my head with beautiful memories of our year together, and memories that went further back too. We held each other's hands as my body left Coda, and I gripped them as tightly as I could before there was nothing left to hold onto.

I found myself in the broken remains of the Vickerdon factory, and for at least an hour I cried at the thought of my oldest friend Josh. The tears were bittersweet, because though I did miss him immensely, I also treasured his memory. He was a person of such purity, he was a beautiful soul.

After a long and tedious stint at the Vickerdon street bank, I finally managed to access my account. The first thing I did was buy a carton of cigarettes before returning to the old factory, I pulled up a chair and thanked the universe for all the love and beauty that I'd had the chance to be a part of. I was even joined by a familiar little face, Marron the cat sat beside my chair as a gave him scratches behind his ears.

CHAPTER 40-

I returned to Endon and spent a couple of months in the newly rebuilt Endon hotel, during which time I found a job at the town library. Eventually, after spending time together over weekend coffees, I worked up the courage to ask Olive out for dinner. We slowly fell in love as the two of us enjoyed at least a hundred dinners together. Sometime later she asked me if I wanted to move out from my main-street apartment to instead live with her and Ryan in her house on the pine tree road.

Three years later I proposed to Olive, and we got married in the Endon town church. The following year we had a healthy baby boy we named Josh, and I love him with all my heart. I love my family, and I'm thankful for the way my life had turned out.

On a rainy Saturday morning I was driving Ryan back from his karate class, we laughed and joked about this and that before getting back home. When we walked through the door Olive asked Ryan how his karate lesson had gone. A deep sadness mixed with joy overcame me as he flexed his muscles and responded.